THE

GIRL

WHO

WOULDN'T

DIE

OTHER SKY PONY PRESS BOOKS BY RANDALL PLATT:

Incommunicado

ALSO BY RANDALL PLATT:

The Cornerstone
Hellie Jondoe
Honor Bright
Liberty's Christmas
The Likes of Me

THE

GIRL

WHO

WOULDN'T

DIE

RANDALL PLATT

Sky Pony Press
New York

Sky Pony Press books may be purchased in bulk at special discounts for sales promotion, corporate gifts, fund-raising, or educational purposes. Special editions can also be created to specifications. For details, contact the Special Sales Department, Sky Pony Press, 307 West 36th Street, 11th Floor, New York, NY 10018 or info@skyhorsepublishing.com.

Sky Pony® is a registered trademark of Skyhorse Publishing, Inc.®, a Delaware corporation.

Visit our website at www.skyponypress.com.

10 9 8 7 6 5 4 3 2 1

Library of Congress Cataloging-in-Publication Data is available on file.

Cover design by Sammy Yuen
Cover image credit Thinkstock

Print ISBN: 978-1-5107-0809-9
E-book ISBN: 978-1-5107-0810-5

Printed in the United States of America

Interior design by Joshua L. Barnaby

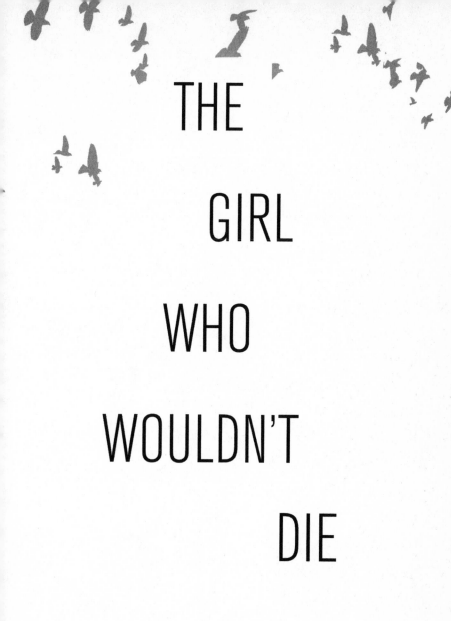

THE

GIRL

WHO

WOULDN'T

DIE

Dedicated
to the memory of the real cigarette sellers
of Three Crosses Square

August, 1939

I.

"IDENTIFICATION?"

I hand it to him and watch his face carefully. He's not my first Nazi.

The young soldier looks at the photo on my forged Austrian student pass, then back at me. "Your reason for entering Poland?"

"My aunt is dying," I say, hoping he can't detect the accent in my German. I might be fluent in four languages—five if I count the street slang my gang uses—but I know my accent shines a Polish light on every word.

"Where does your aunt live?"

"Warsaw."

"When will you return to Vienna?"

"I have final exams in two weeks. I have to be back . . ." I frown at him and add, "That is, providing I can get back. I'd like to finish my second year before . . ." I stop.

"Before what?"

A little smile won't hurt. "I've been in Vienna for two years, sir. I'm pretty sure I know what's coming." I adjust my skirt.

"Yes, well," he says, "these are dangerous times, especially for young women traveling alone."

Don't I know it! These days, a girl needs to know how to defend herself. In five languages. I keep my valise close to my leg and hope he doesn't notice the padding in my skirt hem. Money, more forged papers, a knife.

A soldier pokes his head into the room and says, "There's about fifty more out here, Claus. Quit flirting!"

This Claus looks at me and his face reddens. He knows I understand. I don't smile. I watched these Krauts overrun Vienna and I've had more dealings with them than I'd like to admit. I know I have an edge here. My very gentile-looking smile, this new shade of lipstick I lifted from a woman on the train, these new silk stockings all help. Not to mention my ability to conjure up tears.

"I'm sorry," I say, pulling out a crinkled hankie. "Aunt Bożena is very dear to me. I hope I get there in time."

He hands me back the pass.

There's some sort of scuffle in the hall. I hear a woman cry out and a man make a threat in Yiddish. Others shout in Polish, German soldiers shouting back.

"Is everything okay?" I ask, tilting my head toward the door.

"Yes, yes. Very well, Fräulein, you may go." He pulls a paper off a pad, fills in my name and dates, signs it. Then— ka-chunk!—he pushes down a numbering stamp. I watch over his shoulder. It's a pass in and out of Poland good for two months. Street value? Big.

I rise, and he hands me my valise. If he finds out what's in it, I'll be detained. Or worse. I'm still wanted on two warrants in Vienna. "Please, be careful," Claus says. "And a little bit of advice, if I may."

"Yes?"

"Try to leave Warsaw. In fact, leave Poland altogether. As soon as you can."

I give him a quick look, but then smile sweetly. "Really? Why?"

He smiles back and opens the door for me. "Well, you don't want to miss those exams, do you?" And he winks at me.

"Oops, forgot my hankie," I say, as he follows me out the door and starts to talk to someone in the hall. I rush back in the office and tear off several more passes from the pad and the numbering stamp, pocketing them just as he steps back into the room.

"Find it?"

"Yes, thank you." I dab my eyes, smile, and leave. I walk down the hall against the line of people yet to be processed, and step into the large waiting room. I'm almost there. This train station in Ostrana, Czechoslovakia, is the last checkpoint. Poland is within spitting distance. Then hitch a ride to Warsaw and I'm home free.

But not looking like this.

I find the ladies' room, slip into a toilet stall, and make my change. The prim, innocent school girl goes in, the street ruffian comes out. Thick cotton pants, boots, a baggy sweater over two shirts and my chest wrap. The blonde wig, the cloche hat, the pleated skirt—everything for the school-girl set—gets crammed deep into the trash can after I rip my valuables out of the hem. On second thought, I pull the silk stockings back out. Always a street value. I dunk my head in the sink and wash my face, then grab a towel and hold it over my head.

"Come on, you coward. Look," I mutter, daring myself. The towel slowly comes down.

My hacked-short blonde hair is thick from months of neglect. My skin is ruddy and rough and intensifies my blue eyes. I'm sixteen—aren't I supposed to be blossoming by now? I stand sideways and look at my profile. Flat-chested, scrawny, too tall. My periods still show up unannounced, like an unwelcome maiden aunt.

"So, tell me. Just who are you?" I ask my reflection. "No. What are you?"

The scream of a train whistle reminds me to move out fast. I pull my cap down low, hike up these stolen pants, pull down the moth-eaten sweater, and take one last look. This is the real me—not the Abra Goldstein my filthy-rich Jewish parents tried to forge. No, on the streets they call me the Arab, and I'm ready to reclaim my territory on the shady side of Warsaw. Start up a Warsaw Chapter of the Meet Me in Hell Club and fill it with street kids.

I back out of the swinging restroom door and nearly knock over a well-dressed woman coming in.

"Pardon me," I say, backing away. "Wrong door."

She responds with a bit of a huff as I start toward the waiting room.

Damn! It's that Claus coming toward the men's room, walking with another soldier. I look around. Nowhere to duck into. Quick, think! He'll recognize my valise, if not me! I rush back in the ladies' room, hold my valise against my chest, and lean against the door. The woman looks at me in surprise. She looks Jewish, but then again, I don't. Still, it's my only card. I put my finger to my lips and whisper in Yiddish, "Please . . ." We can hear the soldiers walking outside the door. She dries her hands and looks at me, then at the trash can where the blonde wig is just barely showing. An uneven smile comes to her face.

I listen outside the door. It's quiet. "Thank you," I say to her. I pull out the silk stockings and press them into her hands. Already I've redeemed their value.

"May God go with you," she says, her Yiddish well marked with a German accent.

I peer around the door. The way is clear. If God wants to go with me, fine. Not stopping him, as long as he keeps his advice to himself. God's one of the reasons I'm in this situation in the first place. No, it's more likely I'm on my own.

Just the way I like it.

II.

AFTER TWO DAYS OF WALKING AND HITCHHIKING THROUGH Poland, I'm here. Welcome home, Arab. I hop on the back of a passing lorry and take a deep breath. The scents of the Vistula River off in the distance mix with industrial smoke and it's as though I never left. My gaze wanders north to where my parents' extravagant home anchors an entire city block. The lorry passes a roadside flower stand and the scent of rose blossoms reminds me of the bushes my mother planted when Ruth was born. Ruthie. That little brat fell into my heart the minute she was placed into my arms. Perfect in every way but one: that tiny, sweet, clubbed foot. But oh, Ruthie's smile, her eyes, her everything. Despite myself, I adore that little imp.

I wonder if she'd even remember me after two years. After all, she was barely three when I left. Probably doesn't even have a photograph to remember me by, such was my father's wrath. But if I've learned anything in the last two years, it's that yesterday means nothing. Tomorrow means nothing. Today is everything.

And today, I have an old score to settle. If he's still in Warsaw—if he's still alive—I'll find him. I've been planning our reunion for two years.

I follow all the regular routes, look in our old haunts, hideouts, and meet-up joints. I stroll through Praga Park on the Vistula River and pass familiar places: where Sniper and

I first met, our first flirtations, our first confidence game together, our first holdup.

I thought Sniper was the sun and the moon and the stars in between. Back then, I would have walked through hell for him. And I damn near have. I was thirteen, and a stupid little shit—a gawky, clumsy, stupid-in-love Jew-girl. Eager and willing to run with his gang—to prove myself to him. I know what I saw in him: something different, exciting, even dangerous. But what did he see in me? A dupe. Plain and simple. A lamb to throw to the wolves. And I let him.

I look down each street in this district, our old turf, thinking every thin, tall, dark man I see might be Sniper. I can feel my heart pound. Anticipation of—what, Arab? Revenge or—No! Stop thinking that! Revenge can get a girl killed.

I walk past a café and remember I haven't eaten a real sit-down meal in days. I have some money, but wonder why I should use it when I can see a purse limply hanging off a woman's chair, begging to be lifted.

I bump my valise into her chair, upsetting her.

"Young man!" her escort says. I scramble to set things straight. Kneeling down, I easily slip her purse off the back of her chair. Into my valise it drops and—*snap!*—it's closed.

"I'm so sorry," I say, backing away.

I walk to the next street over, hop a streetcar, take a seat in back, and paw through the purse. I smell the scented hankie —not bad—so I stuff it in my pocket. Hmm, this lipstick is so red! When did that come into style? Not my color—as though I *have* a style! I open the compact. This stays with me. It's as good as eyes in the back of my head! And oh, lovely, lovely cash. Enough for me to live on for days, or longer. I find the woman's identification and pocket that, too. The rest—photos, a comb, tweezers—useless. I leave them and the purse on the floor of the car and get off at the next stop.

I head for one of my old haunts, the Crystal Café. I take a table close to the sidewalk, an old habit—I get an up-close view of the passersby before they get an up-close view of me, and it's a quick escape if I need it.

"Arab?" the waiter asks. "Is that you? It's me, Albin!"

I look at him carefully. Not everyone in Warsaw is an old friend.

"Remember? Spades?" He looks around and whispers, "You know, from Sniper's gang?"

My heart takes a leap at the sound of Sniper's name. I offer him a slight smile. "Sure. I remember you. Good pickpocket."

"Where've you been hiding out?" He hands me a menu.

"Oh, here and there."

"Gosh, I felt bad when you got caught. Never trusted Sniper after that."

I glance casually at the menu. "So Spades the pickpocket is now Albin the waiter. What a world." I grin up at Spades. "Remember when we used to steal tips off these very tables?"

"Got caught, got lucky, got wise," Spades—Albin—says. He nods toward the inside of the restaurant. "Owner gave me a break."

"Well, good."

"You aren't going to . . . you know . . . eat and then take off. Like in the old days? Because . . ."

"Of course not. I don't do those cheap tricks anymore," I say, reaching into my pocket for the change from the purse I just lifted.

"Well, I thought, because, you know, you're dressed like that. Like you used to be when we ran together."

"My wardrobe is being altered," I say, giving him a smirk. "Lost a lot of weight while I was . . . here and there."

"Understood," he says, nodding. "So, what'll it be?"

"Coffee, cruller, raspberry jam." He starts to leave, but I pull him back by his apron. "So, where's Sniper these days?"

He stands straighter. "Oh, around. I see him every so often."

"He still have a gang?"

"Yeah. But—"

"Just tell him I'm back, if you see him."

"Arab, I don't think that's wise. I mean, he set you up plain and simple, and then he laughed when you got caught. Said you didn't have what it takes and . . . then bragged about you . . . you know . . . proving yourself . . . in other ways."

I feel my jaw tighten. Maybe there was a time I would have "proven myself" to Sniper if given the chance, but I never did. I'm going to prove myself to him, all right, but the Arab he meets now won't be the same Arab he remembers.

"And how about Lizard? Ever see him?" I ask, resurrecting another name from my past.

"The Pickpocket Priest?" he asks.

"Some altar boy he made, huh?" We both chuckle over the memories: stealing sacramental wine, smoking in the confessionals, sneaking cash from the donation box for poor children.

Spades smiles and pretends to be swiping away crumbs on the table. "Oh, that Lizard! He's just about everywhere these days. Him and Sniper broke it off after you left. Big fight. Went out on his own. They've tangled a few times, but mostly Sniper stays on his side of town and Lizard hangs out around Three Crosses Square. I think he has about half a dozen little shits in his gang. I see them coming and have to shoo them away, the brats. Sure brings back the old days."

Someone snaps their fingers for Spades's attention. "Coming, sir!" Then, looking back down at me, he says, "Arab, listen. Sniper's far more dangerous now than he ever was. I mean, we were just kids then. He's changed, and not for the better."

"I don't want to gang up with him. Just let him know I'm back. That's all. Just tell him I'm back in Warsaw. I'd like to see him."

I take time to savor my coffee. How long has it been since I had a warm cup? And this jam! I think how lovely it is to be back home, here, this café, Warsaw. Why the hell didn't I come back sooner? I leave Spades a nice tip, compliments of some lady looking everywhere for her purse by now.

I stroll down Sienna Street in the fashion district and take time to gaze into the windows, see what the upper crust ladies of Warsaw are wearing these days. I catch my reflection in the window. I take off my cap and ruffle my short hair. Wonder what my mother would think of me, dressed like this, having been kicked out of school in Vienna, having left with warrants, fines, two arrests, one conviction, no education except the one I earned on the streets. All I really know is the streets. Conning dupes, picking pockets, thieving. I put my cap back on. I need to get a place to stay. And who knows? Maybe I'll scoop up a few kids for my club. Maybe give Sniper a run for his money.

I find a cheap room, settle in, and make my plans.

III.

I'd forgotten how beautiful Warsaw is in late summer. Hot, of course, but I've missed the glimmer off the Vistula, the green of the parks, the rush of people along the sidewalks, the piano music—Chopin, of course—wafting from some music teacher's window.

I hear a horse whinny off in the distance. Ruthie, I think with a grin. Even as a toddler she was horse-crazy. Once I borrowed—well, stole—a pony from a fruit seller's droshky cart. Unhooked the harness from the traces and trotted the pony home. Ruthie on that chubby little pony's back, her shrieks of joy as I led her around and around our block were worth what it cost me. Finally, the pony's owner came, gendarmes in tow, hollering, swearing, shaking his fist.

Maybe it won't hurt to . . . What? Would knocking on the door, stepping inside, really coming home be . . . What am I thinking? My mother's heart was always so weak. I'd just be a thorn in her side—that's if my father even allowed me on the property. Hell, for all I know, Mother's already dead and buried. But what about little Ruthie? What if Mother is dead? Who would be Ruthie's protector then? No, that settles it! I have to see, have to find out. I have to know she's all right.

I walk a few blocks but run into street construction, backing up traffic and people. Ah, my sweet sewers—sometimes the most direct route anywhere in Warsaw. Sometimes the safest. I know the sewers in this district better than anyone.

I slip down a manhole off an alley, wait on the ladder for my eyes to adjust, and assess the sound, the flow of the water, the smell of the industry, life or death—whatever is sloshing through below me.

At first sniff, I feel right at home. Safe. Memories gush back like they're floating atop the foamy sewer water. I was ten when Lizard dared me down into the sewers. Said no girl had ever done it. No girl had the guts. Well, I never met a dare I didn't like. Come to think of it, sewers were the reason I first hacked off my long hair. It smelled to high heaven after I emerged. I can still hear my parents' rage over that! "Proper Jewish girls have long hair." Too bad. Long hair can be dangerous. Someone can use it as a handle to yank you around, pull you off balance. Long hair can get a girl killed.

Something else about the sewers: enemies have to want you pretty damn bad to follow you down here. Sniper and his gang taught me that. Once you get used to the smell and stop thinking about what you're slogging through, once you learn to stop gagging, quit breathing through your mouth, and go slow so you don't trip, it's not such a bad way to get around.

I go a few blocks, using my flashlight to get my bearings and looking for any news signs or warnings other sewer pilgrims might have scribbled on the walls: POLICE PATROLS, TOO WELL-TRAVELED, or BEWARE: FUNERAL PARLOR ABOVE! I hear *plop! plop!* and I feel a couple of rats race across my boots. Damn rats always catch me off guard. Then the rats *plop! plop!* again, back into the water, and I relax. The rats always leave, get on with their work. Unless you're dead. Then you are their work.

I look down the passageway, then at the ladder up. I know just where I am: two blocks from home on Pawia Street.

"Hey, you! Boy! Get out of there!" a man shouts at me just as I shove the manhole cover up and out. Before I can sink back down, someone has me by the collar and he hauls me up onto the street. He whirls me around so the sun's in my eyes and I have to squint.

"It's illegal to go in the sewers! Don't you know it's dangerous and—" My eyes focus and we seem to recognize each other in the same instant. Officer Winicki's face softens. "Is it? Well. Look at you. Abra Goldstein. Or is it still Arab? Alive after all?"

Officer Gustaw Winicki, our neighborhood foot patrolman, has hauled me home time after time. Always lecturing and hinting, but almost as though he cared about what became of me. Sorry to let you down. Again.

"Of course I'm alive. I'm here, aren't I? Just going home, Officer Winicki. No crime in that."

"No, no crime. But you can't go home, Abra."

"I can if I want to," I say, sounding about six years old.

He pulls me back and says, "No, you can't."

"Why not? What happened? Did something . . ."

"No, nothing happened."

"Then why?" I demand.

"Because . . . because you're dead to them." He's looking past me.

"What do you mean?"

"Dead and buried." His voice is now low and soft.

"How can I be buried? I'm right here."

"Come with me." He ticks his head, and I follow him.

We walk silently the half block to the cemetery down the street from our home—past the posh Jewish section and ending in poor man's land. He points down to a gravestone. I kneel down to read it.

What the . . .? In Hebrew, it reads:

ABRA GOLDSTEIN

GONE AND FORGOTTEN

"He buried me?" I ask, still trying to comprehend. "He *buried* me?"

"He buried your memory."

"So, who's in there?"

"No one. It was a symbolic burial."

I brush away some dead leaves and pick up a twig sticking out of the ground. "Who gave the eulogy?"

"This marker just showed up here, about a year after you were sent away."

It hits me. I remember the exact date: the phone call to my father, kicked out of school, hauled before the authorities in Vienna, the three months in jail—one month for each *Reichsmark* I'd stolen.

"There was no funeral, no celebration, no prayers, no . . . what do you Jews call that prayer for the dead?"

"Kaddish," I whisper, unable to take my eyes off my name engraved on the gravestone.

"We heard about your jail time in Vienna. Then, rumors, of course, about . . ." His words trail off. "There was even a report you really were . . . dead."

I stand up and tamp down some lose dirt with my boot. "Abra's dead. Says right there, gone and forgotten."

I look at Officer Winicki, who is offering me his kindest smile.

I return his smile. "And gravestones never lie. But I'm not Abra. I'm Arab." I toss the twig back down on my tombstone, and it pings off to land in the dirt. "So think of me as the girl who wouldn't die," I whisper, feeling my fingernails dig into my palms as I form fists. "Well, at least that answers one of my questions. My father's alive and kicking."

"Yes. He's doing quite well. But your mother . . ."

"What about her?"

"She's bedridden. Has been for these two years."

"And my sister, Ruth?"

"Her limp keeps her from playing with the other children. You know how protective your father is. But there's a governess, and a nurse. Your parents have all they need."

"And now they're rid of what they don't need. I can't believe he did this." I have to turn my back on Officer Winicki and take a breath. No one sees me cry.

"I probably shouldn't tell you this. But, a few times, your mother tried to have me smuggle a letter to you. When your father caught on, he threatened to kick me out of my apartment. Well, decent rent is hard to find in this district."

"Thanks for trying," I say, running my sleeve under my nose, then facing him again.

He puts his hand on my shoulder. "I tried every time. I was there when he washed his hands of you for the last time, remember? Even tore up your birth certificate. Didn't think he'd go that far, but you know your father, Abra. After that jewelry store robbery with that petty thief schmuck . . . what was his name?"

"Sniper."

"Sniper. That's him." Winicki shakes his head. "Worthless street-hound. You know how he'll end up someday."

"There." I point down to my own gravestone.

"Time will heal it all, Abra. Just give it some time. Get yourself a job, clean yourself up, find a good man. Show them you turned out respectable. Prove them wrong. But now? Not now. Your mother is so sick. When you go back, go back a woman. Not . . . this." He indicates my clothes—the only clothes a girl can wear and survive the streets I run in, the crowds I run with, unless she's whoring and needs to advertise. But he wouldn't understand that. "Come on. I need to get back on patrol." He digs into his pocket and pulls out some coins. "Here, get yourself a—"

"No, thanks. I have money." I've done a lot of things, but I've never taken charity and I've never begged. Must be a bit of Goldstein arrogance in me after all.

"Do you need anything? A place to stay?"

"No, I have a place."

"Okay, then. Just give it time."

"Look, don't tell them you saw me."

He smiles kindly. "You have my word, Abra." He backs away and I give him a slight nod goodbye.

Alone now with my gravestone, I try to laugh. So, I'm dead to them. Dead and even buried. Gone and forgotten. Not even a damn memory stone to show someone's visited. I look around and raid an adjoining grave of the rocks placed there, tossing them down on my own grave. I wipe my face and walk back around the block toward our—their—house. Not sure why.

Father always did do well with Mother's money. They own several apartment buildings in this neighborhood. I wonder how many bank boards Father sits on top of, overseeing the Jewish Mercantile League. They all reek of respect like I reek of the sewers.

I slow as I walk by, staying in the shadows. Just one quick look. Just a glance. I pause long enough to listen carefully to the squeaking sound. I know that sound! Now, her sweet voice! That song! I taught it to her!

I look past the high, ornate wrought-iron fence holding in our yard. It's her! Ruthie! Rocking on the wooden horse I bought her with stolen money. Look at her go! I wonder where she's riding to, or who she's riding from. She's so tiny! She's barely grown at all! At five, shouldn't she be bigger? Stronger? But look at her! That porcelain face! We're both blondes, but damn! She's the beauty.

"Well, as I live and breathe. Look who's doing the same."

Sniper! Easy, Arab, easy. I turn around and see we're the same height now. "Think of the devil and his imp appears," I mutter.

"Were you just thinking about me?" he asks, putting his hands to his chest. "How sweet of you." He nods toward Ruthie. "Adorable little girl, huh?"

"Yes. Very," I reply, keeping a chill in my voice, my face in the shadows.

"Word on the street is, you want to see me. I'm flattered. Fact is, I want to see you, too."

"And you just happened to be in the neighborhood," I say, looking behind him in case I need a fast escape. "Nice coincidence."

"Come now, Arab. People in our line of work don't rely on coincidences. Got a great gang now. Sees all, knows all, tells all." He gives a sharp whistle and waves off a man in the distance. The man waves back and disappears into the shadows.

"If I were you, I wouldn't hang around this area. The police are after you." Seeing him here, this close to Ruthie, scares me. Ruthie is none of his business.

He laughs. God, I remember that laugh! Arrogant, confident, dangerous. "If I stayed away from every area just because of the police—well, Arab, you can see that would be impossible. Maybe even unmanly."

I watch his face carefully. This is what I've wanted for two years now. Or thought I wanted. What is he now, nineteen? Twenty? His dark stubble makes his fair skin look all the paler. There's a fresh scar right through his lips, giving a slur to his speech. He has a steely grittiness to him. Much more than I remember. Well, I've got grit now, too.

Ruthie stops rocking and I want to get him away from her, and fast. I start walking toward the nearest bus stop.

"Hey, wait up! You don't just walk away . . ." he calls after me.

I keep walking. I don't like this gnawing feeling inside me.

He catches up, a little out of breath. "So, where you been hiding all this time?"

"Finishing school."

"Well, you 'finished' into a real man-sized woman." He pulls my arm and swings me around. He runs his eyes down and back up. "Or should I say a woman-sized man? Tell the truth, jury's still out about you . . . Well, a couple of boys in the gang, you remember them, Digger and some other kid, found drowned in the river, I forget his name. Anyway, we had us a bet going. She a lezzie or not and who's going to find out?" He pulls me closer to him with a fist in my sweater.

I bat his hand away. "You'd be the last one to find out." My heart's going a full throttle and I can't stop it. I join the line of people waiting for the bus.

"My little Arab. All grown up. You know, let's us go have a nice quiet drink some place and—"

I indicate the flash of diamond on his pinky finger. "Nice ring. Wherever did you get it?"

"Oh, come on now, Arab. You're not going to hold that against me, are you?"

"You set me up, Sniper."

"Nobody put a gun to your back and made you do it."

"You planned all along to throw me to the wolves when you needed an innocent, little sweet thing who just happened to speak Yiddish."

"Can I help it if the old Yid jeweler pulled a gun?" He shrugs his shoulders, mimicking the Jew he is.

"I got tossed away for two years because of you, Sniper."

"Poor little rich girl Abra Goldstein. Got tossed into some sweet boarding school with all the trimmings. Yeah, I heard. Must be nice to have an old man with connections. Anyone else in my gang would have been tossed into Pawiak Prison for ten years. *You* froze, *you* got caught, so you can't hold that against me," he whispers, close to my face. His warm breath reeks of garlic, beer, and tobacco. He pulls me close. "But I know other things you can hold against me."

"You'll never live that long." I glare into his eyes and find all the same perilous opportunities glaring back.

He slowly gives me his now-crooked smile. "Well, can't blame a man for trying. You know, darling, I'm fixed up sweet now. Kinging a good gang. Sure could use you, if you're looking to gang up again." He nods his head toward my old home. "And say, bring along your sweet little baby sister. If she's anything like you, what a shill I could make of—"

I grab him and push him back, upsetting two people waiting for the bus. I shove him again and he stumbles, tangled in a hedge. "Don't you ever, ever even mention my sister, Sniper, or I swear I'll kill you!"

My kick to his groin is hard, fast, and a direct hit. He folds in half, falls back, and writhes in pain, moaning as he grasps his crotch. Love that sound! He's now an easy mark. I rifle through his pockets and take everything—cash, cigarettes, and switchblade. The pinky ring is on good and tight so I leave it for another day.

"Oh, stop whimpering, Sniper. It's so . . . unmanly," I say down to him.

I hop the bus, ignoring the looks from the other passengers. My outfit, my smell, my "I dare you" attitude. I watch the top of my parents' apartment buildings two blocks down disappear into the tree tops. Nothing left for me there. All I have now is the memory of Ruthie's song, the squeak of a rocking horse, an empty grave, and a switchblade.

I pull my collar up, my cap down, and get off at the stop closest to the underside of Warsaw, where I feel right at home.

IV.

AFTER A FEW NIGHTS' SLEEP AND SOME DECENT FOOD, I TURN my sights toward Lizard's haunt, Three Crosses Square. Lizard, with his charming smile and affable manner—always a smile and a nod for the ladies, especially with unguarded pocketbooks; always a joke and a handshake for the gentlemen, especially with loose-fitting rings.

I spot him on some steps, lean up against a pillar, and watch. What an artist! Look how he flashes those newspapers. Wonder what newsstand he stole them from. What is Lizard now? Eighteen? Let's see now—I remember he's a loyal Pole, so no talking politics; he's a good Catholic when it's convenient, so no talking religion. But mostly, I remember he's the best confidence artist in all of Warsaw. Could con a baby out of its mother's arms.

There's a younger boy not far away, attracting customers. Lizard's great with those little urchins. Much more patient that I ever was with the babies in my gang. I grin, seeing Lizard's pockets bulging with other items to sell: candy, cigarettes, lighters, hell, maybe even a moving picture camera or two! It's too hot for a coat but his is there on the steps—his portable department store.

I watch in awe for several minutes. I have to wonder where I'd be now, if not for Sniper, if not for the jeweler, if not for Vienna. I take a few steps closer.

"Got a cigarette for an old friend?"

He whips around and, look there! He doesn't recognize me. I take my cap off and ruffle my short hair. That does it.

"Jesus, Joseph, and Mary!" he exclaims.

"No, just Arab."

"Arab?" The gold tooth he used to brag about is missing. "You're alive!"

"To some I am."

"How long have you been back in town?" He offers me his hand and we shake.

"About a week."

"Well, why'd you take so long to look me up?"

"It's just been a mad social whirl."

"Last I heard, your old man sent you to some ooh-la-la girls' school somewhere."

"Vienna. Wanted to learn how to waltz."

He laughs hard. "Well, I'm glad you waltzed back into Warsaw!" He pulls me aside, taking me in from head to toe. "Look at you! You've grown, you've . . ." He turns me around. "But we need to find you a new couturier. You're getting too old—dare I say pretty?—for this tomboy shit."

"It's what all the fashion-monger street arabs are wearing this season in Vienna."

He hands out a newspaper and takes a coin. "Thank you, ma'am."

"Say, Arab, I've been walking around with a rock in my shoe for some time now." His voice is now low and sincere.

"Well, I thought you'd be smart enough to stop and shake it out, Lizard." I give him a playful shove.

"No, I owe you one. You got to believe me, I had no idea Sniper would put you up to that jewelry job. I never would have introduced you to his gang. Can you forgive me?"

"Ah, don't worry. I was young and stupid."

There's an awkward pause and then our eyes meet.

"Well, we were all young and stupid," he says. "All of us. But hey, let's talk about success, not failure."

"Always the optimist, eh, Lizard?"

"Well, you either laugh or you cry."

"Yeah. And if you cry, you die," I say, my voice a bit harder. A little piece of me wants to show him how much I've changed.

He catches my eye. "Guess you've grown wise, huh?"

"Wise as Solomon. Had my own gang in Vienna."

"Thank you, sir!" he says, selling another paper. "Come on, I know a place. I'll buy you lunch. You look like you could use some meat on your bones."

Lizard hands the remaining stack of papers to the little boy. "And don't take any slugs," Lizard warns him, pretending to bite down on a coin to check it.

The little boy smiles up at him, displaying two missing front teeth. Lizard smiles back. "Okay, just watch, then. And make sure you go find your brother after. He's shining shoes on the corner. I want you off the streets before dark."

The little boy nods, holds up a paper, and lisps to the passersby, "*Ga-sthzety*! *Ga-sthzety*!"

"You've always looked out for your gang, haven't you?" I say as we walk down the steps.

"Wish I'd looked out better for you. Anyway, someone has to watch out for these brats."

"How many do you have?"

"Six. Warsaw has never lacked for orphans and little beggars." He leads us away from the square, down an alley to a cheap alehouse.

We order beer and sandwiches. "So tell me, what's the news on the outside?" Lizard asks. "I mean, you say you were in Vienna? Were you there for the *Anschluss*? Saw the newsreels. Impressive! Tens of thousands of people cheering Hitler's—what do they call it? Unification?"

"Make that a quarter of a million people. Raked in a small fortune picking pockets while they were being 'unified.'"

"You've got to love a distracted crowd," Lizard says, sipping his beer.

"Until you get caught," I say, frowning. "Got a little too careless."

"The great Arab of Warsaw? Thought you said you grew wise. Tsk, tsk."

"As good as any other reason to come back to Warsaw. Except timing has never been my strong suit. Does the expression 'from the frying pan into the fire' mean anything to you?" I say, catching his eye.

"What do you mean?"

"I've seen this." I tap the table for emphasis. "I know what's coming. Take a deep breath, Lizard. What you smell is war. Right over there." I point west.

"Well, we have an army. Air force. Cavalry."

"Hell, there's an image! A horse and a rider up against a German tank," I say, recalling the panzer tanks rolling into Austria by the dozen. "Best you could hope for is a horse crapping on one."

He lets out a long sigh. "You're right. I just don't know what's going to happen to me, mine, my boys. Everything."

"I'll tell you what's going to happen, Lizard. Where there's war, there's opportunity. And I intend on surviving just fine."

"Easy for you to say. You can kiss your father's ring, beg forgiveness, and live back home."

"Hell no."

"Then what? I'll tell you, Arab, there are no jobs here in Warsaw. No legitimate jobs, that is. Military is asking for sign-ups, but I don't think you'll pass the physical, even dressed like that."

I feel a sneeze coming on and reach for the scented hankie in my pack. As I tug it out, my beat-up notebook comes with it. Lizard spots it and pulls it out. I reach for it, but he holds it beyond my reach.

"Well, I remember this," he says, leafing through it. "Your, what, diary? Journal, for your little poems?"

I snatch it back and put it away.

"I thought maybe you'd become a writer or something in Vienna. It's perfect for starving poets, they say."

I scoot my chair back a bit. "I actually learned a lot in Vienna. And it has nothing to do with poetry," I say, leading him away from the subject of my weak and weary scribblings.

"Such as?"

"Learned some new cons. Some counterfeiting. And I don't care how deep a pocket is—I can get in and out of it before the mark even breaks wind."

He laughs. "Same old Arab. Cocky as the Queen of Hearts!"

"So, I'm thinking . . . my skills, your skills, your boys . . . your shining personality, my dazzling good looks . . ."

"Gang up together?"

"Well, I prefer to think of it as a club. Called mine the Meet Me in Hell Club. Who doesn't like to join a club? Bet we can find some fine young men, like I had in Vienna."

"Fine young men? How many 'fine young men' did you 'have'?" he asks, raising his eyebrows.

A bit of a silence. I'm leaving it at that. "So, I hear you and Sniper have a bit of a turf war going on."

He laughs. "Ha! I got a feeling our little turf war is going to be child's play if what you say is true, and the Krauts do set up housekeeping here. How's your German?"

"Excellent, actually. Another thing I picked up in Vienna. So, it's settled?" I say, raising my second glass of beer to Lizard. "Team?"

"*Jawohl,*" he answers. "That and *nein* are all I know. Think it'll be enough?"

"It will be if you stick with me. Only, let's get one thing settled, right here and now."

"Oh great, already the female is calling the shots," he says, giving my arm a shove.

I sit up straighter and look him in the eye. "I'm serious, Lizard. We're fifty-fifty on this. But I warn you, I've changed. A lot. I won't be pushed or bullied or made a fool. Like before."

He cocks his head. "I think you're confusing me with Sniper."

"Just so you know. No one takes advantage of me. Not anymore."

"Uh-huh," he says, running his tongue through the hole where his gold tooth used to be—a habit I see he's formed when thinking. "Well, okay then. Shake?"

"Shake."

"I got to get back to my boys. How about we meet up here in, what, say a week? That give you enough time to get settled?"

"Deal. One week. That makes it . . ." I mentally count off the days.

"September first," he says. "Right here."

SEPTEMBER, 1939

I.

WHAT THE HELL WAS THAT? I SIT UP STRAIGHT IN BED. ALL sounds seem louder in this cheap, rooftop garret. Thunder?

Another huge boom! The whole building rocks! That's not thunder! I grab my pants, haul them on as I trip toward the window. The air is cut by the whine of the air raid siren. Another drill? At what, six in the morning?

The siren clashes with a new sound from the skies and becomes an ear-piercing, steady drone. I look up. The planes appear.

"Messerschmitts," I whisper. God, they look almost otherworldly! Like dozens of flying black crosses in formation. For a second, I'm mesmerized by them.

I look around. Quick! What do I need? My coat, my cash, my journal—stuff it all into my satchel and sling it over my shoulder. What else? I grab my shoes, not bothering with the laces. Already the hallway is filling with confused, half-awake people. I weave my way through them, down the stairs, no eye contact, no nothing. Get out, fast!

Outside, half-clothed people are running in every direction, mumbling, crying, shouting.

Where do I go?

What shelter is closest?

What the hell is happening?

A shell hits nearby. Chunks of brick, wood, glass, and concrete blast up and then rain down and I plaster myself against a building. Back alleys! Come on, Arab. Move! You know where you are! This is my territory. I know every deserted cellar, every vacant building, and every back alley in this district. Knowing is easy, but getting there in this chaos, fire raining down, everything exploding all around me, is another.

Billows of dust and smoke choke the streets. Cars speed about, honking. People scream; a runaway horse nearly levels me. Some people are paralyzed, frozen in horror.

Then, two smaller planes come screeching down, barely missing the building tops. Who knew an airplane could fly so low, so fast, and rain machine gun fire at targets—people targets? Some people—targets—stop to look up, dumbfounded, and they're shot before my eyes.

I feel a tug on my pants cuff. "Help. Help," a woman calls up. She's covered in blood. Her child is in her arms. "Take her. For the love of God, take her!" the woman pleads. "Get her to safety."

The sky grows even darker as the planes circle back around.

"Please! Save my daughter!" the woman cries out, spitting blood. Her daughter is barely moving. What do I do? I can't take her! I can't . . . God, this little girl could just as easily be my Ruthie. The plane is coming in for another pass and I snatch the child up, hold her to my chest, her tiny legs bobbing against me as I run.

I duck in the nearest alley and try to get my bearings. The child moans softly. "Mama, Mama."

I cradle her head to my shoulder. "Sh," I say. I look around and spot a door. I gently set the child down and use a garbage can lid to break the door window. I reach around, unlatch the door, grab the child again, and stop. The cool air brings the scents of fresh cut pine, paint, and varnish. I feel for the first step down, but it's not a step, it's a ramp.

Another crash comes from above. The child whimpers. I feel her warm blood soaking through my shirt. I slowly feel my way down the ramp and shuffle over to the wall. I sit down and place the child on my lap. She's not heavy. Maybe three? Four? I remember Ruthie, sobbing in my arms before I was sent away.

I reach for my pack and feel around for my lighter.

It works on the third click. My eyes sting, but I can see around me. Good God. I'm surrounded by coffins. Well, this place should be busy tomorrow. I damn myself for thinking it. The child's groan brings me back to the here and the now. I hold the lighter over her head, but I have to look away. What can I do? The gash along her shoulder is deep. Too deep. I didn't know blood could be this dark. I take my jacket off and wrap it around her, tying the sleeves together to apply pressure. I hold her to me and rock her back and forth. Her crying has all but stopped.

I light a cigarette and watch the smoke drift off into the warehouse. A long silence. Is it over? Then I hear the loudest boom yet! I protect the girl's head. There is a gust of smoke and dust from the alley above.

Finally, silence, for what seems like an hour. The sirens blast. It's the all-clear signal. All clear, I think to myself. Nothing's all clear out there. I get to my feet, carry the little girl up the ramp, and look through the alley before going out. The crates, cans, boxes are now scattered and smashed up against the walls. I can barely make my way through the rubble. A chalky haze rises like fog in the morning sun.

I stop, looking into the street, unable to take this all in. I lean back against the wall and pull in deep, steady breaths. I look down at the child, now limp and heavy in my arms. Her death rattle came just after the all-clear.

People start milling about, crying, calling, cursing.

I find the child's mother, right where I last saw her, only now a tree branch has fallen across her legs. I kneel and carefully place the child next to her mother—face to face. This is where the child should have died—here, in her mother's arms. I empty the pockets of my jacket, pull out a wad of bloodstained money and the scented hankie, also soaked with blood. I place the jacket over their faces.

I turn my back. Unsteady, I have to lean against the side of a building. I put my head back and look at the now empty sky. Blue, serene, none the worse for wear. Looking up means the tears flow back into my ears and can't wash down my face, cleanse away the splatters of blood, and tell the world how very, very scared I am.

I go back to the rubble in the street. People are milling about, crying, screaming out names, moving debris, dousing fires. Are they moving in slow motion or am I just seeing them that way?

I wipe my face with my sleeve and walk away.

I slip into the safe, dark comfort of the nearest sewer.

II.

"ARAB!"

I turn and look around. I know the voice, but here in all this chaos and rubble . . . "Lizard!"

We're in each other's arms, holding, soothing, holding tighter. "You're all right?" he asks.

"Yes, yes. You?"

"Two of my boys." He shakes his head as though to knock the image out of it. "A shell came through our hideout." His face is contorted, his eyes bloodshot. "Got some glass in my leg and side. God, the whole city . . . Your family? How about them?"

"I got a call through to a neighbor. The whole district was spared. Knowing my damn father, he probably stood outside and dared them to hit him. I can just see him—shaking his fist and warning the Messerschmitts, 'That's far enough!'"

"But this is war, Arab. Maybe it's time to swallow your pride and go back there. Your family has money and connections. Get out of Poland while you can." I remember the passes I stole when I entered Poland—what—a lifetime ago?

"You don't know my father. I'm dead and buried to him. Complete with gravestone. He's not going to let a little thing like a German invasion get in the way of his hate for me. Somehow, he'll come up with a way *I* caused all this."

Lizard offers me a cigarette from his pack. My hands are shaking. As Lizard tries to light our cigarettes, his hand shakes, too. We force a chuckle. "Hold still."

"You hold still!" I return, trying to aim my cigarette toward his trembling match. "I haven't stopped shaking since that first attack." We smoke and look around. Nothing is recognizable. The nightly shelling, the fighting, and the news of the German army fast approaching the Warsaw borders.

"Did your flat hold up?"

"No. Whole building is gone. I got out just in time." I hold back a shiver.

"God, what was it, last night or last week? Time is just . . . Time is—"

"Two weeks, Lizard. They've been pounding us for two weeks!"

"How have you been surviving? Did you get a food ration card yet?"

"I've been combing through bombed-out rooms, homes, kitchens." I look down at my bloodied shoes and take a huge breath to hold down the haunting visions. "Bodies. Getting money, anything . . . off of bodies."

Lizard grabs my hand and his eyes fill. "Come on. Let's just walk. Find a park. Maybe a drink."

We walk across the street, step over the legs of a dead horse, head west. The only thing between us is our cigarette smoke.

There's a park bench, pretty as you please and welcoming, unharmed between two craters where shells have landed. "Oh look. The Krauts missed something," I say, indicating the bench. I look up and yell to the sky, "Oh Adolf! You missed this bench! Yoo-hoo! Over here!"

"Cut that out. Come on, Arab." He pulls me down and we sit, smoke our cigarettes down to our fingertips, and toss the butts into the crater. I see the remnants of a child's bicycle sticking out of the dirt.

"What happens now?" Lizard asks, looking around.

"Well, they say our air force is gone. Leaders have fled. Reports are the Krauts'll be in Warsaw any time. You've seen the posters looking for recruits. You going to enlist?"

"What, carry a pop gun and be a front-line target? No thanks."

"Well, I have my plan. I've got some stashes around town. Going to liberate all the goods I can, find a hole, hunker down, and see what becomes of all this."

"Well, I wish you luck 'liberating' cigarettes. Already the price has skyrocketed." He holds up the pack. "Cost me a fortune."

"The great Lizard bought cigarettes? What's this world coming to?"

He laughs and nods his head in agreement. "I guess I need to step up my game. I just don't know what's going to happen next."

"I'll tell you what's going to happen next. I've seen this all before. The Nazis are going to take over Poland. Maybe they don't get the welcoming committee they got in Austria, but nothing's stopping Hitler now. What's that he says— 'one people, one nation, one leader.' Well, I'm one person in one nation under one leader. Me. And that's just the way I like it."

"Every man for himself, huh?" Lizard says. I can tell by his low voice, his cold stare at his feet, this isn't sitting well with him. "Whatever happened to safety in numbers? Looking out for each other? Thought maybe you and me would . . . take care of each other."

I look at him. No one has taken better care of me than me the last two years.

"Look, I agreed to team up. But I don't need anyone taking care of me. I'm pretty damn good at taking care of myself."

"Well, then maybe you can take care of me." If not for his big grin and batting eyes, I'd think he was serious. "How do you say 'pretty please' in German?"

"Never say that to Germans, whatever you do. They'll get a big head," I say, giving him a playful push.

Our smiles meet and disappear together. "Look, how about you go your way and I go mine, and we meet up at Three Crosses when things settle down? You go take care of your boys."

A last embrace. "Take care of yourself," he whispers in my ear.

I break away, but stop on the corner and turn with a grin. He's patting his pockets, looking for the pack of cigarettes I just swiped.

OCTOBER, 1939

I.

FOUR WEEKS! POLAND IS CONQUERED IN TWENTY-EIGHT DAYS. Has to be a new world record. Not just beaten, not just wounded and humiliated, but vanquished.

I watched those four weeks unfold from my hideout, an abandoned apartment in a building vacated for demolition —ha!—and it's one the Germans missed on their bombing raids. No lights or gas, of course, but I have a few candles and my flashlight. I use them only when I have to.

We get radio broadcasts and one-sheet bulletins almost hourly, handed out on the street and pasted on billboards, light poles, anything. They've either bombed, torched, or taken over our government buildings, even the Royal Castle. Then hospitals, bridges, museums, even park statues get theirs. Oh, these clever Krauts! It's almost like they go looking for our churches, our opera houses, theaters— our entire culture! Then wham! Trucks come through with barkers and loudspeakers, announcing new rules and regulations. Do this, don't do that. Blah, blah, blah. Damn tiring.

The Krauts set up food kitchens, bread lines, and first aid centers, but you need identification and ration cards to use those. Not this girl. I have plenty. I've loaded this place with food, water, and things to barter and trade. I've used these past four weeks to get ready for just this very thing. Any deserted home, any bombed-out or boarded-up business is mine to pillage—sometimes fighting off other pillagers, street ruffians, dogs, and rats.

It doesn't take the Germans long to seize all the news-papers and replace them with their own. Who cares? I can steal Kraut papers and sell them just as easily. Just haul a bundle off a delivery wagon, go two blocks over, and sell them on a corner.

I watch the street below each and every time before ven-turing out. The soldiers, tanks, trucks, horses are arriving by the trainload. Everywhere you look—Nazis, horses, soldiers, lines, announcements. Got to hand it to that Hitler. He's got this invasion thing down to a science.

I slowly move the torn window curtain aside and peer out. The bright autumn sun gives the plaza below a serene glow. The Germans have set up barricades along the boule-vard below, and just a few people are milling about.

Well, this could be trouble: I count sixteen SS soldiers with rifles at the ready across their chests, trotting up the middle of the street. A street vendor quickly turns his cart into an alley. A dog barks, then takes off. Even the dogs of Warsaw already know when to expect trouble.

Two little boys are hiding behind what was once a foun-tain. Their heads pop up as they hurl rocks at the soldiers. One little urchin stands up and shouts, "Nah nah nah-nah nah!" and exposes his backside. He and his buddy fall back behind the fountain, laughing.

"Oh, do not do that, kid," I mutter, fogging up the window.

A rock hits a soldier. He seizes his arm and whirls around. He aims his rifle. The boys screech and turn tail. Then, a fel-low soldier presses his comrade's rifle down, picks up a rock, and hurls it at the boys, hitting one square in the back.

The men laugh. "Nah nah nah!" the one who hurled the rock says, wiggling his own backside at the boys. He and his comrade have to trot to catch up with the others. Now the soldiers split into two groups. One group surrounds the building across the street. The other group trots toward my building.

"Damn," I whisper. Why these dead, empty buildings? What could they possibly be looking for? Move it, Arab!

I stash anything I have out under a floorboard and run into the hall. I'm on the fourth floor. I listen over the stairwell down the center of the building and hear their voices shouting orders.

"Check every room! Every closet! Not just the ones along the boulevard!" I understand everything they say. Thank you, Vienna. Not speaking German can get a girl killed.

Some light trickles down from the skylights. Thank God I know the lay of this building! I run toward the janitor's room. I remember seeing a dumbwaiter there.

But there's no light in here. I grope the wall until my fingertips find the two buttons for the dumbwaiter. Then I find the handle and carefully lift up the door. I close my eyes, as if that can lessen the clinking sound it makes. I listen and only hear faint echoes as the soldiers call back and forth to each other. I heard the crash of doors, shattering of glass. What the hell are they looking for? Couldn't be me! I haven't done anything. Well, not much.

I reach into the abyss of the dumbwaiter, but I can't feel it! Where's the damn cage? I grope around until my hand latches onto the cables.

The voices are closer. On the third floor by now, maybe even the fourth. Footsteps on crushed glass, more orders, more responses. "Did you hear something?" a German asks.

"Quiet!" another snaps back.

I hold my breath. Too close!

Forget the damn cage! I climb through the opening. My foot gropes for anything to get a purchase on. My toes find a ledge. I slip my whole body in, both feet on the narrow ledge in the shaft. I pull the door down, leaving just enough room so my fingers can grasp the rim. My other hand holds on tight to the splintered, greasy cable. It's pitch dark, but I close my eyes anyway, as though that might make my heart slow down, my breathing dwindle to next to nothing.

Footsteps. Closer. I open my eyes and, through the small opening, there's a swath of light being cast through the room. I feel the beam reflect off my face. If the soldier knows where to look—if he sees the tips of my fingers clinging to the rim—I'm dead.

"All clear here!" he calls out. I hear them move on.

I don't even exhale yet. Wait, wait, wait, Arab. Not yet. I'm frozen here for an hour, a day, I don't know, except it's a lifetime. My muscles quiver as my grip begins to loosen, one tendon at a time.

All I can hear now is the groan of this cable and the *drip, drip, drip* of water from some broken pipe below me. I slowly lift the door, an inch at a time. Finally, I grasp the ledge and haul myself out. I melt down the wall and want to dissolve here, massaging feeling back into my cramped hands and legs. How long can a heart beat this fast and not just stop cold?

I've been in some scrapes before, even in the dark, rancid sewers, but never once have I been trapped in a small shaft, the whim of a thin, faint beam of a flashlight deciding my fate.

They say we should know our enemies. I don't know my enemy yet, but one thing's for certain—I sure as hell respect him.

II.

"WHAT THE—?" I GIVE ONE OF THE BACK DOORS TO MY BUILD-
ing another push. Locked? From the outside? I wipe some
whitewash off the side window and peer around. Lumber
and chain. Barricaded. So, those Krauts weren't searching
the building yesterday. They were—what?—securing it?
Making sure it was empty, and then locking it up tight?

Stupid Krauts. There are at least six ways out in the basement of this relic. Child's play.

I walk around the building, and the one across the
street. Everything is barricaded. The streets have concrete
blocks and barriers and even benches facing the street. In
sloppy Polish, they post signs: NO ADMITTANCE, STAY CLEAR,
DO NOT CROSS, THIRD OF MAY BOULEVARD TO REMAIN CLOSED,
PARADE ROUTE.

"Parade route?" I ask out loud, taking down the poster.
"Parade route?" I look down the street, now clear of cars,
buses, horses, corpses.

Then I remember Vienna. Of course! The Germans' victory parade. Oh, those Nazis do love their spectacles! Blocks
and blocks of soldiers in precise formation, parading for
Hitler and his Hitlerites. Can't miss this! I look at the flier—
tomorrow, ten sharp. I go about my errands. Need to get a
paper for the latest news and make sure I have everything I
need for tomorrow.

———

This is the best seat in the house—right out my window! I have a pair of binoculars, a bag of peanuts, and a bottle of beer. Not my favorite brew, but this is war and things are tough all over. To my right, I can see clear down Third of May. They've erected a viewing stand just down the block. I watch as the crowds begin to form. But something's different here. These aren't the flag-waving, cheering crowds of German-Austrians—"spineless whores," I remember one editorial calling them. These are a shell-shocked people lining the parade route—exhausted, defeated, humiliated. Hope Hitler isn't expecting garlands and rose petals. I had no opinion then and I have no opinion now. Political opinions might get a girl killed. I just want to watch Hitler's show-stopping encore.

The viewing stand fills with black leather and caps and boots and back-slapping and saluting officers. Bring on the show! I toss some peanut shells out the window and lean out to see down the street. Just like during that first blitzkreig, I can hear it before I see it. The drums and the brass! Then, coming into view, a troop of flag-bearers, swishing in unison and keeping step to the beat of the drums. I grab my binoculars. The only ones impressed, clapping and smiling, are the Nazis lining the streets and in the stands. The people behind the barricades hardly even move. Even the children stand still and mute. I find Hitler and his staff. At least they're having a good time.

How do they do that? How do ten thousand *Wehrmacht* troops step all in time like that? How long do they have to practice to get it so perfect? How do they even have time to invade a country? Look at those motorcycles and their sidecars! Even men walking their bicycles goose step to the beat of the drummers.

They must have requisitioned every black horse in all of Europe! Even those damn Nazi horses seemed to sweat confidence, lockstepping as one to the beat of the kettle drummer, heads high, eyes straight, nostrils flared.

Then dozens and dozens of long cannons on wheeled wagons pulled by small trucks. How far can those cannons shoot? How many Polish people have they already dispatched? How do the Nazis protect their ears when they shoot them off? What's the kickback on one of those things? How long does it take to polish those sabers to make them shine? Hmmm, are those bridle bits made of real silver? I zero in on one with my binoculars. Wonder what silver goes for now on the black market.

How can the drivers in those panzer tanks see where they're going? So many swastikas on so many flags look like red and black pinwheels on the wind.

It's quite a show. It really is. Even better than Vienna. I'm impressed. Anyone who isn't, who doesn't sit up and take notice, is dead as a dormouse. Might Makes Right. Girls learn that one early on. Meek Makes Weak. Some old con artist, ugly as sin but bright as diamonds, once told me, "Girl, growing wise don't make for pretty, but it makes for old." I'm beginning to understand what she meant.

I raise my binoculars and there he is: Der Führer Ringmaster himself, admiring his troops as they pass for his inspection. He and his high-ranking toadies stand out, shining of new black leather against their red-carpeted platform.

I'll have to remember what the difference is in those uniforms—black, blue, green, brown. Why can't Hitler just pick a color and stick with it?

Oh, I love this part! The troops not only step in unison, they even think in unison. As they pass Hitler's platform, they turn their heads in one crisp, well-timed movement while Hitler *Sieg Heils* them back. "Well done!" I cheer in a standing ovation. "Well done, you miserable *szwabs*." One people, one nation, one leader. Well, Adolf! You've done it again! Please, no encore.

The parade kicks up the white, chalky dust that used to be buildings and streets and God knows what else. Black, red, white—like their swastika. You just have to love a theme.

I turn my binoculars back to the platform. "So, there you are again, Adolf," I mutter, taking a good, long look. He looks older than he did in the newsreels and papers. For a man who's just conquered an entire country in less than a month, I think he should be looking pretty damn proud of himself. Instead, he looks—what, cordial? Chatty?—pointing here, pointing there, perhaps saying, "Keep that park, blow up that church, move the Vistula River so it flows west to east in summer and east to west in winter."

Now the band comes closer. They march up and stop in front of the platform, glowing of spit and polished brass. The men on the platform all rise soberly. I can hear the faint refrains of "Deutschland Über Alles," Hitler's catchy theme song—I remember how it echoed up and down the streets of Vienna.

I scan the platform, looking at each member of the victory committee. If this was the telescope on a high-powered rifle instead of a pair of stolen binoculars, I might have a good, clean shot at him and his leather-clad men. Click. Bang. Dead. Make a note, Arab—get a gun. Chances like this don't come very often.

The faces of the people all seem to look the same. A silent crowd bearing witness with shock and disbelief. Still and all, it's a parade to remember.

I look away for a moment as I scan the newspaper I bought earlier and mutter a new headline of my own, "Warsaw Fucked." Says here we're under the "General Government." "What the hell's that?" I ask the paper. I scan the article for the dos and don'ts and legals and illegals, the rules and other Nazi crap. Makes no difference to me. I have my favorite trio to look after: me, myself, and I. After all, this is war.

When the crowd starts to disperse, I grab some soap in my stash and decide to commemorate this auspicious occasion with a little graffito. I head down and out onto the streets and scribble on the window of an abandoned dress shop:

Hitler arrived

Mustache and all

October five, after the fall

Since that day

Everything's rotten

Hitler's gone

But not forgotten

III.

"YOU THERE! BOY! HALT!"

I stop cold and hold my bundle of newspapers to my chest. People are being conscripted off the streets to scoop up parts of dead things, haul away a rotting horse, or overturn a burned-out car. I've already been stopped twice and told to relinquish something: my thick work boots and then the brown raincoat I'd only that day stolen off a coat rack. Each time, I know I'm being tested. It doesn't take much to ignite these golems, these automatons. I've watched them mow down an old woman for not crossing the street when they approached. They were a lot nicer in Vienna.

So I know how I react, how I smile or don't smile, how I cock my head or bow my head, how I slink, waltz, or march over to the SS officer will set the bar for the rest of my life—which could be only a matter of minutes. What's it to be? Subservience, arrogance, defiance, or—

"Newspaper, Herr *Hauptsturmführer*?" I ask, making my decision. Yes, I know he's just a lieutenant, not a captain, but a little flattery can go a long way. Then I look up and see his face. He's striking! And young. Not much older than me—nineteen, twenty, tops. Arab, stop it! He's the enemy! Damn his looks! Didn't Sniper teach you anything?

"Yes, yes, I'll take ten copies," he replies in excellent Polish, dismounting his black horse, and taking a paper, oblivious of me.

I quickly get hold of my senses. "Ten?" I ask back, keeping my voice low.

"Hold my horse, boy."

I set my bundle down and hold the reins. The horse gives my arm a nudge. Probably the best-looking Kraut horse in the ranks. "They sure issue you beautiful horses," I say, thinking Ruthie would kill just to sit on this animal.

"Uh-huh," the officer mumbles, absently scanning the paper. "He's mine. I brought him with me."

"What's his name?"

"Hummel. Quiet, can't you see I'm reading!"

The horse keeps nudging me and I remember a half-eaten apple in my pocket. "Can he have this?"

Annoyed, he looks at me over the top of the paper. "Yes, yes. Fine." Then, he points to the papers. "How much?"

My mind races. It's such an easy racket confusing a foreigner the value of our currency. "For ten? Um, fifty *zloty*."

"Fifty *zloty*!" He casts me a chilly glance.

Uh oh. He knows. "Did I say *zloty*? I meant *groszy*." I smile sheepishly.

"Even that's outrageous!"

"Well, the cost has gone up since . . ." We lock eyes. My mouth goes dry. "Well, since you arrived."

"And why is that?"

I can smile the wings off flies. "Well, for one thing, newspapers are a rare commodity these days. Seems there's been a slight halt in the supply of paper. Some gossip about a factory burning down. I don't know, I never listen to gossip."

I pause, wondering if he knows what a smile is, but silently begging him to smile. He's the Aryan ideal. Tall, straight-backed, fair of eye and hair, healthy, ruddy cheeks, even sparkling, perfect white teeth. Wears his black uniform as though he were born with it on.

While he's combing through the paper, I force my thoughts back to business. I touch the beautiful silver bit in his horse's mouth. Must cost a fortune.

"And of course, these are collectors' editions," I continue.

"Collectors' editions?" he asks, giving me that cold look again.

"This is history in the making," I add. Then I notice the front-page photo of the cavalry corpsman atop his horse, Hitler saluting in the background. It's this very Jerry. "Well, look! *You* are history in the making!"

Is he blushing? Holding in a smile? "Yes." He rummages in his pocket, hands me a coin, takes the papers, and folds them into the black leather pouch behind his saddle.

"Sorry, sir. Fifty *groszy*."

"Look closer, boy. That is fifty *groszy*."

"Oh yes, I see that now." I pocket the two-*groszy* coin. "Thank you, Herr *Hauptsturmführer*."

"*Obersturmführer*," he corrects. "Best learn German rank insignia, boy. And learn the German language too, if you Poles want to survive in the new world."

"I speak a little German already. Lucky me, huh?"

"Good. I tire of your ugly Polish language."

He looks me over carefully. I know I'm being sized up. Little does the officer know he's being sized up, too. "Are you sure you have enough papers?"

"Yes, these are all I need," he replies. "For the men in the barracks." He indicates the money and says, "Best spend that soon. Deutschmarks are going to become the coin of the realm. And Germany is the realm. Your Polish *zloty* will be used to wipe Jewish asses."

"Well, I've had my broker invest my money in South American and Swiss bonds. Some American cash, of course."

There it is again. The slightest, narrowest, smile. "Too bad. Germany is the future. Not those second-rate countries."

I know better than to argue. Besides, at the rate the Germans are going, I think he very well might be right. I pull out a pack of cigarettes and offer him one. A good customer is a good customer, regardless of world domination, and tobacco transcends race, nationality, and religion.

"Smoke? They're Egyptian." Lie. They're Polish. "I can get you all you need."

He takes one and I notice the fine silver lighter he's pulled from his jodhpurs' pocket. "May I?" I ask. Heavy and engraved on both sides. FRIEDERICH VON SEGEN. I flip it over and read FOR FRITZ. MAY YOU CARRY THE FIRE WITH YOU ALWAYS. MOTHER.

"Very nice," the soldier says, inhaling as though he hasn't had a decent smoke in months. "Very good. Very . . . different, but pleasant. So, you sell cigarettes, too?"

"I can get you anything here in Warsaw. Anything—from a Polish tart to Chopin's heart." It's my standard street pitch.

"Chopin's heart? What's that? Some sort of Polish pastry?"

I know better than to laugh. "No, it's the heart of Chopin. It's entombed over there in the Holy Cross Cathedral. If there still is a Holy Cross Cathedral."

"Just his heart?"

"The rest of him is buried somewhere in France. If you want the rest of Chopin, well, that might take some doing, but I'm your connection."

"Why would I want any part of Chopin?" the lieutenant asks, almost relaxing now.

"Well, I only mention it because I read today that you Germans have outlawed all Chopin's music with the rest of the Polish artists. Guess it's Bach, Brahms, Wagner, and polka bands from now on."

Now he laughs! "I see. No, thanks. Not in the market for hearts today. But I'll keep it under advisement."

"Still and all, it would make a great conversation piece. A little war souvenir. Or a gift, say, for Herr Hitler . . . Der Führer?"

"And you're just the boy to get it, right?"

"For a price, of course."

"I assure you, if it's something Der Führer wants, he won't have to pay for it."

I smile and nod. It's a good point. "Like I said, anything you need. This corner's my usual place. Just look for me here. Tell you what, keep the pack," I add, pressing it into his hand. "I have more. Think of it as a welcome present."

"How old are you?" he asks, his voice harder now. Our tête-à-tête is over.

My heart races, this time out of fear. Polish boys and men are being abducted off the streets for work camps, fighting, or God knows what else. Here today, gone tomorrow. So I reply, "Old enough to smoke. Why?"

"Identification?"

Here we go again, I think. Careful, careful, Arab. Already some Jews I know are in hiding, drifting, fading quietly away, getting out of Poland altogether. We all know about Hitler's "Jewish problem"—which really isn't his Jewish problem but the Jews' Jewish problem.

"Have you seen the lines at the registration centers? And four hours for a loaf of bread?" I hope my cordial manner and shining smile will sway the interrogation. "But I'm not Jewish, if that's what you think." I've seen more than one poor man having to drop his pants to display his circumcision—or lack of it—to German officers. And then won't I be the talk of the barracks?

"Everyone needs to be registered. Everyone," he states stiffly. "You will be issued identification papers and a food ration card and your race will be noted."

I decide to smile. Be the dumb Pole he probably expects me to be. "Well, I'm just a stupid Polish Catholic." I edge closer and add, "But between you, me, and Hummel here, I'm not even sure I'm much of a Catholic."

The lieutenant crushes out his cigarette with his boot and replies, "It's not your religion we're concerned with. It's your blood. So get registered and tell your parents they need to—"

"Oh, my family was called to Berlin," I break in.

"Berlin?"

"Yes, Berlin." I casually exhale smoke. I sense his interest. "As a matter of fact, Father's reading a paper to . . ." I pause. What? ". . . a . . . the Society of Geo-Mediologists. He's an expert in his field. In fact, Hitler's people are very interested in his theories."

"I see. The son of scientist is a common street peddler?"

"Well, that's the whole theory of geo-mediology, though, isn't it?" I try not to look past him at the approaching soldier.

He insinuates himself into our conversation. This one is also tall and very thick-chested and he sports a Hitlerish mustache. I think my heart has dropped into my shoes.

"What's all this?" he asks, in broken Polish. Then, in German, "Hello, Fritz. Are you having trouble with this . . ." He looks me over. "This Pole?"

"No, Herr *Hauptsturmführer*, not at all," Fritz replies. Then back to me: "Continue. What theories?"

"Quite logical and simple, really. How can a brilliant man like my father sire one so stupid, like me?" I stand back and tap my head. "It's confounded science for years."

The imposing soldier doesn't understand Polish, and Fritz translates for him. "He *is* stupid, isn't he?" the intruder says. "Tell him I wouldn't go bragging about being so stupid. Every species weeds out its weak, sick, and old. And the stupid ones, like this shit, eventually do away with themselves. One way or another. It's nature's way."

I nod my head sadly in agreement to Fritz's much kinder Polish translation and say, "Precisely what my father says." I know I'm stepping dangerously close to being "weeded out, one way or another." Worse yet, being plucked.

When the young lieutenant shows his friend his picture on the cover of the newspaper, I take my leave, only to be stopped again by a loud, "Halt!"

I freeze, turn, and slink back. He holds out his hand. "My lighter!"

I try to look inferior and apologetic while reaching into my pocket. I hand it back. "See?" I tap my head again. "Stupid, stupid, stu—"

The butt of the captain's gun along the side of my head sends me spinning.

Not sure how long I've been out. I'm sitting against a wall, blood dripping down on my shirt clear through to my chest wrap underneath. My head is pounding. People walk over my legs, eager not to notice me.

I blink the crusty blood out of my eyes. What's this? I pull at the paper pinned to my chest. I squint to read it.

STUPID POLISH THIEF

I'm damn lucky I don't have a bullet hole between my stupid Polish eyes.

I touch my head, feel the gash, and wonder if my ear is split open.

"Think, Arab," I whisper, flinching. I'm too dizzy to get up just yet. Retaliate? There's a laugh. Defy? Another laugh. I think back on those boys with their rocks—that first small act of defiance, a little boy, sticking his tongue out, taunting a soldier. And that nearly got the little tyke shot in the back.

IV.

OVER THE NEXT FEW DAYS, I CONTINUE TO SELL ON MY CORNER and here he comes back again—the dashing, spit-and-polished, handsome, young, Polish-speaking SS Nazi with the horse named after a porcelain figurine. Fritz Von Segen. I'll be more careful this time. And I do have a little score to settle.

"Hello, Lieutenant," I say. A bandage is still wrapped around my head, anchored by my cap. "Can your horse have a carrot?" I ask. I already know how much he treasures this animal. A little grease never hurts, so I always try to have something for the horse.

"Cigarettes today?" My heart is jumping around. The last thing I want is another "conversaton" with his captain.

"Yes, please. Three packs, if you have them."

Another customer comes, tosses me a coin, and takes a paper off the stack next to me. "Thanks, Arab!"

"Arab?" Fritz's eyes widen. "Your name is Arab?"

"Nickname. Everyone calls me that."

"Odd name for a street kid in the middle of Warsaw."

"No, it's not. See, all us street kids are arabs. You know, street arabs? Or don't they have those in Germany?"

"Not where I grew up."

"Where was that?"

"Bavaria."

I'm imaging one of those alpine chalets with the Alps, skiers, and goats in the background, like I've seen in the travelogues. Where the upper crust vacations.

"Your head," he says, pointing.

"Sir?"

"You're bleeding."

"It'll stop. It always does."

"That lighter is dear to me. But Wilhelm didn't need to hit you that hard."

Well, this is interesting. A conscience? "I'm just glad it wasn't Wilhelm's lighter. I'd be dead, I'm sure."

"Wilhelm has a temper."

"I'll keep it under advisement. I was seeing double for a week. And believe me, I don't need to see double Germans!"

I hand him a Hummel figurine of a horse. "Here. On me. You know, to make up for that lighter episode."

"Wherever do you find these things?"

"Oh, people are selling anything they don't need. I buy from them, triple the price, and sell to you Germans. It's a nice system. Someone has to balance the rising cost of living." Our eyes meet and I tip my cap and grin. "Uh, make that the cost of not dying."

He laughs. "At least you're honest, Arab."

"That's what you think, Fritz," I say back. "You know, you could make a little something on the side if you sold these cigarettes to some of your comrades."

He frowns and shakes his head. "Well, that wouldn't be very fair, would it?"

Fair? Did a Nazi just say fair? My eyes widen in disbelief. I spread my arms with palms open upward and do a complete turnaround, indicating all of Warsaw around us. He gets my point. Smiles and takes his cigarettes. I look at the money in my hand—he's shorted me fifty *groszy*. Again.

V.

It's the first rule on the streets: opportunity makes the thief. The trick is to recognize the opportunity when it hits you in the face. Or maybe I'm still seeing double from being hit on the side of the head. I see double opportunity in those big silver S-shaped bits and the medallions on the bridles of the Nazi horses. And there's one captain in particular I'd love to settle up with.

Problem is, getting around is damn hard now. Cars and buses stop where they run out of gas and there's no such thing as a direct route anymore. What I need is a bicycle. I look everywhere, especially in front of office buildings. I find one poorly hidden in a park, so I'm quick to "requisition" it. Some kid gets a lesson, and I get a bike. After only a little banging and straightening, it rides fairly straight. Unlike the previous owner, I'm going to hide it well and guard it with my life. Who would ever think one's very life might depend on something as common, as simple, as a kid's bike?

A few times I've biked behind the cavalry units to the small, old hotel they've commandeered not far from the Saxony Gardens district. It's close to bridle paths and has a large, modern stable, an indoor riding arena, and a polo field with a track around it. Nothing but the best for Aryan horses, I figure. I know which soldiers exercise which horses on which days. It looks to me like this fierce SS Cavalry Corps consists of nothing more than rich boys and their rich horses, cantering the war away on a polo field, not a battlefield. Pretty nice way to ride out a war.

As I'm returning my bike to this week's hiding spot, I hear the clop of hooves. I run my bike over to the remaining oaks along the street and duck behind a tree. Four SS soldiers. Fritz is one of them. They trot together briskly, posting up and down in perfect unison.

I hop back on my bike and follow them, keeping a safe distance, to a tavern, already designated "*Nur für Deutsche.*" Getting so a conquered girl can't get a decent table at a conquered tavern anymore. Damn nuisance.

I stash my bike and watch the soldiers tie their horses and enter the tavern, leaving the four horses standing genially, barely winded from their trot through the district.

I've been around carriage and delivery horses often enough to know the basics. I ease closer, keeping one eye on the horses and the other eye on the tavern door. I pull out my knife, open it, and quickly go to work on the closest horse's bridle. I slice through the leather strap that connects the bit, including the reins, which fall limply to the ground. Horse doesn't even budge. Same thing with the second and the third. They just stand here, either too well trained to wander off, or too stupid to realize they can.

But the fourth horse issues a low snort when I approach. "Whoa, Hummel. It's your old friend, Arab," I whisper. "Steady." He keeps nuzzling and turning around, going for my pockets, looking for an apple or carrot. I already have three bits, so I settle for slicing the silver buckles from the girth of Hummel's saddle. Then I slice off the black saddle bag and take it for my collection.

Second rule of the streets: never stick around long enough to admire your handiwork. It's just as bad as returning to the scene of the crime or sticking around to watch the fire you've started. So I take my plunder and hop on my bicycle to get myself out of here.

Okay, so I break the second rule. I hear the soldiers coming out of the tavern and, slinking even deeper into the shade of the trees, I pause to watch. None of them notice anything and the horses aren't mentioning it.

Fritz Von Segen is the first to mount. Upsy-daisy! With nothing holding the saddle to the horse, he falls straight back on his perfect German ass, the saddle falling in his face. The other three laugh just as Hummel spooks, rears back, and runs off. Now all the horses are galloping away, stirrups bouncing as they bolt.

Now, no one is laughing. Except me.

I assume they have a nice, long, thoughtful walk back to their cozy quarters at the hotel, carrying what's left of their Aryan dignity. I take off in the opposite direction, a cocky whistle on my lips. Can't wait to tell Lizard. He'll yell at me for playing it so risky, but damn, it was worth it.

I enter my new home hole, pausing to listen for sounds of life on each floor. I close the door, lock it, and reach into the hole hidden behind a photograph of a constipated-looking old woman. I pull out a can of peaches, open it, and bolt down half. I don't know who the old woman is, but all I have to do is look at her and I'm not so hungry. A good reason to keep the old bat hanging there.

I shake the contents of Fritz's saddle bag out onto my bed. *Let's see, what does a man like him keep close?* A small silver flask. I take a sniff, then a pull. Whiskey. And not good whiskey. Probably the same swill I sold him just last week. I recognize the burn as it snakes down my gullet. Lizard can have it.

I pick up a silver locket. In elegant, well-worn engraving I can make out VON SEGEN. I click it open. Each side opens yet again, and there in front of me are the smiling faces of an elegant woman and three beautiful girls. His mother and sisters? I take a close look at the girl in the middle. She looks a little like my own Ruthie. So pretty.

I wonder if I could ever be half as pretty. Who am I kidding? And what the hell am I even thinking? War is no time to be caught being pretty. "Somebody should tell that to Fritzenheimer," I mumble down at the locket.

I click it back together and pick up the next item—a book, bound in leather. Byron's *Don Juan*. I leaf through it. Huh, it's in English. And I'll bet it's banned by the *Reich* in all languages. My eyes land on the title page. Inscribed in an elegant hand, in French, I read:

To FVS
LOVE OF MY LIFE,
HENRI

I narrow my eyes and think about this. I walk to the old lady's photograph on the wall. "How very, very interesting. Fritz has got himself a boyfriend. And not just any boyfriend, but a French boyfriend. So, tell me—how do you suppose an SS Nazi soldier-boy gets himself a French boyfriend?"

I have to smirk at the old woman's expression—I swear her eyes just popped! Guess I'll keep that under advisement, I think, hiding the book.

NOVEMBER, 1939

I.

I'VE STOPPED ALONG THE SIDEWALK TO BLOT MY BLEEDING HEAD. It's been two weeks since my run-in with Schneider, the captain with the temper, but the damn cut pops open all the time. Probably should have gotten stitches, but the lines for even an aspirin go around the block six times.

I continue on my way. Lots on my list today. Taking advantage of the weather—cold, but at least it's not raining or snowing. Now that I've had a few weeks to take it all in, I figure it's time to spread out. I've watched from a distance—noting the places they've set up as offices, headquarters, barracks. They've taken over just about every office building not destroyed. They're rebuilding inns and restaurants and taverns. They're seeing to their own Aryan comfort and safety first. Getting lights, gas, and water. Residents? Wait. We'll get to you. Jews? Forget it.

Part of getting to know my enemy includes knowing where and when they go out on patrol. My notebook is good for more than just my weak poetic scribblings. Far more important than my old angst is my new log: who, when, where, and why the patrols move, even if it's just a guess. Knowing when and where they are means I know where and when not to be, especially the ones on horseback.

I've never been one to keep all my eggs in one basket. I've been dividing up the spoils of my own war: food, identification, cash, and supplies. So I find deserted, safe places to stow my goods throughout the city. I have my home hole—another abandoned apartment building, not far from Three Crosses. I keep most of my stash there.

One hideout isn't far from Pawia Street, where my parents live. Each time I'm there, I check on my family's home. So odd—from the curb, from a distance, it's as though nothing has changed. Most of the buildings here are spared, the factories keep spitting out smoke, buses and streetcars run on schedule, people come and go. This posh district should have been the first to be bombed, I figure. If Hitler's plan was to wipe out his Jewish problem, then why spare this area? Still, I'm grateful. Ruthie is always in the back of my mind.

And checking on her is first on my list. Just to know she's still okay.

"Where're you heading, all dressed up?" Lizard asks, lifting the corner of my blue woolen scarf. I carefully liberated it from a man's coat as he stood in front of me in line for a streetcar.

"East."

"Need some company? Been awhile since I've been 'east.'" He says east like it's a snooty resort.

"Suit yourself." I start walking, and he matches my pace.

"Do you ever wonder what you'd do if you ran into your old man?" Lizard asks. "If you ask me, I think that's why you go east so often. Maybe hit him up for a few shekels."

"Well, I didn't ask you."

"I hear things are getting dangerous over there. So many Jews and all."

"So, you're afraid?"

"No, but I hear women need to be traveling in twos—"

I stop, indicate how I look, how I'm dressed.

"Oh. Right," Lizard says. "I forgot. It's just that . . ."

"You going to yap the whole way over there?" I shake my head and give him a hard look.

We walk in silence. I pick up a few apples off a vendor's cart, and we hitch a ride on the back of a delivery wagon.

"Brings back memories, huh?" Lizard asks, looking around the neighborhood at our childhood haunts. "Remember when you and me first met? You were sitting on a park bench, reading, with your, what was she, nurse?"

"Governess," I say. "Make that warden."

"And you saw me lifting a wallet?" Lizard says, grinning at the memory.

"And I chased after you."

"Thought sure you were going to turn me in or something," Lizard says.

"No, remember? I said either you show me how you did that or I'd tell on you."

Lizard looks off into the distance and thoughtfully sucks through his missing tooth. "Do you ever wonder, Arab? You know, if maybe we're just born this way?"

"What way?"

"You know. Sort of, born bad. Sure confused me back when I wanted to be a priest. Couldn't quite fit those two together. The whole good-evil thing."

"We used to call you the Pickpocket Priest," I say, trying to joke the serious tone out of his voice. He looks down at the apple in his hand. "Look, Lizard, think where you'd be if you were a priest. Is there a damn church even left standing here in Warsaw? Trust me, evil trumps good every time."

"Yeah, you're right," he says, smiling over at me. "And where would those brats in my gang be?"

"That's the spirit!" I say. "Come on, let's go. We can shortcut through the park."

We hop off the delivery wagon and enter the park. This area didn't escape the bombing raids.

"Oh, look. Poor horsey," I say. The statue of some long-dead hero on horseback has been hit directly, by the looks of it. The hero is gone, pieces of him collected and stacked up in a tidy little pile by some idiot.

"What were they going to do, put him back together? Humpty Dumpty style?" I ask Lizard, pointing to the remains.

The horse is a different story. He still stands, looking ahead, unwavering and unaware that he only has two legs left to stand on.

"Remember when we used to use that statue for target practice?" Lizard asks. "A beer says I can hit the horse right on the beak." He winds up his arm with great drama and then flings his apple core toward the sad statue, missing it by a quarter mile.

"You never were a good shot," I say.

"Let's see you do it. Get back here. Girls don't get closer shots."

I wind up and throw my apple core, hitting the horse square in the rump.

"Okay, we'll buy our own beers," Lizard says.

I lead the way toward my old home and we quietly hide, as I always do, in the shadows down the block.

Everything is fine.

"Let's get that beer," Lizard says, pulling me along.

So many shops are closed now, boarded up, many with the finality of that damn yellow Star of David painted across each one. I pause to look inside a window. The shop—or what once was a shop—is torn up, the remnants of a fire visible in a corner. These days it's a matter of wear it, sell it, or burn it. Someone's scribbled on the window with soap: GOING OUT OF BUSINESS SALE! COMPLIMENTS OF THE KRAUTS!

"Don't turn around," Lizard says, looking in the reflection of same window. "Sniper."

I see the reflection, too, now—he's standing across the street. "That's not Sniper. Look how that man's dressed. He's . . . God, that *is* him! What the hell is he up to?"

"What are those uniforms?" Lizard asks.

"Shit. SS," I whisper.

I pull my new scarf up around my face. Lizard pulls down his cap and we both slowly turn around. We watch Sniper chat cordially with the three soldiers. Even laugh.

"Bet I know what he's doing," Lizard says. "He's selling information."

"Bounty hunter?"

"I heard he was getting into the hard trades. Whores, drugs. Look at the way he's dressed. See that?"

We watch the exchange of money. Sniper points to the apartment behind him.

"And he's selling out his own," I say. "My father owns that building. Only upstanding Jewish families in there."

"He'd probably sell out his own mother, the bastard," Lizard says. I recognize that hardness in his voice. He doesn't use it very often.

"Snakes don't have mothers. Sniper was hatched, not born," I remind him.

Lizard grunts a snort of laughter. "Good point."

We watch Sniper and the soldiers share a joke or something. Laughter, back-patting, congratulations. I nudge Lizard. "The irony is Sniper looks so goddamn Jewish."

A scuffle on the sidewalk steals our attention. Soldiers appear, scattering people as they approach us. Then, soldiers from the other direction appear and trot up the steps of the apartment building. More soldiers appear from behind, surrounding the area.

"Uh oh," Lizard says, pulling me into the street to avoid the people beginning to scatter. There is a sudden chaos.

"This way!" Lizard shouts.

"No!" I pull my arm out of his grip. "Split up!"

Traffic is stopped as more people spill into the streets, trying to avoid the same soldiers we are. I glance at Sniper.

"He's seen us!" I say. "Vanish!"

Lizard melts into the crowd in one direction and I try to make my way toward the sidewalk, where I know I can duck into an alley or shop. I weave along, glancing over my shoulder. Damn! Sniper and one of his SS friends are not far behind. Do something, Arab!

I enter through the first shop door I find open.

"What's going on out there?" a woman asks, looking through her shop window at the roundup outside.

"Roundup."

"Oh dear," she says. "Those poor people."

"Got a dressing room?" I ask, pulling a coat off a rack.

She looks back outside. "Oh my God. I don't want any trouble."

"Lady, please," I say.

"Through those curtains."

I disappear into the back of the store. Damn! No back door. A dressing room, small office and storeroom, and a bathroom. I hear the bell on the shop door ring.

"May I help you?" the clerk asks. I hear the fear in her voice. Lady, careful.

"Sir, you can't go . . ." I hear the clerk say. "Ladies only!"

"We're not looking for a lady," Sniper says.

I slip through the stacks of boxes, nearly tipping over a naked mannequin. There's an old desk, stacked high with boxes and papers. I hide under it, pulling more boxes around me. One thing is for sure. I'm trapped.

I hear them pull the curtains aside. "No one here," the SS soldier says in fractured Polish.

"I told you that!" the clerk says. I hear a slap, a scream, her fall.

The bathroom door opens and the footsteps come closer. I hold my breath, remembering the eternity I spent in the dumbwaiter not that long ago. I hear them looking around the room.

"Are you sure you saw her come in here? This is a lot of work for just one street punk. I have to get back to my unit."

"No, trust me, you want this one!" Sniper says.

"Ha! Look at this!" the soldier says. "May I have this dance, Fräulein?"

Damn, I want to look but don't dare to move. What the . . .? From the shadow on the wall I see what I think is the big, bad SS Nazi dancing with the naked mannequin!

"Fine! You stay here and make love," Sniper says. "I'm heading back out. I have work to do." Footsteps, curtain screeching along its track, the bell on the door ringing.

That leaves me and Fred Astaire.

"*Danke*, Fräulein," he says. I'll bet anything he's bowing to her. Then, finally, the same sounds—footsteps, curtain, doorbell.

I count to thirty, then slowly rise from my hiding spot.

I look at the mannequin. I take the coat I pulled off the rack and drape it around her. "Here," I say. "It's cold. Cover yourself up."

I walk over to the brave clerk, who's holding her bleeding jaw. "You okay?"

"I can't wait until those *szwabs* get hell out of Warsaw!"

"Here," I say, giving her a handful of cash. "For the use of the dressing room."

"But . . ."

"No, trust me. You've earned this."

She counts the money in her hand and looks back at me, astonished. "Look," I say, "it won't buy much once the Krauts outlaw Polish money and bring in their own, but see if you can buy your way out of Warsaw. Out of Poland, hell, get out of Europe. And take your naked friend in back with you. She's earned it, too."

II.

FUNNY, PEOPLE WEREN'T NEARLY AS PANICKED WHEN THE weather was warm and the sun was shining. Weather changes everything. Things are getting serious here in Warsaw. Everything is rationed and our meager allotments are getting more meager every day. Supplies have dwindled to next to nothing. The Germans are requisitioning everything—from men off the street to gas cans in garages—for "government work." Inconvenience gives way to concern, concern gives way to panic, and panic gives way to greed. And greed creates black markets. I'm already hip deep. Maybe I always have been. I know what people want, need. I find it and supply it.

Doing my best to keep business as usual. Papers, shoe-shines, cigarettes, knickknacks, anything I can get my hands on to sell on my corner. I'm not the only one in "the trades," by far. Vendors are everywhere, mostly selling family treasures and clothes. Anything.

Each day brings more deportations, more neighborhood cleansings, more roustings of Jews. An empty building is an invitation for the Krauts to barge in and look around for Jews in hiding and take anything they find. As I go about my day—exploring, bartering, requisitioning—I am always aware of the sounds that signal more danger. The bark of a loudspeaker, the pop of a gun, the screaming of neighbors, the shuffling of boot steps—all warning signs that another Jewish family is being hauled away.

Like right now. I stop in my tracks and hide behind a tree to wait this one out. This neighborhood is nice. Before the occupation, probably the worst thing that ever happened here was a stray dog messing with someone's fancy French poodle.

Across the street a soldier is flashing his Luger about and shouting orders. An old man carries an even older woman out to a lorry parked on the street. The man slips on ice, totters, then drops the old woman. He falls into a heap on top of her, nearly tripping the Nazi. The soldier swears and sets down his Luger to yank them up. He tosses them both like sacks of potatoes into the lorry. Then there's a gunshot from inside the building, and the soldier is called to help.

A small, blanket-shrouded head bobs up from the bed of the lorry. The old woman looks around. It's as though she knows I'm here, watching. At first, she looks confused, terrified. She touches her face where a trickle of blood runs down into her shawl. But now a very calm, peaceful smile comes to her face—like old people can look when they come to realize maybe they've lived too long and seen too much. She looks down at the gun at her feet on the lorry's tailgate.

Will the old girl have the chutzpah to reach down? Use the gun? Make a stand? Do something, anything, to save herself? Does she even grasp her fate?

The old woman looks back at me. No, there isn't any fight left in this woman. She's going to be shipped off to hell in a handbasket with the rest of her family. Wait! What's she doing? She slowly, slowly moves her foot to push the Luger until it falls to the gutter below the lorry.

More people are herded from the sidewalk and are loaded in. The old woman grasps the side of the railing, making room for them. Between the folds of her scarf, I see her slight, toothless smile, and her gentle nod toward me. It's a look of victorious surrender, if there can be such a thing. I return her nod, her smile. This is a godsend, and she and I both know it.

I wait until the truck has vanished down the street and things return to normal. People go about their business—some people's business is to ransack the house that family was just hauled out of. As for me, I venture to the gutter and sit down on the curb, keeping the weapon in my sight. I look like just another lost soul sitting in the gutter. Slowly, I use my foot to scoot the weapon closer. I toss my scarf down on top of it, look around again, then pocket the bundle, scarf and all.

I'd like to think that doomed old woman knows her one act of defiance and bravery adds to my small arsenal. Her death, my survival.

I pull a piece of chalk from my pack. I make my tribute to her, the chalk slipping on the sidewalk cement:

THE WOMAN WENT
WITHOUT A WORD
HER SMILE THE LOUDEST
I EVER HEARD

III.

I HEAR THEM BEFORE I SEE THEM. ANOTHER PARADE—ONLY THIS one is different and dangerous and now daily. I blend into the mute bystanders so I won't be run down. It's a parade of Jews, at least a hundred, each wrapped in several thick layers of clothing—so many on the children, they look like fat, stubby mannequins. The adults pull handcarts of what bare necessities they are allowed to bring—bedding, food, clothing—and push children in carriages. Women rush to sell rings off their fingers, bracelets off their wrists, books, silver, furs. Word gets around quickly, and these people already know: Fineries won't be needed. Cash will. I spot a jeweler buying for spit what I know will end up in his shop for outrageous prices. Occupation can be quite an occupation, actually.

I fall into step with a limping German soldier. He looks me up and down. His face is weary, so I offer him a cigarette. He hesitates, looks around, then takes one.

"Where are you taking these people?" I ask him in German.

"Elsewhere," he states wearily. We keep walking.

"All of them?"

"They go to factories."

"Factories where?"

"Elsewhere!" he repeats with a snap. "Work shall set them free." I can tell he has the same cold all of Warsaw is sharing. "You've heard the orders. Male Jews, fourteen to sixty, work." He gives me a closer look. His eyes are red and weepy. "How old are you?"

"I'm not a Jew. In fact, I'm not a male, and I'm only eleven. I'm big for my age." I smile innocently.

He gives me a pitying look as he shakes his head and puts his cigarette to his lips. "My sister's that way. You both better watch it." He coughs out the smoke.

I know what "that way" is, and I change the subject. "Those children can't work. What about those women?"

"They'll find something for them to do. They tell us everyone is going to be fine, if they work."

He stops and we both wait out his approaching sneeze. He lets go, sighs heavily, wipes his nose on his sleeve. "Damn Jews and their head colds!"

"Yeah, those Jewish colds can be killers." I keep a straight face.

He stops and gives me a look of concern. "You mean people die from these colds?"

"For some reason, only Aryans," I say, trying to match his serious tone. "Just make sure you get lots of chicken soup."

"Great. I'll probably end up back home at Stutthof."

"Where's that?"

"Just a little village up by the Baltic. They built a new Jew camp there. My father got work there, and he says they built a wing to study diseases and, hell, make three-legged women, for all I know. Stutthof is the last assignment I want. I'm sick of sick people!"

He coughs, not bothering to cover his mouth. "Goddamn Jews. Can I have another cigarette?"

I press the pack into his hands and watch the procession continue on down the road, off to a factory in a place called Elsewhere, where their work will set them free.

Several military trucks come barreling up the street in the same direction, honking their horns, the soldiers aboard shouting orders to move. I trot away to avoid being run down. More people, more trucks, some with people crammed into the backs. All guarded by soldiers with rifles at the ready.

I hop up on a stone wall to sit and watch.

"Well, I'll be damned. It's my old friend, Arab."

I whirl around, angry I've been caught off guard. Stupid! I'm a sitting duck here! My throat could have been slit and I would have deserved it.

"Go to hell, Sniper." I turn back around and keep watching the Jews' exodus.

"Now this is twice I've offered you the hand of friendship and twice you've rejected it. I'm beginning to think you don't like me."

He hops up onto the wall and sits down next to me. I note his suit is clean and well-pressed. Not the same one he wore the other day. Bounty business must be booming.

"You're getting to be quite the gal about town," he says.

I don't reply. I want like hell to tell him I know all about his filthy new trade. But I hold it in. I won't give him the satisfaction of knowing I'm trembling inside.

"Yes, sir," he goes on. "Seems like everywhere I go, I see you."

"Well, I never go anywhere, so you must be seeing someone else."

"My boys say the same thing. 'Say, guess who I saw today?' 'My, that Arab sure gets around,'" he says, imitating different voices.

He pulls out a knife and clicks it open. "Ain't it a honey? Had to get me a new one." He looks over at me. Clean-shaven, reeking of aftershave, teeth sparkling. He points the tip of the knife to my chin, smiles and says, "Someone lifted my old one. This one's better, though. Gots lots of spring."

He pulls out an apple and begins to slice off sections. He spears one and offers it to me. I ignore it. "I'd think twice, Arab. This might be the last apple in Warsaw, for the duration."

I ignore him. He shrugs his shoulders and stuffs the apple into his mouth, then points his knife toward the street. "You know, who doesn't love a parade? Say, did you see Hitler pass through town? Now, that was some parade!"

A little girl falls in the road, starting off a chain reaction of tripping people. A soldier gruffly jerks them up, butting them along with his rifle.

"Look at that," Sniper says, shaking his head, munching his apple. "Lambs to the slaughter, I tell you. Those Jews are good as dead. Just thank whoever you worship you're blond and blue-eyed."

"I don't worship anyone."

He nudges me. "You could easily be one of those Jewish lambs."

"I'm no more a Jew than you."

"Liar. I knew you when, remember?" He points his knife toward my crotch. "Not only that, you don't got a *shvantz*." I can feel his apple breath on my cheek. "Too bad you can't grow one. This getup ain't going to work forever, you know. Pretty soon some horny Kraut's going to find your crotch and have himself a good old time. Or has that fancy lieutenant already been there?"

"What are you talking about?"

"I've seen you talking to him on your corner. Like hell you're just selling him cigarettes. You wouldn't be the first Jew bitch I know to be under—if you pardon the expression —a German's protection."

"Go screw yourself."

"Look, they want us all dead. I can promise you that," he says, matter-of-factly. "I know. I have connections. Every

fucking last one of us. Dead. Won't matter what you got in
your pants. Hell, six of my gang got picked off the streets for
the work parties. Only one came back and you don't want to
hear his stories about the other five. I heard of one man, had
a rare blood type and guess what? They took it all! Yep, just
drained him dry. Huh," he adds, with a thoughtful smile,
"Wonder what a body looks like without any blood in it."

He looks at a passing line of Germans and flicks the
core of his apple off his knife toward them. Two little boys
run to it and fight over who gets to gobble it down. "I tell
you, Arab, it's a whole new world. On the other hand, this
keeps up, you and me'll be the only operators in Warsaw."
He leans into me and I scoot away. "Hmm, that could be
very lucrative. Maybe we should team up again." He inches
even closer.

I give him the coldest, hardest look I can.

"I tell you, that Lizard is just a cheap punk. You keep
ganging with him, you'll never get anywhere—probably
get yourself killed—all those snot-nosed boys to look after.
Come with me. Where the real men are. After all, this
is war."

"You're right. This is war. And it always has been." I
jump down off the wall and look back up at him. "I should
have killed you when I had the chance."

"Be seeing you, Arab! Think of me as your . . ." He pulls
out a small dictionary, "No wait, wait. Got it right here. Does
us all good to speak German now, you know. Here it is. I am
your *Schutzengel*." He mangles the word.

"I don't need any damn guardian angel, least of all you!"

"Gonna be watching you, sweetheart. Here! Have an
apple on me!"

I turn in just enough time to catch it.

I fade into a busy crowd, wondering why the makeup of one's crotch causes so many problems. Either you're a male Jew with a circumcised *shvantz* or a female ripe for the picking.

Either way, you're screwed.

MARCH, 1940

I.

IT'S BEEN A PRETTY DREARY OCCUPATION SO FAR. THE GERMANS have been busy with upsetting and reorganizing everything for everyone. Every day a new decree! I even wonder if it's to keep our eyes on the right hand while the left hand creates more havoc. Of course, rumors fly around every corner, especially the rumors of a wall going up around the Jewish Quarter. If all us Poles didn't have reasons to hate the Germans before this, we sure have them now.

Holidays? What are those? Days when no one you know gets humiliated, deported, or shot? No, there aren't any holidays anymore. First to go are the Jewish holidays. Every single one of them. Verboten. Done! Thousands of years of history, gone with one tidy German decree. If any Jew dares to celebrate or honor God, or even sing a prayer, it's done like everything else is done in Warsaw—in secret and behind locked doors. And if you're discovered? That'll earn you a front row seat to a firing squad or a one-way ticket to Elsewhere.

Then Hitler puts the kibosh on the Polish holidays. So what's left? Oh, the Germans do love their Christmas! But that first Christmas of occupied Warsaw? Pretty damn sad. No songs sung, no candles lit, no prayers whispered, no food prepared, no gifts exchanged.

Too bad, because December is usually a great month for me and the trades. But our first Christmas of the Hitler Holy Occupation? Pitiful! Pitiful to see people eke out anything in the way of a holiday spirit. I stockpiled little things all fall to sell on my corner through the winter, and Lizard had his boys cut cedar boughs and holly sprigs to make into corsages to sell. Just the smell of pine or a splash of red and green—that's all most people had to honor the season by. The whole season was taken up with survival, anyway.

But our little gang made it through. Me in my home hole, and Lizard and his boys in their church basement hideout. We've gotten this far.

There are some people who think hope springs eternal—or they have an eternal hope for spring. They think food will somehow return, homes will somehow heat, businesses will somehow reopen . . . Well, they are dead wrong. Or just dead. It's nearly spring now, and it isn't getting better—it's getting worse.

I laugh at those eternal, infernal optimists—mostly the few people who still have full bellies and warm hearths. Probably have already sold out to the Krauts.

Then there are still people who insist this can't go on much longer—*As soon as spring comes, wait and see! The world will come to save us.* Well, it's been seven months since Germany flew into town, and no one has even sent a get-well card.

We are on our own.

II.

"Only half a pack?" Fritz asks. Over the months, he's become one of my best customers for weekly cigarettes and whatever else I can pilfer for him, and for his horse—souvenirs to send home to his family. Even through the dreary Christmas and New Year's seasons, Fritz would come to buy, smoke, get his boots shined. Looking at him today, I chuckle to myself. He's almost single-handedly supporting our gang.

He dismounts, slings Hummel's reins over his arm, pulls out a cigarette and lights it, then grimaces as he inhales. "Then again, who wants a full pack of these?"

I'm thinking my Fritzenheimer's usual calm, elegant manner is dwindling right along with tobacco supplies. This occupation thing must be wearing him down, just like the rest of Warsaw. I've noticed the change in his handsome face. He looks harder, older. Only seven months of this, and we're all so much harder and older.

"Look. I have something for you," I say.

"What's this?" He holds up the silver spider I picked up, along with other confiscated holiday items. He holds it up by the fine silver chain. "A spider?"

"It's a good luck. Who doesn't need luck these days?"

"How much?"

"It's solid silver."

"So are the cleats on my boots," he says, unimpressed. "Well, I do have a sister who collects good luck charms. Two *zloty*."

I'm envisioning the smiling faces in the locket. Which sister, I wonder? I watch him dangle the charm. "Well, sisters are special. Tell you what. How about I give it to you and then you give me some information?"

He looks around. "You know, I'm not the soft touch you seem to think I am, Arab."

"Of course. I know that. All I want is a slight nod of your head. You don't even have to say anything. That way, if your Hitler comes and asks, you can honestly say you said nothing."

"Get to the point. I'm on patrol."

"Are the rumors true? Are they—are you—really going to build a wall? Make a ghetto?" I hold Hummel's reins, letting him nuzzle around my heavy wool capote looking for whatever treat I might have for him.

A huge crash—very close and very loud—startles all of us. Hummel rears back and Fritz is quick to grab the reins.

"Easy, boy, easy."

My heart should be used to these sudden noises by now, but it's not. Hummel calms and Fritz looks across the street. He nods to the work party. They're hauling a cartload of bricks and stones, chunks of concrete from the bombed-out church. Loading all of it into the bed of a truck. "There's your answer."

I'm still getting my senses back. "Dropping concrete?"

"Ever wonder what they're going to do with all that rubble?"

I look across the street and shrug. "I don't know. Maybe take it back to Germany and build one of those castles you—"

"Or other things," he says, breaking me off with a chilly glance.

I look at the rubble, the weary men consigned to haul it. "Can I take that as a yes? A ghetto?"

"A ghetto? Heavens, no. Ghettos are barbaric. Just a place where Jews can . . . congregate." He takes another puff of his cigarette and makes a face. "Where the hell are you getting these things? Can't you get anything better?"

"No, matter of fact, I can't. I was lucky to find those."

"Well, work on it, will you? Or I'll have to find another supplier. And tell your gang of pickpockets over there I'm on to them," he adds, pointing to two of our boys, who are stalking a man standing on the corner.

I give a sharp whistle and the boys quickly turn in a different direction, leaving the man untouched and unaware.

"So, tell me, Herr *Obersturmführer*, if you were to build a wall around someplace—and I'm not saying you are—where would that be?"

He pockets the spider, tilts his head east. In Polish, he repeats, "A place to congregate. You're smart. Figure it out." Fritz tosses his cigarette butt, mounts, and rides off. My two newspaper boys are fast on the smoldering butt, fighting over it, then settling on trading puffs until their fingers burn on the last bit of tobacco.

I feel a chill. So the rumors are true. They are going to build a wall, and soon. I look east—toward Warsaw's Jewish Quarter. Where they "congregate." Toward home. Toward Ruthie.

III.

IT TAKES ME LESS THAN TWENTY MINUTES TO WEAVE MY WAY TO this building. It was a high school library not far from Three Crosses, and now it's an infirmary for Polish factory workers. I walk inside and head to the woman at the information desk. She takes one look at me and points her pencil to the back of the room. I look around at the empty shelves—all the books were probably burned by the Nazis. That, or looters burned them for fuel over the winter. No matter how you look at it, the books are ashes now. The shelves may be empty, but this space is full. There are cots in organized rows and only dingy muslin curtains for privacy. The windows are open to the warm spring air, but I still get whiffs of disinfectant and illness.

But look at that! Finally! A tip I got on the street was right. There, at the back of the room—telephones! There are five booths, but the wood doors, the seats, and the phones themselves in four are gone. Salvaged, stolen, who knows?

A working phone is as rare as a leg of lamb here in Warsaw. There are sixteen people in line ahead of me. This could take all day. But I have to find out. Just find out.

There's an old woman—maybe one of the librarians?—who sits next to the queue. On her lap is a cigar box. I grin at her sign: WORKING PHONE—20 REICHSMARK—NO POLISH CURRENCY—ONE CALL. Sure didn't take her long to goose step into the *Reichsmark* world. If I were smart, I'd charge people to stand in line for them, and take any currency. There's a line for everything in Warsaw—even to get buried. I could make a killing.

"Lines! All I do is wait in lines!" a woman in line behind me me says. "Identification cards, food ration cards, passes to get across town to work. By the time I get to the front of the line, they'll close, and I'll have to start all over again tomorrow. Look at this line, and just for a damn phone call! And would it kill them to heat this place? Fucking Germans," she says, holding her hands over her child's ears. "Say, my daughter needs a potty. Would you mind holding my place for just a minute?"

She doesn't give me a chance to say no. Off she drags her little girl. The woman in front of me says, "That woman's wrong to complain. This is all temporary."

"It is?"

"Of course. The Germans don't mean us any real harm."

"They don't?" I'm holding back my smirk. What rock has this woman been living under?

"No. We just do as we're told and things will get back to normal. You wait and see. Say, do you have a cigarette?"

I pull out a pack, one of the six I stole off a counter this morning. "Four *zloty.*"

"I don't want a crateful. Just a cigarette."

I sigh and shake one out for her. She lights it with her own lighter. "See, my husband knows all about Germans. Says they're here just to organize some things, get us settled. Why, deporting all those thousands of Poles from the Muranów district will take months. My husband's with the relocation office. He knows all about these things."

"Why are they moving people?" I ask. This strikes me as odd.

"How should I know? My husband can't tell me anything more. I just know he's got a good job. The paperwork must be enormous! And already the Germans are helping us rebuild the city. Maybe they'll have to arrest a few malcontents, but things'll be just fine."

"Like Jewish malcontents?" I ask her. Let's see just how stupid this woman is.

She shushes me and looks around. "Don't even say that word."

"Malcontents?"

"Jewish," she says, between pursed lips. "It's bad luck."

"Seems to me it's the Jews with all the bad luck." I lean into the wall and wait for her response to that. I've run into hundreds of anti–Semites all too happy to point fingers at Jews as the cause of all their problems. I can't change them. But I can mock them.

"Well, they deserve it," she says around her cigarette. She fans away the smoke.

"Do they? How so?"

"Well, they're always everywhere. Mixing and mingling. Let's just say, I'm happy they won't be in parks, schools, theaters, buses! Well, there's nothing wrong with that."

"So," I wave my hands to indicate the room, the world, around us. "This is all their fault?" I need to keep my voice down. Others are looking our way.

"Well, if Warsaw didn't have so many damn Jews, then we wouldn't have all these lines, all these inconveniences, would we? Can't even get a decent smoke these days." She doesn't seem to care who's listening.

I'm not sure how to respond, or if I should. All I can do is blink at her in disbelief. "You know," I say, my voice low. "I can sell you ration cards and other papers. Can I show you something in a nice work permit?" I indicate my pockets.

She takes a step back. "Well, that would be illegal!" she yips. Then, she looks around. "For what shift?" she whispers. "Our oldest wants to get on the night shift at a factory."

"Oh, drat the luck! I only have work permits for the day shift." I love watching her righteous face dissolve into a flustered embarrassment. There are no differences in the shifts for work permits. One size fits all. I pat my coat hem, where two passes for factory work now safely reside. Just that morning they were in the wallets of distracted men.

The woman and her child come back. But there are several more people in line now.

"Hey, back of the line, lady!" a man calls out.

"Yes, but . . ." She points to me.

I shrug my shoulders. "Sorry, lady."

She exhales a huff, covers her daughter's ears, and curses her way to the back of the line.

The woman in front of me smiles. "Serves her right. Malcontent."

I don't have time for this. I offer the woman the pack of cigarettes for her spot ahead of me and then trade my place further up—four cigarettes for each spot ahead. Finally, I'm next. But the woman on the phone right now is sobbing uncontrollably. Telephones these days aren't for chatting and catching up on family gossip—they're to share bad news. She's talking in Yiddish—risky, here, where the words echo in the bookless room.

I light a cigarette and hand it in to her. She looks at me, smiles weakly, then takes it and smokes. She's nodding as she listens, shaking, and pulling her hair away from her face. Her red hair dye is now a weary pink, her dark roots six inches grown out. Her face is blotchy and her lips are stained with yesterday's lipstick. If she was smart she'd dress like me. Get rid of that ratty fake-fur collar and tweed skirt. Find some pants, sweaters, hats. Cut that hair and start over. This is no time, no place, to put one's beauty on display.

She hangs up the phone and rushes out of the building, sobbing.

My call won't take long. If it rings, good. If the maid answers, better. If the line is dead, I'll get over there fast. I wonder if the telephone operator is on the take, too. Seems like that's a lot of coins to submit for calling just a half mile away. But it's always worth it.

Ringing—good. They have power.

"*Słucham?*" a tiny voice answers.

I freeze. I was always forbidden to answer the phone growing up. That's the maid's job. Surely Father doesn't allow Ruthie to, either.

"Are you there? Say something!" she says. The static on the line makes her sound so far away. "Mama, no one's there!" She sounds a little insulted.

What do I do? Spying on them from a distance, checking up with Officer Winicki and other neighbors, is one thing—but hearing Ruthie's voice is another. There's a rustle of something.

"*Słucham?*" My mother's voice. God, my mother!

Words catch in my throat. The man behind me in line taps my shoulder. "Hurry it up, boy!"

"*Słucham? Who's there? Halo?*"

I can't. I mouth the word mother, but nothing comes out. I hear another rustle. "Do not answer this phone, Ruth! What has father told you?"

Click. She's hung up. Slowly, I replace the earpiece. I stand up and can barely get of the booth out before the man behind me barges in.

Stunned as I am to hear their voices—Mother's and Ruthie's—at least I know. They're alive. They still have electricity. They're still okay.

I bolster myself against the spring chill and set out to find Lizard.

I hop on my bike and pedal toward Lizard's hideout. Now that I know my family is safe, at least for another day, I need to think about what Fritz told me. The Jews, the wall . . . and the cigarette shortage.

I stash my bike and light a cigarette, watching the smoke disperse as I travel in and out of the shadows to Lizard's hideout. "A smoke," I think out loud, blowing on the tip of my cigarette to make it glow. "Everyone needs a smoke these days." I've seen a starving man trade his ration of bread for two cigarettes. A smoke is what a condemned man asks for before facing the firing squad. It's the last thing people have at night, the first thing they want in the morning. Tobacco—the great equalizer on the streets. Even those sturdy, straight, thick Germans don't think of it as a weakness. Supply and demand. Christian, German, Gypsy, Jew. Face it, everyone needs a smoke.

I have my customers to think of. No, I have myself to think of. Ruthie . . . Mother. I have to stay solvent and focused. Bigger, Arab. Think bigger. These Krauts aren't going anywhere anytime soon. Just how do you plan on surviving?

I look around before knocking our code on the basement door of the burned-out church. Three knocks, returned by four. I slip in and tell Lizard my grand plan.

"You've come unstuck, Arab," Lizard says, taking the last cigarette out of my last pack. "I think you're crazy."

"I don't care what you think. I'm going to do it." Lizard has grown just as hard, tired, and cynical as the rest of Warsaw. I miss his positive attitude and cheerful outlook. On the other hand, what sort of outlook can we afford?

"Hunger has gone to your head. I tell you, Arab, you've come up with some wild ones in your day, but—"

"So what are you and your boys going to sell once we run out?" I throw the crushed pack of cigarettes at him. "Once the Germans get their own distribution up and running? Going to sell flowers? Who the hell gives flowers these days? How about newspapers? Who wants to read the German news? Who can even read German, besides me?"

Lizard and I are sitting in the one parishioner's pew we spared from burning over the winter. He rummages through his jacket, pulls out a cigarette, straightens it out, and holds it up. "Want my last one?" He strikes a match, but I blow it out.

He looks at the cigarette as though the solution to our supply problem might be written on it. Or maybe he's thinking about my plan. "All right. You have a solution? Great. But just remember, the more people you bring into our gang the more risks you take. I'm not going to put the lives of my kids in jeopardy just because of some harebrained scheme you've come up with."

"Fine. Tell you what. I'll just put my own neck in the noose, okay? If it works, maybe I'll let you in on the deal." The snap in my voice is also courtesy of our first winter of occupation.

"Don't be that way, Arab. What happened to fifty-fifty?" He sounds hurt. Who can afford to sound hurt these days?

"Lizard, listen. So we made it through one winter. What about the next, and the next?"

"You know this can't last." He crosses his arms—something he does when he's trying to be superior. I ignore it.

"The hell it can't. Those rumors are true! They're going to build a wall. Cram all the Jews in there—and why, do you suppose? Wars need factories, and factories need workers."

"Other countries will come to our aid."

I stand up and point to the world above our basement. "I am sick of people thinking others are going to come save us, Lizard! Where are the Brits? The Americans?"

"Fine, fine. Let's not get into politics."

Our eyes meet. For some reason that strikes us both as funny, and we break out laughing. Here, in the basement of a bombed-out church, our country overrun by Germans and Soviets, our Jewish population evaporating before our eyes, our whole Polish life destroyed in a matter of months . . .

"You're right," I laugh. "Politics has nothing to do with this!"

I leave, intent on my mission, but with a tiny kernel of laughter still nestled under my ribs. If it can't be food, laughter will have to do.

IV.

"WHAT DO YOU WANT?" THE WOMAN ASKS WITH A GROWL, peering suspiciously through the cracked-open door.

"I want to see the owner. Or the manager," I say, smiling through the crack.

"Gone," the woman says with a guttural laugh. "Along with everything else. Now you be gone, too!"

"This *is* the Arizona Cigarette Company, isn't it?"

"No cigarette company here. Go away!"

But I put my foot in the door. "Please Madam, wait. Look at me, I'm no threat. Just looking for . . ."

"I know what you're looking for," she continues, opening the door a little wider. I see an ocean of young, ghostlike faces behind her. "A handout. Does it look to you like I have anything to spare?"

"Well, maybe I can change that." I wink down at a curious toddler clinging to her mother's skirts.

"Who are you?" the woman asks. I notice one hand is gripping an iron skillet. "I don't recognize you."

"That's because I'm new to the district."

"So are the Germans," she says.

"And that's just what I want to talk to you about," I say, hoping my smile might charm, maybe even relax her. Truth is, I hate having my back to the street for more than a few seconds. "Maybe I could come in, and we can discuss a business arrangement. It's chilly out here."

"It's no warmer in here."

She pauses again. I know it's just as risky for her to trust me as it is for me to trust her. But just then, a baby wails and an older child calls out, "Mama! Pawel did it again!"

The woman quickly turns and goes into the room, leaving me at the door and able to slip in. Of course, I've seen a lot worse in the last several months . . . starving families, sick children, grandparents abandoned because no one could, or would, care for them. But the home is dark, cold, and damp, and there seems to be a coughing child in every corner.

The woman gathers up a baby and begins cleaning his face with her long apron, murmuring soothing words. Her eyes, narrow and suspicious, land on me standing there, hat in hand.

A boy, maybe my age, holds two of the blue and white armbands now imposed on all Jews. "Mama, here. Your armband." He also looks at me with caution.

"Put those damn things away, Yankev!" his mother growls. "This isn't Hitler." She turns back to me. "Can't you see I have enough to keep me busy here?" She squints at me. "What sort of 'business arrangement'?"

"You make cigarettes, don't you?" I point to the factory and warehouse behind the house.

"Used to make cigarettes. When they took away my husband, they closed the factory. When was the last time you saw an Arizona Cigarette in Warsaw? Or Morwitans, or Nobles? When did you last have a decent smoke?"

"That's my point. May I sit down?"

The child in her arms settles and the woman says, with raised eyebrows, "You have five minutes. No more."

I quickly explain my plan. "So, if we can get that production line working again, I can sell every cigarette on the black market," I conclude, running my tongue over my teeth in the hopes that my smile appears brighter—not girl, not boy, just confident. Five more curious children have now relaxed in my presence.

"And what about the Germans?"

"What about them? They'll be our best customers." I wave my hand as though they are a minor inconvenience. "You know what they say: Better a good enemy than a bad friend."

"You know Jews aren't allowed to have their own factories in Warsaw anymore. No business at all! Not even a rag-and-bone cart. The rations they give us couldn't feed a half-dead pigeon. Seven children I have, and they want all of us to starve."

I wonder if I should tip my hand, tell her I'm just as much a Jew as she is. But I think better of it. "They want all of us to starve. But who says we must?"

"Adolf F. Somebody," the woman answers drily. "And you know what the 'F' stands for."

I smile at her and like her at once. "Shall we go look at the factory? Mrs. . . . ?"

"Praska."

"Mrs. Praska. Can we get inside the factory from here?"

The woman adjusts the baby on her hip and leads me through a closet, then down a dark hallway. She opens the door to the factory and lights two overhead kerosene lamps. Her children follow close behind in a flock.

When my eyes adjust, I can't believe what I see. Bales of tobacco stacked clear to the rafters! The assembly line is dusty, and little paper packs of cigarettes dot a conveyor belt. In my eyes, they are stepping-stones to better days.

"You mean they didn't take any of this?" I ask.

"The stupid dogheads didn't even know what sort of factory this is. They just showed up one day, demanded all the men come out, took our cash box. Said any business run by

Jews is outlawed. They cut the electricity line and warned me to leave."

"But you haven't left," I say. That shows gumption. Grit. Just the qualities I admire.

"And I won't until they throw us out. We can hide here just as well as anywhere." She indicates the factory around us. "They might as well have taken a torch to it. This factory is useless to me now. I can't feed my children tobacco."

"Mrs. Praska," I say confidently, "this is far from useless. How many people does it take to run the line?"

"My husband and I and two men. It's a small line. The machine does most of the work."

"I can make all the arrangements. I'll bet this fellow right here can work, can't you?" I ask the tall, thin boy standing protectively next to his mother, arms crossed.

The boy just stares at me coldly. "They'll find out and shoot us all."

But the woman passes the baby off to him, picks up a pack of cigarettes, and shakes one out. My lighter is out fast.

She inhales, exhales. She smacks her lips like a connoisseur might sample wine. "The tobacco is stale."

"So what?" I say, taking a cigarette and lighting it. "A smoke's a smoke these days."

"What happens when they find me running this factory? I have children to worry about."

"Why would anyone have to know?"

"Mama! Papa would say trust no one! Especially this street ruffian!"

"But this ruffian has connections," I say. "If we can start up that assembly line, I can sell every cigarette at five times the price you did before the war. Maybe ten!"

"Mama, no. You saw what they did to the Kaplans last month! Shot, one by one, while they begged for mercy!"

"The Kaplans were stupid," she says. "Everyone on the block was warned. Those weren't real Red Cross workers claiming to help us poor Jews. The Kaplans were stupid and fell for it!" Then, to me, she says, "It takes money to buy our way out of Warsaw. I hear the rumors about the ghetto in Łódź. One here in Warsaw soon. They'll find us and make us move there, and we'll lose all this anyway. *Umbashrien!*"

"God won't forbid it, Mrs. Praska."

She looks at me, the slightest trace of a smile coming to her face. "You speak Yiddish?"

"Only when it's convenient. Those aren't rumors, Mrs. Praska. I know it for a fact. They've already marked off the Jewish Quarter. Started stockpiling supplies. Rocks, bricks, boulders—anything they can get their hands on—to build their wall. Hell, there won't even be a gravestone left in all of Warsaw. And Adolf F. Somebody isn't building walls to keep the stray dogs out."

"But I don't understand. Why? We're good people. Good citizens."

"It's . . ." I search for the word. ". . . convenient, to have all the Jews in one place. But even people in a ghetto need their cigarettes. I tell you, I can sell every cigarette you can make me."

She looks at me. "Take advantage of your own people?"

"I don't have a people," I answer, dodging her question. "That's what makes me good at what I do."

Mrs. Praska is looking at me carefully. I take a slight step back. Never good to have anyone look too closely. "Come with me," she says, leading the way back into their living quarters. "Yankev, stay here with the children."

"Mama!" he hollers. "You'll get us all killed!"

She closes the door to the factory passageway and leans against it, looking at me with a cool assessment. "Who are you?"

"A common thief with uncommon skills."

"What's your name?"

"Call me Arab."

"Arab," she repeats, as though it's the first time she's ever heard the word. She comes closer. "Take your cap off, Arab." She smells of tobacco, as though her years of working with it has infused it into her skin.

I do. I had my hair cut just a few days ago. I always keep soot on my face, urchin-like. She walks around me. "Arab, huh? An Arab helping a Jew. Interesting."

I'm beginning to feel uneasy. I wonder if I've backed the wrong horse—as that horse is now backing me into a corner. She has a commanding presence. Not one to trifle with.

"It's just a nickname. Now, do you want to talk business?"

"You're a girl, aren't you?" she says, folding her arms.

"Do you want to talk business?" I take a wide stance and glare back at her.

"You can fool a lot of people . . . Arab . . . but you can't fool nature." She points to my crotch. "That's a pretty big calling card you have there."

I follow her gaze down and see the dark red blood soaking my pants crotch. I feel something warm snaking down my leg. So much for what I'd assumed were hunger pains.

"Look, Mrs. Praska. It makes no difference what's between my legs. All that matters is I can help you and your children—me—all of us. I can make it happen. My sex has nothing to do with this."

She smiles and offers me another stale cigarette. "Are you done?"

"Look, you're a businesswoman, and . . ."

"Sit down." She indicates the filthy, overstuffed chair. "Wait." She hands me an even dirtier rag. "That's my best chair." I put the rag down and sit on it. She smiles, pats my leg. "I love you already, Arab. But if you're set in going about this war as a boy, you'd better let me get you some raspberry leaves."

"It's tobacco leaves we need, not . . ."

"Two cups of raspberry tea a day and that . . ." She points to my bloodstained pants, ". . . won't be such a calling card. I can fix you up."

"It's a deal, then? Partners?"

She gives me her gnarled, red hand. "Partners. But Yankev, my oldest, needs to know. I depend on him for so much now."

We go back into the factory.

"Yankev, we're going into business," Mrs. Praska announces.

"With him?" he shouts, pointing at me. "You can't be serious!"

"With her," Mrs. Praska corrects. "And you are not to tell anyone about us, her, or anything. Is that clear?"

"Her?" Yankev echoes, even louder. The baby he's holding starts to cry and leans toward its mother for comfort. "You take this bum in off the street and believe what . . . she? . . . says? Are you crazy? Girls can't even save themselves, let alone us! And girls bleed!"

He points to my pants. I've heard enough. I walk toward him, noting I have about an inch on him. He's thin, lanky, and shaking, almost blue in his righteous paleness. Was this the son my father always hoped for? "This arrangement is between me and your mother. And any time you want to square off with me, that's just fine. All Jews bleed when shot, Rabbi, so don't spout your pious Jewish bullshit to me."

He looks to his mother. "What would Papa say?"

"Papa is dead. It doesn't matter what he would say. I say we do this."

"What will it take to get that line up and running?" I ask, walking past Yankev, making sure I bump his shoulder as I pass.

She points to the light fixtures overhead. "Electricity. They cut the power months ago. Not only do they want us to starve, they want us to freeze in the dark while we do it."

"If I can get the power back on?"

"How?" Yankev demands, crossing his arms. "Flip a switch?"

"In a manner of speaking, yes. I have connections. Mrs. Praska, first thing is I'll arrange to brick and board up the windows. Then sound and light won't be able to escape, and this factory will look just as deserted and cleared out as every other Jewish business."

We go back into the house and set up a plan. I can feel Yankev's eyes on my back. He is going to be trouble, I know.

The plan is simple. She and her older children will work the factory. Then I'll be in charge of selling the cigarettes in plain paper packages on the streets of Warsaw. Our customers won't care what brand they are or where they come from. My motto: a smoke is a smoke.

"We'll make a killing. I promise you."

"That will be a nice change," she replies, smiling.

Before I leave, she gives me a pair of her husband's wool trousers, taking my bloody pants. She gives me a small box of raspberry leaves. "At least in a dead neighborhood I can take whatever I can find. The Kaplans had a greenhouse, God save their souls."

"And ours," I say, pocketing the leaves as I turn.

"Arab?"

I turn back.

"Don't worry about my Yankev. Our secrets are safe."

V.

IT'S TAKEN SOME DOING, BUT I FIND MY ELECTRICAL CONNEC-
tion, a genial fellow I've been selling cigarettes to. He used
to work for the utility department before being conscripted
to rewire bombed-out buildings for the Germans.

He climbs a pole and rigs a connection to the block. His
reward is twenty packs of cigarettes, a few American dollars, a pair of boots I stole, and perhaps the grim satisfaction
that he's committing one small act of defiance, ensuring his
own supply of cigarettes as a bonus.

Yankev and I raid cellars for bricks and pull the boards
off other Jewish businesses. Together we brick and board
up the factory. But Yankev nearly knocks me off my ladder
as I paint a big yellow JUDENREIN across the front and sides of
the building.

"What are you doing?" he hollers.

"Keep your voice down," I growl, grabbing the bucket of
paint back from him. "Careful, that paint was hard to find."

"Traitor!"

"Shut up, Yankev! You don't know me well enough to
call me that! Don't you see? This just shows other Germans
this place has already been deloused of Jews? *Judenrein*—
free of Jews! It might as well say 'Go away—no Jews here!'
Think, Yankev! Just think, for a change."

He glowers at me while I finish it off with a huge Star
of David.

It warms me to the marrow to know we, a bunch of Jews, just might get away with it, right under the Germans' straight Aryan noses. There's something supremely ironic—even humorous—in it. So much so, I paint in lopsided Hebrew on a sidewalk in Three Crosses Square:

CHRISTIAN GERMAN GYPSY JEW
DOESN'T MATTER WHICH ARE YOU
BUY A SMOKE, HAVE LOTS TO SELL
LET'S ALL SMOKE
OUR WAY TO HELL!

VI.

"HMM, THIS IS DIFFERENT," FRITZ SAYS AFTER I SELL HIM ONE of the first packs from the resurrected cigarette factory. There's finally been a lovely spring thaw, and everything seems to smell better, fresher, greener. Finally.

He looks at the plain paper wrapping. "What brand?"

"My supplier is testing a new tobacco mix."

"Much better. Yes, much better." He inhales deeply, smiling. "Something I've been meaning to ask you, Arab."

"Anything, except who my new supplier is. Hitler might claim them for his staff, and then where would you and I be?"

"You know, I studied several languages in school. I wonder how someone like you manages German so well. And I've heard you talk to your street urchins in Yiddish."

I turn around, displaying my deplorable clothes, and says, "Why, yes. My wet nurse was Jewish. And our cook was German. The upstairs maid was French. What an education."

"And you being the idiot child of geniuses." He takes another pull of his cigarette, holding in his smile.

Change the subject, fast! He's beginning to get too close to things about me. But it's not like my hand doesn't have a few cards to play. "You know, I can get you . . . other things," I bait.

"Such as Chopin's heart? Ah, Chopin . . . a heart that made music like his is probably still beating," he says, almost lyrically. He looks off into the distance, as though hearing the delicate notes of a piano étude. "But I prefer Wagner. Can you get me some Wagner recordings?"

"I'll work on it. Until then, how about some poetry? Just the other day I got my hands on a lovely old edition of *Don Juan*."

He looks me straight on. "Did you?"

"Leather-bound. A bit worn, but still in good condition. Do you like Lord Byron?"

"Not necessarily." His stance changes a bit. "You know, Arab, usually by your age, there's at least some peach fuzz. And your voice . . ."

"What about my voice?"

"You should be singing baritone, not alto, by now."

We stare at each other for a moment. What are our eyes telling each other? "Oh, so now we're talking opera?" I ask.

He casts me a wry glance. "Yes, of course. Wagner, remember?"

Okay, so he knows I'm a girl. That's Problem B. Problem A is what my life hangs on: my race. But I have two sweet aces up my sleeve—Lord Byron and Henri.

"Can you detect a slight hint of mint in that cigarette?" I ask, changing the subject again.

"Yes, now that you mention it."

"You have a delicate palate, Herr *Obersturmführer*. They stack every other bale with sacks of mint."

"Very nice. I'll take all you have to spare."

I'm not about to tell him we used a mixture of Lysol and kerosene to clean and grease the rolling machine.

"About that copy of *Don Juan* . . . How about I hang on to it for you. In case you change your mind."

"I'll change my mind about the time you grow a *schmekel*," he says, flicking his cigarette into the gutter. "See, I speak

Yiddish, too. Oh, and while you're at it, change your blood."
He smiles back at me.

"If anyone can, it's me."

"That reminds me. I met a friend of yours."

"I have a friend?"

"Tried to sell me some information."

My heart thunks hard. Easy, Arab. "Really? What was his name?"

"He didn't give it."

"And did you buy this information?" Keep it light. You know what this is about.

"No, his price was too high. Especially for information I already have."

"Well, good. Hate to see you taken advantage of."

"Anyway, he said he has a message for you."

"Shoot."

"Yes, that was the message! He wanted you to remember there are sharpshooting snipers everywhere."

"Yes, so they say. Always got to be looking up, then, don't we?" I keep looking east and he keeps looking west. Well, now we know. We both hold each other's nooses.

No more is said about it. I wonder if this is what they call an accord. A small peace between a Nazi and a Jew, right here in the middle of a war.

"And that reminds me. Just got in some excellent brandy."

"Brandy?"

"Odd about brandy—every day it ages, it becomes more valuable."

Another officer is approaching us on horseback and Fritz turns on me. "And if you don't cross this street when you see me coming, Polish pig, you won't live to regret it!" he shouts, taking his Luger out of its holster. I bow my head and slink away. If I had a tail, it would be between my legs.

"Von Segen! Quick! Follow me!" the captain shouts. I recognize him. Wilhelm Schneider. I still have the scar on my head and the sign STUPID POLISH THIEF to remember him by. Several more officers bully their horses through the crowds on the sidewalk.

Fritz mounts Hummel and they trot down the street, scattering pedestrians and cart vendors as they go.

"What's happening?" a young woman coming up the sidewalk asks me just before I can slip into the shadows.

A dozen more soldiers run to the intersection, stopping all traffic and rounding up every person on the street. I see she has her Jewish armband sewn onto her sleeve. I rip it off.

"No, I'll be arrested!" she cries, picking it up.

"You'll be arrested anyway."

"Jews are being shot for not wearing these! Look, you've ripped it!" she continues. "Now I'll have to go back home and fix it." I try to stop her, but she insists on continuing on down the street toward the commotion.

"Stupid woman! Go ahead! Run back into the burning barn!" I shout after her. I look around. Where have all these people come from? Nazis have rounded up dozens and are pushing everyone into the streets. I turn and weave my way through them to get out of here.

I head down an alley and come back out two streets over. Finding myself right by the Crystal Café, I hide in the shadows I know so well. Oh, God, I don't like the looks of this.

The soldiers, each armed with a rifle, point, butt, and use their weapons to herd the group of seventy or so people. The soldiers examine papers and weed people out, pushing others out of their way. Several dozen are lined up along the curb. Onlookers pop their heads out of windows, emerge from their stopped autos and streetcars, and watch with a vague, helpless curiosity.

The breath of excited horses, sturdy soldiers, and con-fused people mingle and fill the spring air. I catch the ter-rified eyes of the woman whose armband I ripped off. She's trying to convince an officer all her papers are in order and shaking her loose armband up as proof.

"Count off by threes!" Schneider commands the Jews left standing on the curb. They do as they are told. *"Nein! Auf Deutsch!"*

"Eins, zwei, drei . . . eins, zwei, drei . . ."

Oh God, there's Spades. Oh please, Spades, don't be called out. I sink lower behind a hedge.

"Dreier! Step forward!" About a dozen people step out of the line. Including Spades. "The rest, go there, with that man!" Then, to Fritz, he shouts, "These idiots don't under-stand. Translate, *Obersturmführer.*"

Fritz steps forward and reads in Polish from a card. "There has been some illegal activity in this district. There has been theft of German property. To make it perfectly clear that we will not tolerate any activity by subversive Jews, we are ordered to take appropriate action."

With that, Wilhelm Schneider takes out his Luger and trains it from head to head of the men and women lined up. People are crying, pleading, praying. Oh God, he's going to do it!

I see their plan and I know their action. We onlookers aren't the target. Today. I come out of the shadows. Spades and I lock eyes. God, his face, his eyes! I close my own eyes the minute I hear the pop of the gun and the fall of his body. Next, it's the woman with her armband still crumpled in her hand. Then, Schneider signals his troops and *pop! pop! pop!* A volley of accurate shots, the remaining *dreier* crum-pling to the pavement, falling silently on one another like so many armloads of hay on harvest day.

The street is silent. No shouts of horror. No wrath, no indignation, no protest. Just silence. The Germans quickly move to restart traffic, usher away those Jews who are lucky to have called out *eins* or *zwei*, and within a numb instant, all is normal on the street—people walking along, gingerly stepping around the bodies; cars and streetcars continuing, and the Germans returning to their patrol, after propping up three of the bodies against a wall as a warning to everyone. A woman in the middle of two men. Laughing, a young soldier places one hand of each dead man on the woman's breasts.

If it wasn't for the unlucky dozen lying dead, a few pockmarks on the wall of the café, blood congealing on the sidewalk before it can slip into the anonymity in the sewers, no one would be able to tell anything has happened.

I'm frozen. I've seen the bodies, I've seen the roundups, I've heard the gunfire. But now, here in this café, where I've sat so many times. Spades. The woman with her useless Star of David.

Finally, I duck around a corner and dissolve into the back alley. Then I stop cold, not sure of what I'm seeing. There, crouched down, leaning against a building, forehead resting on his folded arms, is Fritz, his horse's head low next to him as though consoling him. It reeks of fresh vomit. Fritz is breathing hard. I back away, but I step on a piece of crushed glass and it echoes through the new-dead silence. I stop. He looks up.

He stands, pulls his Luger out, and aims it at my head, hand shaking. I put my hands up and slowly back up a few steps. His crushed face is contorted and anguished, no longer handsome and dashing. His eyes are red and his face is wet with tears.

"Are you as good as your word?"

"Yes." I try to look at him and not down the barrel of his Luger.

"You never saw this," he growls, teeth clenched.

"Saw what?" I make a feeble attempt to smile.

The Luger slowly comes down, and he wipes some spittle from his chin.

"I'll see about that brandy." It's all I can think of to say.

Writers write of irony. The brandy I have to sell is the same brandy I stole off a German delivery truck I was pressed into unloading just a few days ago. How could I not liberate a few bottles? So . . . I am the reason for the roundup. So . . . those twelve people lying dead in the street died for my sins.

If Christ died for gentiles' sins, then twelve Jews just died for mine.

SEPTEMBER, 1940

I.

SPRING AND SUMMER HAVE PASSED, AND NOW, AS FALL approaches, I realize how much I've changed. The massacre was months ago, but I can't get the images out of my mind. I think that's what Hitler wants. He wants us to stand by and silently witness—the wall going up, the deportations, the massacres, the randomness of life here in Warsaw— hell, in all of Europe now, for all I know. The only news we get is ground out by the Nazi propaganda machine. Anyway, I don't have time to worry about Europe.

But these nightmares—not like me at all. I close my eyes and see those twelve dead people, gunned down because of a torn armband and some Nazi's rage over a few bottles of stolen brandy. How will I ever forget those faces, that woman without her armband, Spades . . . all lined up against that café wall?

And my family—any of those twelve people could have easily been my family. Maybe even my baby sister, since Jewish children are granted no quarter. The first thing I did that night was make an angry gash in the wall of my home hole—one gash for each life lost. I smashed the bottles of brandy and pledged then and there I was going to avenge those lives—if someone doesn't take mine first.

Those gashes are the last things I look at each night and the first things I look at each morning.

The Germans are good as their word, I'll give them that. They started building the wall in April. Did they ever!

Nine feet high with shards of glass cemented into the top. Concertina wire coiled on top of that. This isn't a friendly, backyard fence, the kind that makes for good neighbors. The roads in and out of the Muranów neighborhood, the Jewish quarter, are barricaded with barbed wire and thick beams. They take on the appearance of checkpoints with guard towers. One thing's obvious: without a work permit or a pass, once you're "quartered" there, don't plan on coming out the way you went in.

In one way or another, I've checked on my family all summer, even though, between the construction, and now the cutting off of streets and alleyways, it keeps getting tougher to get over and back.

"How long has it been since you heard anything?" Lizard asks. We're sorting out packages of cigarettes for our boys to sell to the work crews as they head back from building the ghetto wall. "Maybe the phones are just out of order."

"I called six days in a row. No, something's happened."

"Did you call your neighbors?"

"No phones anywhere. So I'm going over. You don't know my father. He'll get himself and Mother and my sister killed. He gives orders; he doesn't take them. Besides, it's not my father I'm worried about. It's my mother and sister."

"Isn't your mother always sick? Maybe she's . . ." Death has become so second-nature in everyone's thoughts. Lizard catches himself. "I mean . . ."

I try not to visualize my mother getting tossed onto a truck like the old woman with the Luger, to be hauled Elsewhere. No work will set old women free.

"Could be. But then there's Ruthie. The poor kid's got a club foot. And you know what the Nazis think about imperfection. And if she's becoming anything like me, well, you know what a mouth I have." No work is going to set her free, either.

"Well, maybe he can buy their way out. And doesn't he have a lot of influence in the Jewish community? Aren't they letting the Rabbis and the muckety-mucks take care of their own?"

"I don't know. That's why I'm getting myself over there today." I resist the urge to light a cigarette, knowing we need to keep our supply for selling and bartering.

"When will you go? Mrs. Praska says half her kids are sick, so production might be slow for a few days."

"Damn Krauts sure caught on to the sewer system. Have you seen them welding some of the covers closed? Damn inconvenient."

"You're asking for it traveling the sewers these days. Watch out for kerosene or poison gas. If they suspect anyone's down there, bombs away! You're on your own in the sewers. Just you and the rats."

"If this war has taught me anything, it's the value of careful." I smile at him, but he's not smiling back.

"Still, I think you better think this over, Arab." Lizard slings several canvas bags of cigarettes over his shoulder.

"I have thought it over, and I'm going."

"Well, just remember there are all the Praskas, and me and our boys to consider. If you get your head blown off, what about our operation here?" He grabs my hand and catches my eye. "I mean. I don't know what I'd do without you."

Now is no time for this sort of talk, I think. "Well, Lizard, you'll muddle through somehow. You know where my hideouts are, you know where I stash things. If I don't come back, you can have everything." I pull my hand away from his. "Fifty-fifty becomes one hundred percent."

"Let me know the minute you get back. Promise?" Now he smiles, but there's concern in his eyes.

"I'll come here first thing. Won't even stop for a beer."

II.

I STUFF SOME SUPPLIES INTO MY CANVAS BAG, WONDERING WHAT I should take on my trip over to the ghetto side. Luger? What if I get caught and searched? That's going to look a bit suspicious. On the other hand, it also might save my life. I decide against it and put the gun back into the hiding spot in my hideout's wall. I decide to take my knife instead—easy to hide, and useful in many ways.

I sling my bag over my shoulder and head out onto the street, looking both directions before I round each corner. While I make my way across town, I think about bigger things—my family and just how the hell I should approach my father. On the streetcar, I remember how his anger controlled so much of our family. On the side streets, I remember how my mother seemed powerless. In the sewers, I remember how I have always looked out for just myself.

As I pause before a shop window and look at my reflection, I see only little Ruthie looking back. I wipe some sewer goo from my cheeks and pinch some glow into them. Sunken cheeks are all the rage these days—something I'm doing right, at least. Everyone is suspicious of chubby cheeks.

I run my hand over my head, feel something, pluck it out, then put my cap back on straight. I fuss with the scarf around my neck, trying to look halfway feminine.

Just like all the other times I've come to check on them, I hide across the street. Already this neighborhood is in disarray. Garbage is piled up along the streets, gardens are untended, abandoned belongings are stacked in the yards of the neighborhood houses. There he is! Up the block. It's Tuesday—rent collection day. I take a breath for courage, come out of the shadows, and cross the street.

He sees my shadow and holds his cane up. "I don't want any trouble!"

Then his cane slowly comes down, and we stand staring at each other. Who is this man? I know I've changed, but I'm shocked to see how much my father has transformed. Thin and bent and gray. A forty-seven-year-old ancient man. The once-zealous glow in his face is replaced by a desolate look of hunger and fear.

I open my mouth to speak, but nothing comes out.

"Abra!" He gasps my name, like evoking a ghost. He steps closer and stares into my eyes. "But . . . you're dead," he whispers.

"Only to you, Papa." I relive what I felt—the horror, humiliation, the damn anger at seeing my own headstone.

"Two years now, dead. Who are you really?"

"Father, it's me. Your daughter, Abra."

"I have no daughter Abra. Only Ruth. Abra is dead and buried."

"Shall we go dig up that grave and see who's not in it?"

He totters and catches himself with his cane. I make no move to help him.

He glowers at me again, as though refusing to recognize me. "They told us! We heard stories. Stories of disgust and filth! Stories of shame!"

"I didn't come here to discuss my death, or lack of it."

He starts to speak again, but then turns abruptly and hobbles toward the house.

"I've come to help you and Mama. And Ruth."

"No. No. Go away. We don't need your help. We are fine here. Leave us in peace." He starts toward the front walk again. I notice the entire iron fence is gone—pulled up for scrap, no doubt.

"You call this peace?" I shout, following him. What am I expecting? That we'll fall into each other's arms and beg forgiveness? There's no room in war for forgiveness.

He grabs the stair railing and takes each step up slowly. When he gets to the top, he looks down at me. It's as though he has no idea what to say. His eyes are oddly vacant. Then, slowly, tears form, magnified by his glasses. I've never seen my father cry. My own eyes suddenly sting. He might be broken, but he is my father.

"Father. Papa. Let me take you out of here."

"This is our home." He opens the front door. I follow him up the steps. Instead of being greeted by a maid, I'm met by a blast of stale, hot air. I look up the staircase and hear footsteps.

I stop at the threshold. "May I come in?"

He looks at me closely, almost as though he still doesn't believe it's me standing here. "You've come this far. Back from the dead, even," he says, his voice just a weak rasp. "You may as well come in. For a moment."

I step inside and look around, inhaling the emptiness, then follow him into his study—bare now of paneling and furniture and books.

"Papa, let me take care of you."

"A man takes care of his family. A daughter does what she's told."

"Maybe before. But Papa, everything's changed."

"We are fine here."

"Don't you see what's happening? Don't you look around you? Do you think they're building that wall to keep the riffraff out? They're building it to keep the riffraff in! *We* are the riffraff." I struggle to keep my voice low and calm.

"Speak for yourself. I am a man of no small consequence. No small influence! Even the Germans respect authority."

"Only their own."

"God will keep us safe," he says, almost as a prayer.

"Yes, I see what a superb job your God has been doing around here. Doesn't God help those who help themselves?"

"Always disrespect! I was right. Abra is dead."

"Please, Father, this has nothing to do with me. I came here to help you!" Is it all going to come down to his damn sense of honor, propriety, and stubbornness?

"I am not stupid! I know what's happening! I am ready! I have Red Cross satchels for us and gas masks. I paid five hundred *zloty* apiece for us to get typhus vaccinations!"

"I could have gotten you those for half that," I say, almost under my breath.

"The cellar is stocked with supplies. I have money to bribe officials." He walks to his desk drawer and pulls out a small, blue envelope. "And just in case, I even bought cyanide tablets. Cost over three thousand *zloty*. We'll all die here, if need be."

I stare in disbelief. "Kill Mama? Kill Ruthie?"

"If need be," he says. The envelope shakes in his hand. "If need be."

I grab the envelope, shake out a tablet, and examine it under the light of the window. I lightly put it to my tongue.

"No, Abra, don't!" He grabs for it.

I let the taste settle, then pop the tablet into my mouth and chew it.

"What are you doing? That's—"

"Aspirin. You spent three thousand *zloty* for aspirin. German aspirin!" It's the item of the season on the black market.

I hand back the blue envelope. "If not for you, then for Mother and Ruthie. Let me at least take them away. I can hide them on the other side. I have connections. With Ruthie's blonde hair, I can easily get her forged documents. She'll be safe with me."

He shakes his head. "Turn her back on her faith and become a goy like you? And what life do you offer? Begging? Pickpocketing? Thieving? What other skills do you have to pass on to your sister? I shudder to think."

I'm ready for that, and I let it pass. Besides, he's right. I've stolen, lied, cheated, caused the massacre of twelve innocent people, and am already planning my own sweet revenge. I need to keep my voice low and controlled. "Open your eyes. Have you heard of a ghetto, Papa? Do you even know what one is? When they finish that wall, close those gates, and cram every Jew in Poland inside this place, then you . . ."

"I have money!" he shouts.

"Polish money! You might as well use it for toilet paper!"

"You do not raise your voice to me!"

"Stubborn fool!"

Oddly, he smiles. Three years ago he would have smacked me into next week for such a comment. "So nothing changes, eh, Abra?" He puts the blue envelope into the drawer. "God will provide. And what God doesn't provide, I will! All this will pass."

We stare at each other. "You have your mother's eyes."

"And my father's stubborn streak," I reply, almost without thinking.

Another small smile.

"I want to see Mama."

"She's sick in bed." He blows his nose on a filthy handkerchief. Again, our eyes meet. I'm beginning to understand. He almost reads my thoughts. "Cancer."

"And Ruthie?"

"In school, of course."

"What school? They've closed all the schools."

"We have teachers and we have cellars. See? We're not so helpless here. *Komplety.* Secret school."

"Where?"

"Right downstairs. But you may not see her. It would only confuse and upset her. Some things must be left alone. You may look in on Mama, but I've just given her morphine. The pain, the drugs, they confuse her. She won't know who you are. See her, then please, go back to your half of the world."

I start for the stairs. "No, this way."

"But Mama's room . . ."

"Rented now. All the rooms. Rented."

He leads me to the room off the kitchen—the one that was once a maid's room.

Mother is sleeping soundly. Like Father, she seems to have shrunk. Once a beautiful, hearty woman, she's now a small, wheezing form. Bottles of medicine line her bedside table. I wonder which of those are counterfeit and worthless.

I kneel down next to her bed and stroke her once-glorious blonde hair, streaked with gray and swept back in long, frazzled braids. I lift her hand, kiss it. Her eyes flutter open, and she looks around the room, unaware I'm at her side, holding her hand. Finally, her eyes find my face. She inhales a breathy gasp.

"Who are you?"

"It's me. Abra."

"No, you're not Abra. Abra is . . . is . . ." Her smile vanishes as she stares at me. "Abra? My Abra?"

"Yes, Mama."

"Are we all dead?" She grabs my hand.

"No, Mama. Mama, listen, I can save Ruthie. You have to tell Father. I can save Ruthie."

"What's happening?" Her vacant, sunken eyes dart about the room. "Is it over? Have they left?"

"Mama, listen. You have to tell Papa I can save Ruthie. Do you understand? Mama, look at me!"

Her eyes fall on my face and the smile returns. "My Abra. Back from the dead. I knew you'd come home. I've always known you'd come home."

"Mama! Please, please listen! Tell Papa! Tell him to let me take Ruthie!"

She searches my face. "You need a bath. Tell Helena to draw you a bath."

I put my head on her bed and fight back tears of frustration. "No, Mama. Please."

I feel her hand on my head. She's found the scar. "What is this?"

"I walked into a door." She'll never know about her stupid Polish thief.

"You must watch where you're going." She gives me that wonderful smile I remember from childhood. She nods her head, ever so slightly. "Yes. Yes, I will tell Papa. When the time is right, I will tell him."

"Now! Tell him now. Mama. I can take her now."

"Take my Ruth? No, no, no. I can't allow that. But maybe, after . . . after . . ."

"Promise me, Mama. I'll come back, and then I can take Ruthie out of here. I know I can save her."

She grasps my hand in hers and brings it to her lips, kissing my fingertips. "Papa says everything will be fine. Just fine. And Abra? Make sure the gardener is watering my roses." And she drifts off to sleep, a small smile of contentment on her face.

I kiss my mother's forehead and tell her I love her. "Yes, Mama." I walk toward the door, as close to defeated as I've ever felt.

I know now I can't save my father. And I can't save my mother. But, by God, I will save my sister!

I walk past my father. "I can get you more morphine." I reach into my coat and set some papers down on the table. "Here. *Ausweis* and *Kennkarte*."

"I forbid German words in my house!"

"It's just identification. This is a work permit, Papa. That's why they call it a life ticket."

He looks at the portrait of my mother, painted when she was young and stunning. "God will provide," is all he says.

I leave through the kitchen door, ignoring several strangers who are cooking over the stove, and continue down the walkway toward the cellar's side door. I peek in and see only blankets hanging. But I hear voices beyond. The school room.

Ruth and I always had a secret signal. It's a gruff clearing of our throats that started as a teasing imitation of our father. Then it became a warning that our father was close by and to stop whatever mischief we might be up to. I wonder if she'll remember it.

I slowly open the door, and very slightly clear my throat.

"Ruth, sit down." It's an older woman's voice.

"I have to go to the bathroom," Ruth says. I recognize the lilt in her voice when she fibs.

"Ruth, the bathroom is upstairs."

"I'll go around outside. My father doesn't want anyone disturbing my mother."

"Very well. Be quick about it. And don't think you're going to get out of the spelling test, either."

"Okay. But I know all the words," she says.

The blankets split open, but she stops cold when she sees me. Then, she slowly limps around me, as though inspecting a horse at auction. I kneel down. "Ruthie. It's me. Abra."

"Abra who?" she asks, a frown holding in a smirk.

"Your sister, that's Abra who. Have you forgotten your own sister?"

She put her hands on her hips. "You lied! You said you'd come back."

"And I am back. See? What, no hug for your sister?"

"No! You said you'd bring me a treasure. Where's my treasure?"

"Well, you just come with me," I say, picking her up and carrying her outside to the old tire swing hanging from an ancient oak. I reach into my satchel and pull out a rag doll. Ruthie doesn't need to know where or how I got it. The child I took it from no longer needed it.

"Thank you!" She embraces the doll.

"Now am I your sister?" I ask.

Again, she gives me a once-over look. "I'm not so sure. Papa says not to talk to strangers."

"I'm not a stranger."

"I don't know. You look pretty strange," she says, reaching for my cap. "You look like a boy."

"I know. I like to pretend. And you know what?"

"What?"

"I can run really, really fast in pants."

"Mama won't let me wear pants. She says it's not ladylike . . ."

"And sometimes it is. But not now. So, am I your sister?"

"Yes!" she says, throwing herself into my arms.

"Now, you have to hide that doll from Father, understand? He doesn't know I'm seeing you."

"Why? Oh yeah, you're dead. I forgot."

"You're six now. A big girl. Can you keep a big girl secret?"

"I like secrets," she says, now cradling the old doll.

"Good. We're going to need lots and lots of secrets."

"Ooo, you stink," she says, grimacing at the smell of my shirt.

"Ruthie, now listen very, very carefully. Put the doll down and look at me. Do you know the cemetery where grandmother Goldstein is buried? Just over there?"

"Uh-huh, but I don't like it there."

"Ruthie, you know the mausoleum?"

"What's a . . . masso linoleum?"

"The stone building with the iron fence around it?"

"It's scary there."

"No, Ruthie, listen! I can leave you more things in that place."

"Candy?"

"Yes, and maybe medicine. Or money, or food."

"Why? I don't like it there. Can't you bring it here?"

I tuck some stray golden hairs back inside her scarf, loving this little opportunist. "No, Ruthie. This is just a game of hide and seek. You can hide something for me and I can hide something for you. It'll be fun, and Father will never know. I have to go."

"Take me with you!"

"Not today, Ruthie. Mama needs you now. You need to take care of Mama."

"Father says bad things and he yells at me. Everything is all different. I don't like school. I have to share everything!"

"I know. I'm going to fix that. You must be patient. I have a lot to do to find us a home someplace safe. Until then, you're safe here. But Ruthie, I have to go." I catch her up, hug her, put her down. "But remember, I'll bring food and clothes, and where do you go to find them?"

"That scary place," she says, pointing toward the cemetery.

I start up the walkway. I stop to wave and she waves her doll's little hand goodbye at me. She turns and limps slowly back to the cellar door.

NOVEMBER, 1940

I.

OVER THE MONTHS PREPARING FOR WINTER, I KEEP THINKING of Aesop's grasshopper and the ant fable. No wasting time for us as we take advantage of the warm fall weather to raid, stockpile, trade, and steal everything we can get our hands on. I've been able to find streets in and out of the ghetto that are not yet barricaded, but it gets harder and harder as the days wear on. I make as many exchanges as I can with Ruthie. Cheese, a toy, fruit, earmuffs. She leaves meager findings in exchange—a purple crayon, a broken plate, a book pulled out of a burn pile. Each time it's harder to get through, as the wall slowly wraps its arms around the ghetto. That leaves the sewers, but even those are more and more difficult to slip into and out of. They have stepped up the patrols around and inside the ghetto.

Side roads in and out of the ghetto are cut off entirely, now leading only to dead ends of high walls, broken glass, and barbed wire. On the main roads they've build thirteen gates that squeeze traffic into long lines. Sometimes those with work permits, the factory outworkers, have to wait over an hour to get their passes inspected to get in and out.

The old cemetery close to my home is only a short sprint from a sewer opening. But as the building crews work that area, I have to be extra careful. I've even been pressed into service for three rainy days—mixing cement, hauling gravestones, and adding them to the wall. I helped haul my own gravestone and entomb it in the wall. With my own hands

I packed cement around it. I was careful to place it so the engraving faces out. If I'm going to be gone and forgotten I don't want anyone to forget.

The Germans have announced they're going to officially seal off the ghetto by the middle of November. I can almost feel the sense of struggling humanity close in around me when I manage to sneak inside. How many people can they fit in here? Every day, truckloads of people come. Roundups herd more in every day. At what point will the walls collapse from the bulging population?

Like always, the Germans are as good as their word. The gates close on November 15th, right on schedule. The sentries and checkpoints are set. Men with scopes and rifles watch from towers above, men with guard dogs patrol below. Only German soldiers, Polish police, Nazi officials, and factory workers are allowed in and out. Still more Jews in. God, where do they come from?

For weeks I've been getting things in order for Ruthie. Everything is ready. Ruthie will stay with Mrs. Praska as soon as I forge her papers. Lizard and I nearly got ourselves killed stealing a sick little girl's Aryan identification, birth certificate, and passport—worth gold!—in a Kraut infirmary. A flirty little nurse friend of Lizard's looked the other way. A Nazi doctor called the security police and we barely got out the back stairway. A doctor, for God's sake! So much for "first, do no harm"!

All that's left is getting her photograph, and that I'll get once I have her here on the Aryan side, safe and sound. I'll kidnap Ruthie from my parents—at gunpoint, if I have to. It's been weeks since I've made it back over, now that it's nearly impossible. The sewers are just as dangerous as the streets now. But I have everything I need.

———

I barely recognize our old street, buried under a layer of filthy snow. Our house, the grounds, seem out of a different world. A whole wing has been torched! Total strangers answer when I knock on the front door. I look behind them. "The Goldsteins?" I ask. "Where are the Goldsteins?"

The man starts to close the door, but I force it open again with a shove. "I asked you, where are the Goldsteins?"

"I don't know," he says. A cadre of small children, bundled up to their noses, peek around the corner of our once-lavish parlor. I can see laundry hanging across the room. The smell of piss fills the entry hall.

"This is their home! Where are they?" I demand.

"Who is it, Josef?" a woman asks, shoving her children aside.

"My parents! My sister. The Goldstein family! Where are they?"

The man steps away from my grasp. "We were brought in two days ago. Shoved in here like cattle through a chute. There are four other families just in these two rooms! I don't know who your family was. And I don't care! I have my own to worry about!"

"Josef, show some compassion," the woman says, coming into the hall and looking into my face. "We're sorry. We don't—"

A voice from the darkness down the hall breaks her off. "I know. I was here."

I push my way past the man and his wife. "What? What happened?" I ask the woman on the stair. She steps out of the shadows and I'm taken aback by her face. I can't believe she has the strength to talk, let alone stand. Even in layers of clothes and a blanket around her shoulders, she can't weigh more than eighty pounds.

"It was the middle of the night. It's always the middle of the night."

"Where did they take them? Did you hear?" I feel a panic rising up deep inside me.

"The Nazis never say. They just took your father. I heard the commotion. The old woman was dead, I don't know, maybe for a few days. That stupid old man went looking for an undertaker. That's probably how they knew to come after him." She tries to laugh, but only coughs. "Bodies being carried out by oxcart and he wanted an undertaker! Can you believe it?"

"Then what?" I demand. I want to shake the woman until she tells me that Ruthie is here somewhere. That she's hiding, playing a game!

"Then I heard him yelling when the soldiers came. I was sure they'd just shoot and be done with him."

"My sister, the little girl?"

"If she was with him, they took her, too, because she's not here."

"Someone turned them in." Another man comes out of the darkness and puts his arm around the tiny woman. His voice is clogged and thick. "Said he was stirring up trouble. Could have been any one of us here. You can only cram so many people into so small a space. And people will do anything for a few more ration cards."

"*Ach!* It was a bounty hunter," Josef says. "Money to be made, betraying good people, murdering little children. How much worse than a Nazi, a bounty hunter? How is it you think we got tossed in here?" He spits on the floor.

"What does it matter? They'll come back for all of us. It's just a matter of time. If the Nazis don't get us, typhus or pneumonia or an infected splinter will. Come, Josef, prayers," his wife says, following the sound of a child's cough.

I don't want to believe any of this! "No! Someone here must have . . ."

The emaciated woman shuffles back into the light with a photograph, slightly torn. "Here. Is this your sister?"

I hold it to the light. It's Ruthie—my heart leaps at her smile! The writing in the corner dates it: Ruthie's birthday, two years ago. "Yes," I whisper.

"My son found it behind a dresser. At least you have that. Such a beautiful child."

I feel my eyes sting. Why did I wait so long to come? Why wasn't I here to save Ruthie? All I needed was her . . . photograph . . . for her forged papers. I have the photo, but Ruthie's gone.

"*Lech l'shalom,*" the woman whispers to me, as though saying it out loud will bring the walls down around us. They all smile, turn their backs, then disappear back into the parlor, leaving me in the entry.

I walk down the steps. Numb, I walk back onto the street, clutching Ruthie's photograph, damning myself every step.

How did I let this happen? I should have been here! I look down at the photo in my hand. Ruthie! Every cell in my body screams. I kick slats off a fence, pull viciously at some bushes and throw the broken twigs and leaves into the air— anything to keep from crying out. If I can just stay angry at myself, I won't be able to cry.

But I know in my heart, in my soul—if I still have a soul—I can't afford to mourn. I might just as well walk around with a target painted on my back as cry. Law of the streets: you cry, you die.

Survive today. Cry tomorrow.

I head back to the Aryan side, shoving the memory of my parents behind me. But not the memory of Ruthie.

II.

I CRAWL BACK INTO MY HOME HOLE ON THE ARYAN SIDE. DON'T count what's gone, I tell myself. Count what I still have. I pull out the piss can from under the bed. Nestled under is another can—where I keep folded money. Coins rattle so I hide them in toes of shoes and false pockets of clothes. I keep Mrs. Praska's money along with the other important spoils of my war hidden in a hole in the wall, concealed by strips of wallpaper. Now, I pull it all out to make sure the rats haven't pilfered anything important. Even rats are on the take by now.

A soldier's binoculars, slipped right off his shoulder as I bumped into him.

Two bottles of wine, heisted off of café tables.

Six pairs of boots in escalating sizes, some spit and polished, some bloodstained, taken from men who no longer needed them.

Three fine, silver SS bits.

A numbering stamp that looks like any other, but has the eagle and swastika symbol.

Money in several currencies, earned on the streets, picked from pockets.

Twenty or so sets of false identification papers, some bought, some stolen. One for a six-year-old Aryan girl, just waiting for a photo to be attached.

Three *Ausweis* work permits, now priceless on the streets.

Several passes for clearance out of Poland, also priceless.

The coup de grâce: three German Army identification cards.

And, of course, a leather-bound edition of *Don Juan*.

My eyes land on the photograph of Ruthie. "God, look at you. So beautiful. So . . . so . . ." My whispers trail off. I open the locket to see Fritz's family smiling out in their shining, Aryan smiles. Also beautiful people. Loved, beautiful people.

As if to introduce them, I set the photo and the locket side by side.

Then it comes to me. I know what to do with these treasures.

I know Fritz exercises his horse on Saturdays, so I know exactly where to find him. Just him and his precious Hummel. The track around the polo field is a slushy, muddy oval. I watch from the knoll as Fritz canters his horse. Hummel's black coat is striking against the piled-up snow on either side of the track. The sun glistens off the ice-encrusted polo field. The horse puffs out steamy breaths like a dragon.

I toss a snowball in front of Hummel. The horse shies a bit and Fritz looks up to see me approach.

"Aren't you a bit off your own turf?" he asks. "*Nur für Deutsche.*"

"Yes, but the sun belongs to everyone," I say, patting Hummel's nose. "May I?" I pull a slice of apple out of my coat pocket.

"Go ahead."

We listen to the sound of the horse's bit jingle as Hummel crunches the apple.

"I'll bet you didn't come all this way to give Hummel an apple."

"You're right. I came to trade."

"What could you possibly have to—" He catches himself, looks down at me, and smiles as I hold his book up. "And what are you asking in exchange?"

"Information."

He looks around the field, dismounts, hands me the reins. "Here. Walk my horse so no one gets suspicious." He walks a few steps ahead of me and lights a cigarette.

"So, tell me about this trade."

"I need to know what happened to my family."

"You have a family?"

"Fritz, they were in the ghetto. And now they've been taken away."

"I'm sorry," he says, low enough for me to think he truly is.

"But you must be able to do something."

He exhales a small laugh. "What makes you think that?"

"Because . . . because you're not like the others."

"I'm sorry," he repeats, not looking at me.

"But there must be ledgers, accounts, names. Even numbers."

"Oh, there are numbers," he says. "Keep walking. I see some men just inside the stable."

I follow him into a paddock off to the side of the stable—out of eye and earshot. He loosens Hummel's girth and slides the stirrups up high under the saddle seat.

"What do you mean, numbers? Where do they take everyone?"

"Look, Arab, we are not talking hundreds or thousands. We're talking millions."

"Millions of what?" I shake my head. What's he talking about?

He lights a cigarette, exhales the smoke, and looks at me. "Jews, Arab, you fool. Jews from all across Europe! Hell, Hitler would bring them over from America if he could and don't think he isn't thinking about it. Don't you see? There are no names anymore! There isn't time for bookkeeping! God, why do you make me spell it out?"

"No, you have a way of finding them. I know you do! Here's the address. I've written everything down so you can find—"

"You're not getting this."

I pull out the photo of Ruthie. "Now, here's a photo of my sister. Her name is—well, it's all on that paper." I hold up Lord Byron. "You get your book back when you tell me where I can find my sister."

He shakes his head, pulls a brush from his saddlebag, and begins wiping the mud off Hummel. "How could someone as smart as you be so fucking stupid?" he asks, his cigarette bobbing off his lips as he speaks.

I pull him around and show him the picture again.

He stops and takes the photo. I pull out the locket, open it, and hold it next to the photograph of Ruth. "Ruth sort of looks like this girl here, don't you think?" I point to the youngest face in the photo. "Blonde, blue-eyed."

He takes the cigarette out to clear the rising smoke out of his eyes. I watch his face. He looks first at Ruthie, then his own sisters' photos, then back to Ruthie. He tosses his cigarette to the ground where it hisses as it hits the snow. "She's very pretty. Looking Aryan, maybe she'll be okay. Like you."

"Fritz, they took her away!"

"Arab, I'm just a spit of grease on the cog in this whole damn wheel!"

"What would Henri say to that?"

He pauses, looks out over the treetops, and whispers, "It doesn't matter what Henri would say. Henri's dead." He looks at me, his face now hard. "Taken away in the middle of the night, Arab. He was just a number, too. If I could help you, I would. I'd do it for Henri and I'd do it for your Ruth."

I toss his book and the locket down at his feet. The muddy slush envelopes them. Fritz kneels down and picks them up, knocks the mud and snow off. He stands up and stares at me. I take a step back.

"So there you have it, Arab! You're a Jew and I'm a god-damn faggot! We're both doomed. Just like your Ruth. Just like my Henri! So there you . . ."

Fritz stops and follows my horrified gaze beyond him. He turns and freezes. The soldier behind him has heard every word.

My Luger is out of my pocket in an instant. Fritz makes a grab for the gun.

The shot echoes off the polo grounds, leaving us with only the sound of birds scattering above.

The intruder, shot through the face, dead before he hits the ground. Before he can ever repeat what he's just heard.

Fritz stares at me.

"He heard you, Fritz! He heard everything!"

The shock in his face finally smoothes into a stern, jaw-flexed scowl. "Go! Now!"

I pocket my gun and run off as fast as the snow will let me.

I make it back to Three Crosses Square and scramble into my hideout, numb with grief. Not over the boy's life I just took. Grief over the girl's life I can't save.

III.

I STRUGGLE TO OPEN MY EYES. THEY'RE CRUSTY AND STUCK together. I blink tears into them. The glorious moment of fog vanishes and it all comes back to me . . . I see my old home, the near-dead woman, the news, Fritz . . . the dead soldier.

I count the twelve hash marks I've made on the wall over my bed. One for each innocent I saw massacred on the street, that day so long ago. I take my knife and make an X out of the first hash mark.

My first kill. Eleven to go.

I change to a heavier coat, wrap a wool scarf around my head to hide my face, and head out. Winter makes for easier disguising.

I hitch a ride on the back of a lorry toward Mrs. Praska's. I owe her a visit, and her weekly cut. The day is sunny, but very, very cold. The glare hurts my eyes and the chilly air numbs my face, making me cold all over.

I hop off the lorry and head west, careful to peer around every corner before I round it. I come into a spot of sunlight. Damn it! Beggars everywhere I turn!

"Please, sir?" one little boy asks. Three of the fingers of his glove are missing and his tiny hand shakes. A smaller child stands behind him.

I ignore them, go half a block, then stop. I clench my jaw to give me strength against their penetrating eyes. The boys huddle against the wind, trying to warm themselves in the sun.

"Jesus, Joseph, and Mary," I growl, borrowing Lizard's favorite expression. "Danger all over Warsaw. Think of your own hide!" I curse myself as I walk back to the children.

The two boys look up. The older boy pushes the younger one behind him. "I don't want any trouble," the child says, jutting a brave chin out. I remember my father telling me the same thing.

"Oh, you don't, do you? Well, that makes a million of us!" I snap, rummaging through my coat pockets, then pulling out six packs of cigarettes. "Look, these aren't to eat, you little brats, but just do what I tell you, okay?"

The younger boy reaches for the cigarettes with a grin. "Hmm, cigarettes . . ."

The older boy slaps his hand. "Stefan! Mama forbid us to smoke!"

"Yeah, but . . ."

"Shut up!" the older says, shoving him back around. Undoubtedly brothers. He points to the cigarettes. "What do we do with those?" he asks me, a look of suspicion on his face.

"Take these cigarettes over to the Three Crosses Square. You know where that is?"

"Mama said we should never go there. She said . . ."

"I know where it is!" the younger brother pipes up.

"Good. There's a newsstand there. Ask for Lizard. He'll show you what to do. Are you Jews?" I ask.

"Mama said we're too young to be Jews," the little one states. "I'm eight and Lorenz is ten."

"She said we didn't have to wear those armbands," the older one, Lorenz, informs me.

"That's why they took her away," the little guy says, now frowning.

"That's not what I asked you," I say sternly. "Are you Jews?"

The older brother carefully replies, "Yes, are you?"

"Look, you, you're never going to make it out of here being stupid! Never tell anyone you're Jewish, or else you're dead! Got that?" I stuff the cigarettes into the boys' hands. "Now, get going. Ask for Lizard. Think you can remember Lizard?"

"I can!" the younger says, venturing a peek up at me.

"Shut up!"

"I don't have to!"

I kneel down to the level of the younger brother. Something in his sassy defiance warms me, just a little. It also scares me. "Listen . . . what's your name?"

"Stefan."

"Listen, Stefan. This is a very scary time. You have to do what your brother tells you so you can stay together, and maybe even find your mother, okay?"

"Okay," he whispers. His little hand pulls down my scarf. "Are you a girl?" He turns to his brother. "Hey look, Lorenz, he isn't a sir, he's a her. You got any kids, lady, because we might need a . . ."

"Stefan!" his brother shouts. "Shut up!"

"I don't have to!"

"Look, never, ever, either of you, ever tell anyone you're Jewish or that your mother has been taken away." Then, I turn to the older brother. "Lorenz, was she taken away by the soldiers?"

"Two weeks ago." His eyes well up with tears. "She hid us in the linen closet, and when we came out, she was gone. Then some old man said we had to leave our apartment."

Little Stefan spits on the ground. "I'll kill all the Nazis. Wait and see if I don't!"

"You and what army?"

"Me and the army of God!"

"God took his army out of town a long time ago," I reply, re-buttoning my coat. "Now, are you Jewish?"

"No!" the boys answer in determined unison.

"Then what are you?" I ask gruffly, folding my arms like I'm a Nazi interrogator.

They look at each other.

"Hungry!" the younger one replies.

"No, you're a Pole. Got that? Just say you are a Catholic Pole. You might find a church still standing and learn about Jesus."

"Is he giving out food?" Stefan asks.

"I said shut up, Stefan!"

"I can't! Mama says I got too much chutzpah to shut up!"

"Look, kid, your brother's right," I say to this feisty little tyke. "Shut up. Chutzpah can get you killed. Now, who will you ask for at the newsstand?" I quiz as I start to back away.

"Lizard!" the boys reply, their brotherly voices in a gentle harmony.

I am nearly out of voice range, but I heard the young one call out, *"A sheynem dank!"*

I cringe at his Yiddish.

"Yeah, thank me in hell," I mutter, thinking they'll probably never live to see 1941.

IV.

I CONTINUE ALONG THE NEW ROUTE I'VE MADE TO OUR CIGA-rette factory. I have several paths I take, depending on the day and what's happening. The last thing you leave any-where in Warsaw is a track. Hell, even a scent! The entrance into the factory is now through the chute to the coal cellar that we keep hidden by leaves and brush. The overhangs and eaves above the chute were the first sections of the house the family cannibalized for firewood so snow falls straight down and covers our entrance. If snow can be a blessing, it can also be a curse. To keep tracks in the snow to a mini-mum, I walked along a path of boards, jumping from one to another.

"I see Pawel is better," I say, handing Mrs. Praska her cut for the week and touching the baby's cool cheek.

"And just where the hell have you been?" she demands, adjusting Pawel on her hip and pulling me inside. The faint light hits my face. "You look like death."

"Tending to family business, not that it's your con-cern," I snap. I haven't told her anything about my family, about Ruthie.

"I see," she snaps back. Her five younger children gather around me as I give each a piece of Christmas candy. "And for you," I say, handing Mrs. Praska a vial.

"Morphine? Where . . . how?"

"What's our agreement?" She doesn't need to know I stole it for my mother. That she, my father, and my sister are gone.

"Ask her no questions and she'll tell you no lies," Yankev answers.

"You can't tell what you don't know," I snap back at him. "You're looking hearty, Yankev. Seems eating agrees with you." I pat his stomach. "But don't get too fat. Nothing's more suspicious these days than a fat Jew."

Yankev steps back, as though my touch is poison. I know Yankev and I have a day of reckoning ahead of us. But we all have bigger problems just now.

Mrs. Praska pours tea. "What's the news out there?"

I spare her the details, like I always do. "Winter. I would steal you more coal, but the competition is pretty steep this time of year. Every cellar has been raided. Most of the furniture is gone, too."

"The street is lined with trees," Yankev says, pointing toward the side door.

"Nothing like a tree stump to point the way to a family in hiding. Just follow the trail of sawdust."

"I know places out there," he goes on. "And I know how to cover up a trail."

"Well, just remember this, Yankev. While you are out there proving me wrong, there are six children and a woman here knowing I was right."

Little Michal, the four-year-old, hauls over a burlap sack of recently rolled cigarettes. "Did you get the special ingredient?" I ask Mrs. Praska.

"I harvested it myself, from dear Mrs. Kaplan's greenhouse. Bless her soul. To think, we used to tease her about her herbs, medicines, and cures. Dried oleander. I cut the mix myself. Fifty-fifty, just like we decided."

I snap off a piece of straw from a broom in the corner and hold it up to her. "Shall we split a straw on it?"

She snaps off a piece and I offer the straw to Yankev.

"Did you tell him?" I ask Mrs. Praska.

"Yes, she told me," Yankev barks. "Oleander is poison. You're going to get us all killed with your stupid plan!"

"Only our special customers. *Nur für Deutsche*," I say, lifting the sack and ignoring Yankev's opinions. Mrs. Praska and I share a wicked smile.

"Each pack has a tiny purple crayon mark on the bottom," she says, her face alive with mischief.

"Two in each pack?"

"By a fluke of chance," she says. "Or luck of the draw. Whichever you choose."

At that, I hold up my straw. "Secrecy?"

She touches her straw to mine. "Secrecy."

We both look at Yankev. He hesitates, then touches his straw to ours. "Secrecy. Mother, look what Arab is doing to you."

"Arab is not doing it!" she screams, pointing outside. "The Krauts! They are doing it! They do this to me, to us all!" She turns to me. "Be careful this time. Very careful."

"Lizard and I have it all planned out. We're going to spread the boys all across Warsaw so, if this actually works, no one can connect the dots and suspect us." I pick up the other burlap sack. "And these?"

"For Jews and Poles," Mrs. Praska says. "See? The drawstring is black."

Yankev escorts me to the door. "Did you do the inventory?" I ask him.

"We're getting low. What are the chances you can steal a tobacco shipment?"

"Don't think I'm not working on it."

"Is there anything the great Arab of Warsaw can't do?" He tosses down his straw.

"Yes. Plenty."

"Well, I'm sick of the way my mother worships you. Arab this and Arab that. If it wasn't for Arab, we'd all be dead." He mimics his mother's voice. "Now this." He points to the sacks of cigarettes.

"Yankev. This is what I do. You were right about me the very first time you met me. I'm nothing but a common gonif. A stupid, bleeding female at that! If any of us gets out of this alive, you can take full credit for everything. You can be the hero, because I'm just saving my own hide. You have family here, but out there it's every man for himself—so you might be thinking about your own hide!"

His face changes. "I did. I did save my own hide. The day they came to arrest my father. I ran and hid in the attic. Like a scaredy little girl." He turns away from me and bows his head, sniffs, then turns back around. "Yeah, I'm the big hero."

I see his tears. God, I do not need him breaking down. Not now. You cry, you die.

"Yankev," I say, pointing to his family in the apartment, "where would they be without you? Your God helps those who help themselves. It is written."

"My father didn't believe that."

"Yankev, your father is dead. Just get used to that. You have the rest of your life to enjoy your guilt."

"Sometimes you make me sick!" His face changes. "Then sometimes you make me . . . ashamed. You're . . . I mean . . . you're just a girl."

"No. I'm just a Pole, Yankev. Doing the best I can with what I have. And right now, I need you to open that door and see if it's clear." I pick up the burlap sacks.

He opens the door and looks outside both directions. "It's clear."

I pause, touch his shoulder. "Yankev, your family needs you. Forget your father. Just follow the living."

His face hardens again. I know that face. I know he's holding back tears. He nods, and he closes the door behind me.

V.

IF THE MARKET FOR CIGARETTES ON THE ARYAN SIDE OF Warsaw is brisk, the market for them on the ghetto side is fantastic. But that damn wall! So inconvenient! Getting into the ghetto means it's the sewers or it's nothing. They can weld shut some of the covers, but the sewers can't be bricked up—blood, piss, shit, and puke all need to return to the sea. A law of nature even the Germans can't break; even they have blood, piss, shit, and puke. And the sewers guzzle it all, regardless of what race it spews from.

There are others in the sewers, of course, but each day there are fewer and fewer. Some partisans, some underground resistance workers, even some who whisper of an uprising.

"*Dror Hechaluc,*" the kid says, following me after I come out the sewers. He isn't the first to try to recruit me.

"Armed youth resistance?" I say back, looking him up and down. "Armed? With what? Peashooters? Slingshots?" I laugh and continue on.

"We'll get guns! Come and join us."

"Join you? Why? I have nothing to rise up against! But here!" I toss a pack of cigarettes to the boy with big ideas. "For your last smoke, when Goliath lines you up against the wall. Good luck, David."

I continue on alone.

Most people subscribe to the safety in numbers theory. Not me. Especially not after those twelve people were assassinated, counting off by threes. I believe in a solo act. I learned this artful dance long before the Germans arrived: pretend to look into a store window to watch the reflections behind you; sneeze into a handkerchief or stoop to pick something up to hide your face from a passerby; hold up a newspaper with pin holes punched through and it looks like you're reading, not spying. A shard of broken mirror can save your life, help you see around a corner, behind you, signal your accomplice, reflect a spot on your enemy, slice a throat.

The roundups and searches and deportations to the ghetto or to Elsewhere are so commonplace by now, I don't think anyone even takes the time to watch, shake their heads, and mutter "How horrible. How horrible." They may as well have issued horse blinders, the way they—we—turn our heads and look straight ahead. If I don't see it, maybe it didn't happen. Maybe I won't remember it.

"Thought you'd like to see this," I say, plopping a newspaper down in front of Mrs. Praska as she sits with her brood around the kitchen table.

"You know I can't read German. I don't suppose it says the Krauts have changed their minds and are leaving Poland," she says, gently bouncing Pawel on her knee.

"Well, not exactly. Here, let me read it to you. 'Mysterious ailment claims lives of six patrolmen.'" I catch her eye.

"Oh, dear," she mocks. "Do read on."

"'Fourteen others seriously ill.'"

She puts her hand to her mouth and shakes her head. "What a world."

"Wait. It gets better. 'Rare Jewish disease suspected.'" I let that sink in.

"How horrible," she says, her smile widening. "I certainly hope they find a cure."

Mrs. Praska and I gloat. She brings out a bottle of wine she's been saving for a special occasion and allows each of her children a sip. We have killed six Germans. We drink a toast to those Mrs. Praska has avenged—her husband, his foreman, and her four neighbors, the founders of our feast of revenge. We drink a toast to those I have avenged—half the Jews I saw shot at the Crystal Café.

When I get home I'll mark off six more hash marks on my wall.

Seven down. Five to go.

DECEMBER, 1940

I.

I STOP COLD, HALFWAY UP THE FOURTH-FLOOR STAIRCASE TO MY apartment, remembering I have to use all five senses to survive. Feel the atmosphere, smell the enemy, see around corners, hear thoughts, taste danger. Then intuition kicks in. I look down the hall of the fourth floor and inhale. I smell trouble. Cigarette smoke. I glimpse a black uniform in my room. I can hear him lifting things, looking in drawers. God, what have I left out? Nothing. I'd never leave anything out in plain sight. Not in this hole or any other. Everything is well hidden. Except . . . oh God, the piss pot! Did I remember to empty it this morning?

Okay, Arab, what will it be? Fight or flight? I've gotten up here undetected. Can I get back down? No, too late, I'm here. I slowly set down my pack and pull out the Luger.

"You there!" a voice calls through my doorway.

I raise the gun and aim it toward his face. The click of the safety is deafening. His hands spring up as he slowly backs further into the room.

I follow him, keeping my gun high and steady. With a start, I recognize him—Captain Wilhelm Schneider, the very same who ordered the execution of those twelve Jews. The man who shot the woman because I tore her armband off. So, how does a man like that react when a gun is pointed between his eyes? What does he say? What does he do?

He does nothing. He stands frozen; he doesn't blink. He doesn't even breathe. The smoke from the cigarette between his fingers wafts up.

"What did you say, Herr *Hauptsturmführer*?" the other soldier asks from the adjacent room.

Now I have two. Wilhelm Schneider and Fritz Von Segen.

I point my gun at Fritz. He raises his hands.

I glance around the room and see they've rifled through everything.

"Well, well. The information was correct. It *is* your little cigarette seller, Fritz." Schneider says.

Fritz looks at me, knowing full well I understand German. "*Ja, ja,*" he says.

"Well then, this is your problem, Von Segen. Do something. These people can be bought off. Work a deal," Schneider says, never taking his eyes off the tip of my gun.

"I'm afraid you've been discovered, Arab," Fritz says in Polish. "This could get very ugly."

I turn to the captain. "Open the window." My German is quite succinct. He hesitates. I step closer and put the gun to his chest. "*Jetzt!*" He tosses down his cigarette and lifts the window up. I tell him to climb onto the sill.

"Arab," Fritz says, seeing my plan. "Arab, don't—"

The captain looks first at Fritz, then at me. Horror and disbelief cover his face. "You miserable Polish pig, you are dead!"

"Probably, but you first. Jump!"

He stands frozen in the frame of the window. He looks at Fritz as though he's supposed to do something. I train my gun closer and pull up the breech block.

"*Bitte, bitte,*" he pleads. Then, "Fritz, for God's sake!"

"Jump!" I shove my gun into his gut. It's enough to put him off balance, and he falls out. I hear the thump as he lands on the snow-covered alley below.

I look out the window. Down at the crumpled body of the Nazi officer.

"Why didn't you just shoot him?" Fritz asks. "Too messy?" He nods to the Luger in my hand. "You could have shot us both and still have enough for a few more. It seems to be your sport of choice this season."

"I had to do it," I mumble. Then I look hard at Fritz. I turn the Luger on him. "How did you know to look for me here?"

"Put the gun down." He shakes a cigarette out of a pack and offers it to me.

"How did you know?"

He pulls up a chair. "There are snipers and snitches everywhere."

"Sniper," I whisper.

"Schneider pays the snitch, then collects the German bounty himself. Simple commerce. Everyone gets a little something."

"Except the Jew."

"Except the Jew," he repeats.

I put the Luger on the table next to all my stashed belongings—evidence of my trades.

"Don't worry, Arab. I had no idea this was your hideout."

"So, what will your report say?"

"What report? We aren't even on duty. He ordered me to come with him."

"No one knows you're here?"

"No. But there'll be an investigation, once they find his body. Are you going to kill someone every time we meet? Because, if so, we need to set some ground rules."

"Fritz, that soldier at the stables heard everything you said! We'd both have bullets through our heads! This is war, you know. We are enemies. That's what enemies do—they kill each other!"

"I know," he says with wistful sigh. "That private at the stable would have turned in his own brother if it meant a promotion. We're all enemies."

"How did you explain it? That man at the stables?"

"I didn't. I just walked back to the barracks and let someone else find him."

"Then all's well that ends well," I say.

"No, it's not. I hate to be . . ." He seems to search for the word. ". . . indebted to the enemy. Makes for a very complicated war." He goes to the window and looks down at Schneider's body.

"And I've just complicated it even more," I say.

"Schneider deserved it. I hated him for his *eins, zwei, drei* method of execution. What he forced us to become. He was the worst of us." His face has lost its healthy ruddiness, I notice. Just like all of us in Warsaw. We are all becoming shades of gray. "Schneider was a killing machine. The Nazi ideal."

"He's more ideal to me now." I look down at my hands and pick at a scab. "Funny. When I first met you, I thought you were the Nazi ideal." He gives me a curious look. I wonder if he's insulted or flattered.

I stand up. "Come on, follow me out of here."

I lead him downstairs and see him safely to the delivery entrance. He pauses at the door. "It's a clean slate now, Arab. From now on, it's a new war. It has to be. Things are changing. It's a new war."

He smiles weakly, wraps his black muffler about his face, and trots off toward the street.

I go back upstairs, gather up my things. I can't stay here any longer. Not with "snipers and snitches" out there. Fritz's parting words stick in my head as I pack. "Great. A new war," I mumble. "I was just getting used to the old one."

I make an X in honor of Captain Wilhelm Schneider on my wall. I pause to look at the hash marks. With the tip of my knife, I count the eight X's, wondering if a stab of guilt will ever pierce me over the Germans—the enemies—I've killed. No, guilt needs to be reserved for those who count. My only guilt is over Ruthie.

I take one last look at the body of the captain, four stories down in the alley. Seeing the frozen splatters of blood, watching a lowlife creep up, inspect the body, kick it, rummage through the pockets, then yank off those prized black leather boots, spit on the body, and run off is . . . it's . . . can I say it? It's joyful. Joy to the world! As the Christians sing.

No guilt. Joy.

What bothers me, really bothers me, is . . . deep down inside, when I'm this weary and sins are easy to confess . . . I'm liking this. They drum in your head that revenge belongs to God. But it's oh so sweet when it's all mine.

I know what I've been, but oh God, look at what I'm becoming.

II.

"YOU KNOW, ARAB, WE CAN'T TAKE ON ANY MORE," LIZARD says. He points the tip of his knife to our gang of boys. There's eight of us, altogether. "It was easier in summer when there was more food to swipe, more people out and about. But this snow, this weather. Eight's the limit. I know you're hurting about losing Ruth. We've all lost people we love, but that doesn't mean we can afford to go picking up every stray we find."

He goes back to slicing the loaf of bread into eight equal parts. "Come on, get some bread," he calls out to the boys, who appear in an instant from every corner of our new, larger hideout. This old house is perfect since it's closer to our "distribution center" in Three Crosses Square.

"I mean, Stefan and Lorenz are great little brats," Lizard goes on, crumbs from his crust of bread falling out of his mouth.

"They speak Hebrew and Yiddish," I say. "That's helpful. Besides, what was I going to do? And look how they seem to fit right in. When have you seen a more budding pickpocket than that Stefan?"

"Just promise me, Arab, no more. We can't afford to feed any more. And I don't care what their street potential might be."

"You know, there's something else we can't afford." I reach inside a small cupboard and pull out a wad of turquoise material. I shake it out and twirl the fine silk shawl, complete with fringe, around my shoulders.

"Arab . . . that's . . ." Lizard says, reaching for it.

I step back. There's a price tag hanging from the label. "House of Andre. Paris, France. Ooh la la."

"I mean it, Arab! Give that back!"

"Just tell me you stole this and didn't pay . . ." I look at the price tag. "Twenty!"

"Arab!"

"British pounds? So right here is something we can't afford!"

"Give that back!"

"I thought we weren't going to exchange presents this Christmas."

He finally grabs it away and bunches it up. "We're not. That is, you and I aren't."

The smile falls off my face. "What?"

"I mean—God, Arab! That's not for you," he says, his voice low.

"Well, certainly not Mrs. Praska," I say. "She'd never wear anything so . . ."

The look on his face tells me I am so, so wrong.

"It's not for you. It's for someone else."

"Who?" I manage to ask. I can feel my face redden with embarrassment—humiliation—jealousy?

"Irenka. Oh, come on, Arab. Don't take it that way. You and me have never . . . you know."

"Who's Irenka?"

"Remember that cute nurse over at the infirmary? The one who helped us get the identification? So we could forge that pass for your sister?"

Another sting of memory. "Oh. I thought she was just a passing fancy," I say, trying to recover.

"Oh, she passed my fancy some time ago."

I smile and point to the shawl. "Um, good. I mean. Great. I'm glad you've found someone. I assume she's someone you can trust."

"As much as anyone can be trusted these days," he says, putting the lovely shawl away. He comes over to me. I feel like such a damn fool! "And yes, I did steal it. I'd never jeopardize our survival by spending money on anything so trivial."

I smile back at him. "Okay. I know. It's okay. I was just joking—having some fun. Teasing."

"I know," he says. The boys are starting up a boisterous game with a small rubber ball. "Hey you!" He catches the ball and tosses it into a corner. "Quiet! Get your coats and get ready to move out! We have cigarettes to sell! Papers to filch! Shoes to shine! You too, Lorenz! And Stefan, quit pulling his hair!"

They pile out, leaving me alone. I pull a box out from another cubby hiding spot. I open it and finger the meerschaum pipe I've stolen for Lizard. What a beauty! I put it in my knapsack. I'll have it sold in no time.

I try to laugh off the whole incident. Even though that shawl is probably the most beautiful thing I've ever seen.

I layer on my sweaters, coat, muffler, scarf, and hat. Just when I think I know everything, I find out I don't know shit. I think about what Fritz has told me. He's oh-so-right. So goddamn right. It's a very complicated war.

Once I'm safe in my new hiding spot, I pull out my notebook, light a short candle, and begin to write.

WHAT'S WHITE IS BLACK
WHAT'S BLACK IS WHITE

SHADES OF GRAY
THROUGHOUT THE NIGHT
WHAT'S RIGHT IS WRONG
WHAT'S WRONG IS RIGHT
THE STRONG SURVIVE
THE WEAK DON'T FIGHT
BUT LOVE SURVIVES
DON'T ASK ME HOW
DON'T ASK ME ANYTHING
DON'T ASK JUST NOW

III.

"HEY, ARAB!" A SMALL VOICE CALLS OUT. "WHERE YOU BEEN?"

I grab the boy and shove him up against the wall. "How many times have I told you to keep your voice down?" I growl into his ear.

Little Stefan looks up at me and repeats in a whisper, "Hey, Arab. Where you been? Lizard's been looking two days for you!"

"So what? He doesn't own me." I admit to not wanting to see Lizard. Not after I humiliated myself over a stupid, frilly, girly scarf.

I let him go and look around the area. "Getting stuff done. Which is none of your businesses, that's where! Where's Lorenz?"

"He's not Lorenz. He's the Lion. I'm the Jaguar!"

"You're nothing till I say you are," I say, walking ahead toward our den.

Stefan scampers after me. "Uh-uh," he calls out. "Lizard said we could pick our own street names."

"Well, Lizard doesn't king our gang! I do!"

"How can a girl be a king?" he persists. I grab his arm, put my nose to his, and bark, "Who's the boss?"

"You are."

"Who got you into this trade in the first place?" I let go and keep walking, forcing him to struggle to keep up with me.

"You, Arab."

"And who makes cigarettes for you to sell?"

"You."

"Who taught you about crowds and pockets?"

"You."

"Who taught you to have eyes in the back of your head? To look up for pigeon fanciers?"

"I had a friend who kept pigeons," he says, trying to change the subject.

"No, you little idiot! German snipers up there on the rooftops!" I point a finger gun down at him. "*Bang!* You'd make a perfect little target. And you'd wake up with your head decorating the top of a lamppost!"

I stop fast and Stefan, not watching where he's going, piles into me. I turn, bend down to look at him. The color has gone out of his face. "I don't want to decorate a lamp post," he whimpers.

"Well, you will if you don't do what I tell you! Got it? Where's your brother? Why aren't you setting up a pitch?"

"They cut the power at the factory again. Mrs. Praska said to cool our heels." He lifts a snow and mud-caked boot. "Hell, Arab, my foot's already half froze!"

I have to laugh at him—Stefan does have his innocent charm. I hate to be reminded of Ruthie, but there it is. "All right. Let's meet at the den. Go find Lorenz."

Lizard answers my knock at our new den. I come in, walking past him. "Just where the hell have you been?" he asks.

I ignore him and slice myself a piece of bread. "I don't owe you any explanations."

"Well, a guy gets worried, you know."

"Don't waste your worry on me," I say, disguising the twinge of jealousy in my voice with a slight cough. "So, what's going on?" I ask, changing the subject.

"The electricity's still out at the factory, there's no cigarettes to sell, and the gang is bored to death. Frankly, so am I. And usually at Christmas time, there's so much action out there."

"It's no fair, neither! Those Krauts get lights and Christmas trees and all the good stuff!" Lorenz says, picking up on Lizard's complaint. "We don't even get a Menorah candle!"

From the back of the den I hear Stefan singing an old Jewish folk song. "Stefan! Stop singing that! What have I told you?"

"You didn't say I couldn't sing."

"Who sings Jewish songs?"

He looks at his brother, then at me. His face scrunches in anger as he hollers, "Jews! Damn it! Jews!"

"And what are you?" Lizard asks him. "Stefan! What are you?"

"Mad as hell!" he shouts.

"Who at?" Lizard asks.

"Everyone! I like to sing! Those Catholics sing, and so do the Nazis. How come I can't?"

"And just what do you have to sing about, anyway?" I ask him.

"Nothing, and that makes me mad, too!" Stefan says. "We used to sing. Remember Lorenz? For parties Mama and Papa . . . had . . . and . . ." Hardened as the boys are getting, they still have their moments of mourning, following by stoic chins and cast-aside tears.

"Oh, go ahead and let him sing. Sing us a song," Lizard says.

When Lorenz hesitates, I give him a shove toward his brother. "Just keep it low. Don't want to tell the world we have Jews down here."

They sing us a version of "The Dreidel Song," first in Yiddish and upbeat, then slow and in Hebrew. I've heard a lot of versions over the years, but the brothers sing in a lovely, sweet harmony.

Lizard and I latch eyes.

"I got an idea," Lizard says "It's Christmas time."

"But that's not a Christmas song, Lizard." Then, my eyes widen. "Oh!"

"Boys singing on the corner. People might toss a coin or some bread. It's worth a try," Lizard says.

Lizard knows the songs, and I know the German words. The boys are quick studies and we start teaching them the ones they already know the tunes to: *"Stille Nacht," "O Tannenbaum,"* and *"Still, Still, Still."* The other boys are soon joining in, making quite a chorus.

Lizard and I step outside for a smoke.

"Guess who I ran into today," he says.

"Who?"

"Our old friend, Sniper."

My jaw tightens. I haven't told Lizard about my run-ins with Sniper, or Fritz and Schneider. The two dead Krauts. Any of it. Don't need him rushing to my defense—or worse, avenging me. That's something I want all to myself. But I was hoping when Sniper sold me out to Schneider it put him off my trail. "That schmuck? Hoped he'd be dead by now."

"No. In fact, he's looking quite the dandy. Even snappier than when we saw him in the ghetto."

"Did he ask about me?"

"Well, that's the funny part. He said he was going to miss you. Heard you were arrested."

"And what did you say?" I try to sound casual as I sit, fiddling with my buttonless cuff.

"Well, I told him he must have heard wrong. Unless there's something you're not telling me."

"There's a lot I don't tell you," I mutter, visualizing Schneider's crumpled body.

He steps closer and looks into my face.

"What?" I say, glancing up.

"Something I've been meaning to ask. Did Sniper . . . Did he ever . . . get you?" Lizard asks, his voice low and soft.

"What do you mean, 'get'?" I narrow my eyes at him. I think I know where he's going with this.

"You know. I mean, did he, because he always bragged he was going to . . . get you."

"You mean fuck me? I'd kill myself first! Then I'd kill him!" I issue a weak laugh, afraid it's a bit too feminine.

Lizard grasps my hand. "Because, you know, Arab, if he did, I mean, I'd kill him. I'd kill anyone who did you any harm."

"Should I warn Hitler?"

"Come on, Arab. I'm serious. You know how much I think of you. I couldn't love my own sister more."

"You don't have a sister."

"Well, if I did."

"Thanks, brother."

He takes his hand back and even seems a bit embarrassed. "Well, anyway, we'll keep an eye out for Sniper."

I feel an uncomfortable need to change the subject. "Hey, those brats sound pretty good in there."

We go back inside and the boys give us their first performance. Their voices blend like angels!

"Why didn't you tell us you two can sing?" I ask.

"Why didn't you ask?" Stefan replies.

Lizard shoves me. "And just think, Arab—if you join them, people will pay you to stop singing! We'll be rich!" I form a fist and take a sisterly swing at him, which he easily ducks, laughing.

So we have Lorenz and Stefan singing on the street corners. Their sopranos are a perfect pitch and their serious faces a perfect ploy to distract and maybe even comfort people our second Christmas of the Nazi occupation. Who would think two little Jews could sing Christmas carols so earnestly, so passionately? Perhaps because, even at eight and ten, they know their lives—our lives—depend on it.

If we don't have goods to sell, the other boys join them, adding to the harmony. Even groups of German soldiers gather around the singing boys. Away from home and loved ones. Hell, even a Kraut has a home and loved ones, somewhere—mothers and sisters who pray for them, sweethearts who write to them, fathers and brothers who brag about them. Do they know these street carolers are Jews? Do they care?

IV.

"STEFAN! WHERE DID YOU GET THIS?"

"I lifted it off of that tall *szwab* who buys cigarettes on Mondays. You know the one."

"Lorenz sang and I lifted. It's probably worth a million *zloty*!"

I look at the inscription. How many times have I tried to walk away with this very same lighter? Fritz's lighter. Now handed to me by my little street Arab. It's the best present I've ever received.

"Except, you know what?" Stefan says, lowering his voice. "There was this man who sort of followed us."

I look around the square. The snow, the people rushing about, the sad attempt to resurrect a holiday, the soldiers. Nothing unusual.

"Did he have a uniform? A soldier?"

"Nah, just a man," Lorenz says. "At first, I thought maybe he saw me lifting the lighter, but he didn't say or do anything. Just sort of walked away."

"Well, remember, you don't talk to anyone who looks like they're following you," I say, but I'm thinking about Sniper and his black book.

I give the boys more cigarettes and get them set up. With this sudden break between snowfalls, people will be filling the square. But I don't go far, just stand in the shadow of a storefront. I'm not leaving the boys alone.

There. Who's that man? I come out of the shadows and stand between him and my boys. "Stefan, Lorenz, get behind me."

"That's the man," Lorenz whispers up to me. I step closer to meet the man, eye to eye. Gentile, I think. Blue eyes behind wire-framed glasses, fair hair, rosy complexion. New here. Too healthy. Careful, careful, careful.

"We're selling cigarettes, nothing more," I say in German. I open my coat and display a fresh load of cigarettes bursting out of the inside pockets Mrs. Praska has sewn for all us street sellers.

"Cute kid. Is he your brother?"

"Cigarettes or not?"

"Yes, please."

I use Fritz's lighter to light one from the pack he buys and watch his face as he exhales. He coughs a little. "Hmm, I think I detect a hint of tobacco in this."

"Things are tough all over," I say. He looks out over the area. He wants something besides cigarettes, that's sure. He's not leaving. "I haven't seen you in this district before. Come home for the holidays?" It's a standard street joke.

"Well, yes, in a way," he replies. His German is perfect and I feel a deeper chill. Out of the corner of my eyes, I look him over. Clean coat, fur collar, thick leather gloves, felt hat— and galoshes! Who has money or time for galoshes? And he's young. Soldier-boy young. Bet he's not over twenty. What's he doing here in Warsaw, dressed like this? Young German men are conscripted. This one looks like he should at the very least be prepping for final exams at some university, not smoking with the likes of me on the streets of Warsaw. Something's not right here. I button my heavy coat and plunge my hand into my pocket, reassured by the cool tip of my switchblade.

"Well, enjoy your smokes. I sell on this corner most days."

"So my sources are correct? You're the cigarette seller they call the Arab?"

I try not to react. Plenty of people know me, know where and what I sell. I grab Stefan's collar. "You and Lorenz go start some songs on that corner. The factories let out soon. Now!"

Once they're gone, I step closer to the stranger. He takes a step back. "So, just who the hell are you? And what sources are you talking about? Believe me, stranger, I have my gang right around the corner, so—"

Stefan and Lorenz are singing now. The stranger cocks his head toward their music. "They going to sing me to death?" He smiles. "I mean you no harm."

"You have your cigarettes, then, so get lost!"

I walk toward the boys, and the man sloshes through the snow after me. I turn on him again, but he puts his hands up. "My name is Otto Braunsteiner. I work for a small but well-funded charity—"

"Charity! There's a laugh! You've come to the wrong city and the wrong country, Braunsteiner! There's no charity here."

"Perhaps you'll let me finish."

His eyes are soft and a bit magnified by his spectacles. They seem almost peaceful—or maybe just innocent. I cross my arms and take a stance. "Talk."

"A well-funded char—let's call it an organization—in America who . . ."

"America!" I interrupt again. He exhales heavily. "Where's America? On the moon? They don't even know Warsaw exists. Fuck America!"

"America will come. Until then, I have come." He flashes a smile of youthful confidence, so rare now in Warsaw.

"So what does that make you? The Messiah?"

He chuckles. "Hardly. I don't believe in any of that crap."

"But you think you can save us poor, suffering, dumb Poles from the big mean Nazis? Go home. We don't need your help."

"I've got a job to do, and I've come to do it," he states, as plainly as if he's the exterminator come to check the rat traps.

"Look, stranger, no one wants into Poland. Everyone wants out of Poland."

"I don't want to talk here on the streets. Can I buy you a beer?"

"Your club or mine?" I turn away. "I have no time for charity, America, or strangers."

He pulls me back by the arm, an action I repay by pushing his chest and threatening a fist close to his face. But he's not scared. Damn it, I think he's amused.

"I can help you save the boys."

My fist slowly comes down and I examine his face.

"What makes you think this Arab would want to save boys?"

"But you have been. The cigarettes." He nods toward the sound of the caroling. "The singing. The newspapers, shoeshines. We heard about your work here."

I laugh and walk away, but he keeps my pace. "There's a laugh. I know this Arab fellow you're talking about. He has no 'work' here—not like you holier-than-thou do-gooders think when you think 'work.' Arab's work here is to save his own skin—and so far, it's been working just fine. What he doesn't need is you and some guilt-ridden garden club of rich old ladies poking their high-society American noses into his life."

"Well, you seem to speak for 'this Arab fellow' pretty well."

"He and I used to play on the same polo team. Until we ate our horses."

"How old are you? Eighteen? Nineteen?"

I ignore him, keep walking.

"Someone said you might be as young as fifteen or sixteen," he continues.

I round a corner.

"Some sources say you're a boy. Most agree you're a Jewess."

That stops me cold. "How the hell did you 'hear' about Arab? What have you heard? Who from?" He might be working with Sniper or some other bounty hunter. And you don't need a uniform to be a Nazi.

"If I revealed my sources, we'd all be dead."

Again, I push him against a boarded-up Jewish shop, click open my switchblade, and hold it threateningly. "That could be sooner than you think, friend!"

"Well, they *all* said you're tough as nails."

"Who?" I growl close to his face.

"The Gestapo," he squeaks out, leaning away from my knife. "They have a file on you."

"So what? They have a file on everyone."

"Not like yours."

"I think I know who your 'connections' are," I hiss, giving him a harder shove.

"You don't have a clue. Go ahead. Slit my throat . . . Abra."

"What did you call me?"

"You heard me. Yes, I know your real name. I paid dearly for it, in American dollars, no less. They're quite sought after. Just like you. Now, if you could lower that knife just a little and look in my right coat pocket."

I ease up and pull out the folded papers. I glance at the Gestapo file. Well, what do you know. It's complete with two photos of me—the schoolgirl Abra and Arab on the street— past arrests from before the occupation, charges both real and trumped up. Contraband, trafficking, black market, enemy of the state, female. Jew. All the way back to the jewelry store robbery, then to Vienna and back again.

The knife comes down. "How did you know to find me here?"

"Not everyone here in Warsaw is a Nazi, a Pole, or a Jew, you know. We have our sources. We know who's fighting, who's resisting, who's saving children. I've been watching you for some time."

"And you think I'm going to just trust you? A dog-head stranger named Braunsteiner? Just shows up here with these big plans to save the world? Think again, Messiah."

"Look, Arab," he says, becoming deadly serious. "It's only a matter of time before the Germans haul you in."

"They have bigger fish to fry."

"Do they? Look, neither the Gestapo or me gives a shit about why you're saving these children. All we care about is that you are," he adds, sounding a lot harder now. "The Germans want it to stop and we want it to continue."

"What do you want?" I have to struggle to keep my voice low.

"We want you to help us save the children."

"With me between you and the Gestapo? Oh no, Herr Messiah. I'm not going to be your Pied Piper with a big bull's eye painted on my back." I pocket the Gestapo papers. "But thanks for these."

I walk away.

"I heard you can get just about anything here in Warsaw," he baits.

"Yeah, let me know if you want Chopin's heart," I say over my shoulder.

"They say you've kept your gang alive and well for over a year, Arab."

I stop. "Listen, whoever you are. I make and sell cigarettes. Some even have tobacco in them. The kids help me. If they help themselves in the process, so be it."

"They say you know the ghetto sewers better than anyone."

"The sewers?"

"Yes, those things full of shit under our feet. The ones that run into and out of the ghetto."

"You mean to get children out of the ghetto through the sewers? So they end up back here, just to be rounded up again? There's a joke!"

"No. We don't mean to get the children out of the ghetto and over here."

"Then what?"

"We mean to get the children out of the ghetto, out of Warsaw, out of Poland, and out of Europe. We have operatives all across occupied Europe by now."

"Well, good luck to you—and your damned operatives and connections and rich Americans. I'm sure they'll all file letters of protest when the Nazis put you up against a wall and blow your head off, Messiah. Now, if you don't mind, I have cigarettes to sell."

"In case you change your mind, I'll—"

"Don't hold your breath," I mumble. The street is filling with outworkers returning from the ghetto factories. I have cigarettes to peddle.

V.

"WHAT HAPPENED?" I DEMAND, CRASHING INTO MRS. PRASKA'S apartment. "Lorenz said Stefan's hand was blown off!" I go to the bed, where Mrs. Praska is finishing bandaging his hand.

"Just the tips of his fingers," she says. "Thank God for the morphine." She closes her sewing kit.

Lizard holds up a tackle box. "And fishing line."

"Is he dead?" Lorenz asks, his face ashen, his eyes wide and tear-filled.

"No, no. Just asleep. He'll be fine," Mrs. Praska says, giving Lorenz a warm hug.

"Tell me how this happened, Lorenz."

"We were . . . well, sort of begging. Sorry, Arab, I know you don't like us to beg."

"Just tell me what happened!"

"Anyway, a lady was going to give him something and . . . and . . . then there were all these soldiers on horseback. One told Stefan he had something for him and to hold out his hand and *boom!* His fingers were on the street! There was blood everywhere and then Lizard found us and . . ."

"I packed his hand with snow and got him here as fast as I could," Lizard said. "God, can that boy scream! Hope he hasn't ruined his singing voice. Anything to drink around here, Mrs. Praska? I could use a shot of something."

—

Over the next few days, I think long and hard about what to do about it. An eye for an eye, a tooth for a tooth, a hand for a hand. What's a child's hand worth here in the middle of all this horror? Nothing. Absolutely nothing. But I'm not going to let it go completely. I want the man responsible to know I'm hunting him. Make him look over his shoulder. Never know when he'll be in the crosshairs of the enemy's gun.

"I'll say one thing about you, Arab. For a girl, you sure have balls, coming here. Are you even aware these are officers' quarters? The enemy officers' quarters?" He shakes his head and starts up the steps.

I grab his arm and pull him back down. "Fritz, one of your drunken polo club chums shot three fingers off the hand of one of my boys!"

"I know," he says, exhaling cigarette smoke with a long, tired sigh. "I was there."

"And you let it happen?"

Fritz looks at me, his face almost frightening with its chilly lack of expression. "Who do you think I am? I have no power here. I can't find your sister, I can't save your boys, I can't save you. Christ, I can barely save myself."

"All you have to do is show me the man, Fritz."

"I can't do that."

"That little boy is eight years old! Three fingers! Just gone!"

"He is alive, Arab! Think! For the love of God, let it go!" he says through gritted teeth, as though he's ready to explode. And I don't care.

"He's only eight!"

"And he won't live to be nine if you're dead!"

We stare at each other. He whispers, "We just received new orders. There's to be more deportations. They want this city swept clean of everyone who doesn't serve our needs. You Poles are expendable, Arab. Don't you see? Why do you think we've wiped out your schools, museums, your intelligentsia? Your whole fucking culture!"

I have no reply. He's right—bit by bit, everything Polish is being destroyed, buried, or carted off. He looks away. "And this is only the beginning. I tell you now, Arab, I can't protect you. I've been promoted to captain, and still I can't protect you. I have a job to do. I warn you. Let it go." His face, his voice, are now different.

He's right, I think, watching him disappear into the silvery, silent night. The goddamn Nazi is right.

But I won't—can't—let it go. I have to do more. Something about this has hit me deep inside. I can't save my parents, so be it. I can't save Ruthie, so be it. Go after me, fine. Go after Lizard, fine. But go after one of the boys—that's war. The coward who did this is going to pay. God knows, he won't be the first Nazi I've dispatched.

Another snow storm is hitting us and the silence it brings helps me think. Bundled, I walk the streets, glad not many people are out and about. If I don't have to worry about my own safety, I can think more about my boys' safety. I can think about revenge.

But I keep hearing Fritz's words, his warnings, I keep seeing his hardened face as he said "I have a job to do." So do I! I have . . . a job to do. It hits me! That Braunsteiner man! He has a job to do, too!

I find Otto Braunsteiner reading a newspaper inside a union bakery, close to my usual corner. The paper slowly comes down as I take a chair across from him. I'm no fool, though, and I trust no one. My Luger is in my coat pocket, but pointing right at him.

He smiles, as if expecting me. "Will the boy be all right?"

Somehow, I'm not surprised he knows about Stefan. "We've taken care of him. He'll mend."

"Well, good. So, what can I do for you?"

"You said you're going to take children out of Poland."

"Going to try."

"I have two boys I want you to take. I'll pay whatever it takes."

"I don't want your money, Arab," he says almost jovially, giving me a calm, confident, almost arrogant, smile. "I want you. I need your connections, your savvy, your knowledge, maybe even your charming personality."

We assess each other for several moments. "On second thought, I don't think this is such a good idea," I say, "Look at you. You're just a kid yourself. What do you know?"

"I admit I'm young, but I know plenty. Someday I'll tell you."

"But you don't know Warsaw. Look, the reason I'm not dead or wishing I was is because I take advantage of their greed, their nasty habits."

"And you do it so well."

I'm growing exasperated. "All I want is for you to take two boys out. Just two. Then I won't bother you again."

"What are you going to do for me if I do that for you?"

"All right. Tell me what you need."

He leans toward me. "I need someone to help me get as many children as we can out of this fucking war. That's about as clear as I can make it."

"Well, I'd like to know how you plan on doing it. You don't know the Nazis like I know the Nazis."

"Yes, I do. After all, I am a Nazi," he replies calmly.

I feel the hairs on the back of my neck rise. "I'll drop you here at this table if you've been setting me up." I remove the safety. His eyes meet mine when he hears the click.

"You don't need that, Arab. Look, we're not all evil monsters. Resistance comes in many forms and languages. Like you."

"I am not resistance!" I tick my head east, toward the ghetto. "Probably a quarter million crammed into—what?—maybe a thousand acres, and even they aren't fighting back!"

"You'd be surprised."

A waitress comes over. Her apron looks like it hasn't been washed since the Germans marched in and her hose have so many runs in them I wonder why she even bothers. "You Polish?" she asks me, her words as weary as her face.

"German," Otto replies, with a snap of Aryan authority. "Another coffee."

"Because we can't serve Poles," she adds, still looking at me. "I can't even serve me here." She sort of smiles and brings over another cup, filling it with something that resembles river water and tastes just about as good.

"Shall we put politics aside and talk about the children?" Otto says. I hesitate. "And perhaps you can do me the favor of putting the safety back on your pistol. It makes for a very one-sided conversation."

"All right. Tell me this big heroic plan you have."

"We've done this before in Austria and France," he begins. "We have operatives on every leg, from Palmiry forest up to the Baltic. Safe houses, barns, basements, studios, whatever we can arrange. The plan is to establish an underground route."

"Underground? Then building a damn tunnel would be easier," I say. "Look, it's a long way to the Baltic. How many things can go wrong between here and there? And that's just assuming you can get children out of the ghetto."

"Everything can go wrong," he says. "Which is why we need to plan things very carefully. But we know what hasn't worked in the past. And our contacts and operatives by now are seasoned and willing. The deeper Hitler has gone with his 'Jewish problem,' the more determined we have become."

"Rhetoric," I say. "Give me details."

He pulls out a sheet of paper, unfolds it, and crudely sketches a map. He writes PACIFIC OCEAN on one side and TEXAS on the other.

"Uh, Otto? Just how far are you taking these children?"

"If someone finds this piece of paper, the last thing they'll think is 'This is really the Baltic,' and 'This is really Warsaw.'"

I have to nod in agreement. He sketches more and by the time we finish our beers, he's filled me in. Still, I'm not convinced.

"You're counting on a whole lot of luck there, Messiah."

"Look, we can fine-tune this as we go along. There are always going to be hiccups."

"Hiccups? Ha!"

He touches my hand. "Arab. Hear me out. This will work. We put our heads together, I know this will work." He casts me a beguiling smile. "With a little luck."

There isn't that much luck left in the entire world. Let alone Warsaw.

VI.

I'VE ALWAYS BEEN WARY OF THE TYPE OF COURAGE THAT COMES with allies. But even a loner like myself can't do everything on her own. I count my allies on one hand: Mrs. Praska, Lizard, and perhaps Otto Braunsteiner. As long as I don't put all my trust in any one person, as long as I have my rat holes—back door escapes to save my own hide—then maybe we can make a team.

I find this new ally, this Messiah, on my corner waiting for me. I tap him on the shoulder. "Okay, I'll do it. Merry Christmas."

He spins around and grins. "That's the be   present I've ever gotten! Shall we start planning? My p   le are ready any time. Come on, let's have some coffee and talk."

He walks off and I watch him before following. What am I getting myself into? I wonder, catching up to him.

We start to map an escape route for his big exodus. I diagram escapes, come up with a backup plan, and then a backup plan to the backup plan.

Backup plans. What good are those? I recall my father's backup plan for suicide-surrender with his cyanide-aspirin. I smile at the vision of him—swallowing two or three tablets—lying down to die with honor, à la Masada, and wondering why he's suddenly feeling so damn good! Others might kill themselves rather than being taken alive, but not me. Not the Arab of Warsaw. Not even Abra Goldstein.

"So when do I meet this famous gang of yours?" Otto says. "I have to get word to my people—where and when and how many—pretty soon, Arab. We're hoping for sometime in the first two weeks of January."

"I'll set it up for tomorrow. Remember, if they're not with us, the whole deal is off."

"I remember."

"Can you find Krasiński Garden? There's a playground where we can meet."

"I'll find it."

"And I'll be in charge. If my gang says thumbs down, you find yourself another partner. After all, I just want to get two kids out. My partners probably don't want to risk their necks helping you. Whatever happens, that was our deal. Right? Two kids."

We convene in the covered picnic area in the park. Someone has tried to brace up a log wall and there were probably people living in here until the snows started to hit us so hard. But it's been a quiet, safe place to meet, far from eyes and ears.

Lizard and Yankev stand leaning, arms crossed, against the one good wall. Neither are happy about meeting here, but I am not taking Otto to the cigarette factory. Not yet, if at all.

"Come on, where's this hot shot you've been yapping about?" Yankev asks. "It's freezing here and I have things to do."

Otto has been standing in the shadows, and now he steps out. "This is Otto Braunsteiner," I say. "I call him the Messiah. You'll see why."

"Does this Messiah buy or sell?" Lizard asks, his voice low and skeptical. "He must be some savior for you to take a chance bringing him here, Arab." He walks over to him, taps his chest. "Where'd you dig up this choirboy anyway, Arab?"

"Easy, Lizard. He's okay."

"Well, I don't like Messiahs. Especially ones who fraternize with the enemy."

Silence.

"Keep talking," I say, watching Otto's expressionless face.

"I recognize him, Arab," Lizard says, circling Otto. "Saw this 'Messiah' and that Nazi polo player of yours. Chatting like old chums over a smoke. Isn't that right?"

"Yes, that's right," Otto says, his voice steady and unchallenged. "The captain stopped me and asked for my papers. It's what they do, you know. Surely all of you have been stopped and questioned. So I showed him my permits and then admired his horse."

"So let's see them. Show us your papers," Yankev says.

Otto sighs, pulls out his wallet, and hands Yankev a paper.

"I don't read German," Yankev says, handing it to me.

"General Government Department of Utilities."

"In case your toilets back up." Otto looks at Lizard and smiles. "So think of me every time you flush a toilet."

"That won't be hard," Lizard says. "So, Arab, where did you find this Messiah? Walking across the Vistula? Or at the morgue raising a few dead?"

"I didn't find him. He found me."

"Sounds like a fucking *szkop*!" Yankev growls at me, pointing at Otto. I watch Yankev's face. Hardened? Braver? Or just angrier?

"I warned you we're not your common garden-variety Poles," I say to Otto.

"Speak Polish, dammit!" Lizard says.

"And I am not your common garden variety '*szkop*,'" Otto says to Lizard, his Polish impeccable.

He tells them about the well-funded American charity, the underground links and connections, the goal of getting as many Jewish children as possible out of Poland and into safe hands throughout Europe, England, and the United States.

While Otto describes his big plans, I watch Lizard and Yankev. Their reactions are nearly identical to mine. Nothing breeds skepticism like diminished odds.

"And why should we risk our skins to save total strangers?" Yankev asks. It's a good question.

"Because they're children," Otto states.

"So are we," Lizard quips. "Least, we were before the Germans marched in."

"Well, then, you should do it because you can," Otto replies, offering each of us a cigarette. "Here. American."

I pull out my silver lighter and offer it to Otto. "Allow me. SS."

He turns the lighter over in his hand and smiles. "And because you and your gang are very, very clever."

I turn to Yankev. "What do you think?"

"Too risky."

"Let me tell you about Auschwitz," Otto says.

"For political prisoners and dissidents," Yankev says with a dismissive jerk of his hand. "All Nazi fearmongering and propaganda."

"The hell it is! I've been out there. It's called the final solution for a reason. Fuck Nazi fearmongering and propaganda, Yankev! The fact you're a Jew is a slight inconvenience to Hitler."

I want doubt. I want all the what-ifs out in the open, because I'm still not sure if we should team up with this well-dressed Nazi stranger who has all the identifications and American connections. "You know, Messiah, not all the Jewish children in Warsaw are in the ghetto," I say.

"I have six brothers and sisters," Yankev says. "What about them?"

"And what about our gang?" Lizard asks. "If we get anyone out, it's going to be them, not some half-dead brat from the ghetto who'll probably die on you. Or worse, give you away."

Otto takes a thoughtful puff of his cigarette. His eyes land on me. "I did agree to your two boys."

I feel Lizard and Yankev's eyes on me. "Stefan and Lorenz. I want them out. You don't have to go along with anything. If this man says he can get them out and safe, then I'll do what I can."

"I say all or nothing," Yankev says.

"But you and your gang are surviving here. They're not." Otto points in the direction of the ghetto. "You and your gang have cigarettes to sell. What do they have? Nothing."

"We'll run out of tobacco by March," Lizard says. "What will we sell then?"

"Pretty soon we'll being selling sawdust-and-cabbage cigarettes. Even the Germans won't smoke those," I add.

"I say we save our own. You say you have people outside Warsaw to take ghetto children to England and America. Keep them safe. Why not our children?" Yankev says.

Otto tosses his cigarette down. "We have found," he begins slowly. "We have found that work of this nature is . . . easier . . . if carried out by strangers. If . . ." He looks into each of our faces. "If something goes wrong, then each child stands equal odds of survival."

"In other words," Lizard snaps, "no favorites."

"In other words," Otto counters, "no heroes."

"In other words, forget it!" Yankev says. "My own come first! How can they survive if I get my head blown off trying to save strangers?"

"He has a good point, Messiah," I say. "So why not? Why not take our children—all our children—first?"

"We can only take so many. A dozen—tops—at a time," Otto warns. "It's not as easy as 'Quick! Run! Get in the truck!' and *bang!* we're suddenly sipping sherry on the Queen Mary to England. Things have to be coordinated the entire journey. Transports need to be arranged. Underground connections notified. Children can't walk all the way to Danzig. And the documents. We need forged documents, birth certificates, passports."

"Most of our gang already have their papers," I say. "Yankev's family doesn't. They've been in hiding for over a year now. They're too Jewish-looking to even bother with forged documents. They could never pass for Aryan."

"Leave that to me. I'll be able to make arrangements," Otto said.

There's a silence. "There's something else you need to know." Otto's voice is now low and troubling. "No babies. In fact, no one under four."

Yankev looks stunned. "Leave the babies behind?"

Lizard and I exchange glances. He knows. I know.

"A crying baby," Otto explains softly. "Well, a crying baby or fussing child could get us all killed."

"Mother will never agree," Yankev says. "She'll never split us up."

Otto smiles. "That's her decision. Let's let her make it." He looks around. "All right, it's agreed, then. Your children first, then we work together to get as many out as we can. But remember, when things go wrong they go very, very wrong."

"Don't tell us about when things go wrong! You don't look to me like you've even suffered a hangnail," Lizard says.

Otto approaches him. I move to separate them.

"I've been working Nazi resistance in Germany since just after Hitler became Chancellor in '33. I was thirteen. I speak German, Polish, English, and French. I knifed my first Nazi informant when I was about your age. It's what I've been trained to do." He gestures at the room around us. "Do you think this all just happened overnight? Hitler just woke up one day and said, 'Gee, I wonder what Poland's like this time of year?'"

Silence as we all assess him.

"There is resistance! Planned, organized, financed resistance! Only we call it *Widerstand*. I should know. I grew up with it. My father is—was—a highly respected industrialist in Germany. He died defying Hitler. They hung my mother alongside him. I was in London at the time, or they would have hung me, too. I stayed there, allied with the resistance, and I learned. When I did go back to Germany, it was to prepare and organize all of this." He takes his glasses off and polishes them casually. "One on one, I could take any of you. Two on one might be tougher. Three on one, well, I'd like to think you'd fight fairer than that."

Otto points at me. "And don't think just because you're a girl I'd give you any quarter, Arab."

I'm not sure if I should be insulted or flattered. "And don't think I'd take any quarter, Messiah. When things are at their worst, it's every man for himself here. I hope you understand that."

A light dusting of snow has begun, and the skies foreshadow more to come. We shake hands. My army of four.

VII.

NEW YEAR'S EVE AND OUR SECOND MEETING—HARDLY A party—is not going well. The bitter cold seems to heat tempers, not cool them down, especially in this small, stuffy office of a cigarette factory. Yankev has caught a cold from one of his siblings and Lizard's friendship with his nurse has hit a snag. Serves him right. This is no time and no place for romance, turquoise shawl or not. Mrs. Praska cradles a cranky child. None of us has bathed in weeks. Food ration? A laugh. Sleep? What's that?

"Hear her out," Otto says, quelling the argument that's brewing. "Arab says she has a plan, and I want to hear it."

"What does a dog watch when he finds a rat?" I ask.

"What the hell does that have to do with anything?" Yankev snaps.

"Yankev," his mother warns.

"A dog will watch the rat hole," Lizard says. "Get on with your point."

"Right. And the dog is too stupid to know every rat has an escape hole somewhere else. Which is why the German guards watch the gates in and out of the ghetto like a dog watches a rat hole."

"Some Nazis are at least as clever as rats," Otto says. "Some have been known to be more clever."

"*A broch*! They're all stupid!" Mrs. Praska swears, repositioning the baby.

"But I have the escape hole. I know it well. There's a cemetery not far from where I grew up on Pawia Street. On the northwestern side of the ghetto." I show them the map I've drawn up. "Messiah and I agree, it's easier getting into the ghetto than getting out. But here, you see how the cemetery faces the route Otto has planned? His people will meet us in a small village south of Palmiry forest, up here."

"What village?" Yankev asks.

"No names," Otto says. "The less details known, the less the chance of discovery."

"That makes no sense at all! Why not just take the children out from this side?" Yankev demands.

Another good question. "Because all the major roads have checkpoints," Otto says. "If we get stopped and inspected— the orders are for Jewish children to be taken into the ghettos, not out of them. Anyway, we need little more than a path, a trail, maybe a small farm-to-market road. We can't chance taking any main roads. But it's all in the timing. My people have to know, to the meter, where to meet. To the minute when. I'll need lead time to make sure the connections are lined up."

"How? Just how do you signal your contacts? Light a bonfire? Send up a flare? Drop pamphlets from a plane?" Lizard asks.

"I have my ways. And so do they." Otto points north, toward his so-called connections. "Arab, I thought you said your people would be cooperative."

"Well, now that they bring it up, just how do you contact your connections? I hear the telephone and telegraph lines are all tapped."

"If you can even find a working telephone," Yankev says. "Ours stopped working during the siege."

All eyes are on Otto. "Don't you think it's interesting?" he says. "All the bombing, the fires, the destruction . . . you'd think more of those damn pigeons would have been killed. Yet, everywhere you go—bird crap!"

"What's that got to do with—" Lizard stops and looks up. I smile. "Homing pigeons?"

"Don't be stupid," Otto says, giving me a sly wink. "Those went out with the Great War."

"All right." Lizard points to my crude map. "We get the children into the ghetto, and then what? Hang around the bistros, attend a few soirees until his people give us the high sign?"

"Yes. And what about the matter of that nine-foot wall?" Yankev asks. "Or haven't you noticed? The guards, the machine guns. Those German dogs would just as soon rip your leg off as piss on it."

"Let Arab finish," Mrs. Praska says.

"My family is buried in this cemetery." I tap the map. "Hell, *I'm* buried in this cemetery," I mutter. "Headstones were used for a section of the wall."

"How do you know? That's in the ghetto," Yankev challenges.

"I've been there a hundred times." I'm starting to tire of Yankev's doubts. "Haven't you ever wondered how I get our cigarettes sold over there?"

"Bribe the guards," Yankev answers. "Hell, drop them by airplane for all I know. Who knows how the great Arab of Warsaw does anything?"

Lizard and I look at each other and sigh. "The sewers," I reply flatly.

"The sewers!" Yankev shudders. "Well, I'm not going through any sewers. And neither are they!" He points toward his family. "Not after all the horror stories I've heard!"

"I said let her finish!" Mrs. Praska barks. "What about the cemetery, Arab?"

"I had to help them build that section of wall using Jewish headstones."

"Desecrate a cemetery?" Yankev gasps. "I would have died first!"

"No, you wouldn't have, Yankev. You'd like to think you would, but you wouldn't. You do just what the gun at your head tells you to do."

"Can we save the morality lecture for after the war?" Otto cuts in. "What's this section of wall have to do with our plan?"

"Like I said, I was forced to help build it last spring. It was pouring rain. That section was behind schedule and the Krauts were pressing to get it finished. We got the headstones in place, all right. With lots and lots of watered-down cement. I'll bet that section will practically melt into our hands."

"And who do we have to thank for that miracle?" Yankev asks with his usual snort.

"A lot of rain, diluted cement, and some wet, overworked, impatient soldiers," I reply, exasperated. "I also know hiding spots. The cellar of my parents' home is a maze of secret passages, storage rooms, and cubbyholes. I know that district like you know that face," I add, smiling to Mrs. Praska and the child whose face she's cleaning.

Yankev glares at me, disbelief in his eyes. "And you get there by the sewers as though it's just a day on the Vistula!" He points toward the ghetto. "And those aren't the Walls of Jericho, Joshua! Sure, the children will go into the sewers. Sure, they'll keep quiet. Sure, they'll be safe. Well, not with my family, you don't!"

"Yankev!" his mother says sharply, disturbing the little one who's finally asleep on her lap. "You disgrace me! We are saving lives. Our lives."

"Not Pawel's!" Yankev shouts, pointing to the two toddlers playing in the corner. "Not Hanna's! They're too young. Or did you forget?"

All eyes are on Mrs. Praska. Her face is hard, her jaw flexed as her gloved hand caresses the baby's delicate, chapped face. Finally, she says with resolve, "I will save all I can save."

Yankev stands up. "I'll be packaging cigarettes. You heroes figure it all out."

"Remember, only ten cigarettes in each!" his mother calls after him.

The atmosphere eases immediately after he leaves. Mrs. Praska sighs. "I apologize. Yankev is . . . young and very angry. But he might be right about the children going into the sewers. For generations we've told them monster stories about the sewers, just to keep kids out of them."

"The sewers are only as a backup," Otto says. "I'm going to escort the children into the ghetto through the gates."

"We need a trial run, though. Stefan and Lorenz," I say. "They go first."

"All right. Bring me their papers. I want to make sure they're good enough to get past the checkpoints. Do you have recent photos?"

"I can get them. There's a photographer's booth in the Square. He's making a killing taking souvenir pictures of German soldiers posing with those schmaltzy painted backdrops of the Alps," I reply.

"Can he be trusted?"

I glare at Otto for his stupid question. "I don't do business with anyone who can't be trusted!"

He understands my challenge. "No, you don't. Now, where should we meet?"

I give him the directions of one of my old lairs, close to Three Crosses Square. Allies or not, I'm not giving away the location of any of my current holes. "Give me three days," I say. "I have to go over and make sure the cellar of my parents' home is still secure."

"Then that means Friday, January third. Two o'clock? That'll give us enough time to go over the plan so when the workers coming out of the ghetto, we'll go in. The gates are always hectic at five. Plus, it'll be dark."

"And who will take care of Stefan and Lorenz? Are you going to just dump them in the ghetto to fend for themselves?" Mrs. Praska asks.

"They can hide there just as well as they hide here," I say.

"What about your Yankev?" Otto asks her. "Will he help?"

"He's a good boy, but—"

"He doesn't have what it takes," I interrupt. "I'm sorry, Mrs. Praska, but he doesn't have the courage. Or maybe he's the only sane one here. Fact is, we can't count on him."

"I know. I know," she whispers. She goes to the corner and picks up Pawel, her youngest. "But I don't love him any less. I'd rather my son a living coward than a dead hero. Make the plans. I'll handle Yankev. But, if this works, I want as many of my children to go as you can take." She repositions the child on her lap. She looks dreamily down at the sweet face, nuzzles him close to her breast and says to him, "Don't we, my precious? Don't we?"

So, it's set. We have our first plan. I have a lot to get done.

JANUARY, 1941

I.

I SPRING INTO ACTION, GETTING IDENTIFICATIONS, FOOD, AND supplies ready for our test run. Lorenz and Stefan have their photos—it took three tries thanks to their camera mugging, the brats.

Next is securing the cellar at my parents' old home. The upper stories have even more people packed in like sardines, but the cellar—cold, dark, and hard to get into—holds only garbage and memories. Like everything else in Warsaw, it's been ransacked. The rows and rows of preserves my mother kept are gone; barrels of rags, old clothes, and outgrown toys are tipped over and rummaged through. The storage rooms are raided and riffled through. It's as though giant rats have had a field day in the cellar. But it will be the perfect hiding hole for several people.

We're packed and ready to go. I look at my watch. We agreed on 2:00 p.m., but it's already 2:30. Otto is late and I'm beginning to get nervous. How could our plan fail before it even begins?

When I hear the three knocks on the door of our meeting spot, I breathe easier. But as always, I have my Luger close at hand. I draw it slowly and knock two back. It's answered by one knock, and I unlock the door.

A man stands, back to me, in an German SS uniform. I put my gun to his neck.

"Don't move an inch," I hiss.

"I never argue with a female holding a gun," Otto says, as he slowly turns around, grinning.

"Otto, you scared the shit out of me!"

"I never let my back be to the street." He quickly steps inside.

He takes a brief look around and his eyes land on Stefan and Lorenz, frozen and staring at Otto from the shadows. "What's with them?"

"Probably has to do with how well that uniform fits you," I say, pocketing my gun.

"Don't ask me how I got this uniform."

"Arab, who's he?" Lorenz asks out of the recess of the room.

"Didn't you tell them?" Otto asks.

"I don't tell anyone anything until it's over."

"Good, then no one realizes it's gone to hell in a hand-basket," Otto quips, winking at the boys. "Which is which?" he asked.

"The tall one is Lorenz and the shrimp is Stefan."

Otto kneels down and says softly, "Stefan, Lorenz. My name is Otto. Stefan, how is your hand? Does it still hurt?"

Stefan looks warily at me. "It's okay," I assure him. "He's a friend. You can tell him."

"No," he answers in a low, cautious voice.

"The hell!" Lorenz pipes up. "He complains about it so much *I* feel it!" He gives his brother a shove.

"You boys did good to be afraid. Men dressed like me are bad. But I'm only pretending," Otto explains, still kneeling.

"Why, Arab? I thought you said we're going away," Lorenz asks.

"I'm going to find you brand new homes far away from all this," Otto says.

"I want my old home!" Stefan announces. "And I want to find the dirty *szwab* who shot my fingers off and shoot off his *shvantz*!"

"He absolutely cannot act like that, Arab," Otto says, hard and serious. "He has to be quiet and frightened. Subservient." He grits his teeth and seethes, "Occupied!"

"Stefan," I order. "Cry!"

He forces dramatic tears. "Lorenz, look like you have a gun to your head." Lorenz is not only a perfect-pitched soprano, but also a hammy actor. His sweet face is instantly filled with an ugly terror.

I've dressed the boys in rags and smudged their faces with dirt to make them look like they've spent the last year in hiding. I've even pinned yellow Stars of David on them.

"Good enough," Otto says. "Now, let's go over our plan one more time. Quiz me on my route through the ghetto."

We make our way over to the gate on Leszno Street. It's one of the busier gates into the ghetto and the lines are already long with patrols and workers returning to and from the ghetto at five o'clock. The fact that it's still the Sabbath means nothing. Steam rises through the street as all of humanity mills about, impatiently waiting to have their cards checked by the guards operating under dim lights. More to our advantage.

I look around for a vantage point. The snow has been plowed along the street, so I climb the small mountain of ice. From here, with my binoculars, I can see what's happening. I watch as familiar faces and ranked officials are signaled on through with impatient gestures; others are stopped and checked. Still others, tired and anxious to get anywhere but the streets, just push their way through. I look around for Otto and the boys and finally pick them out of the lines. Otto has each boy by the collar and escorts them, shoving people aside. If Otto Braunsteiner isn't a Nazi at heart, I think, he sure as hell is a damn good actor.

They get through the first checkpoint, but are stopped by a second guard who calls them back. It looks like Otto's being asked for papers. Stefan and Lorenz are now struggling to get free of Otto's grip. God, so much for subservience. This isn't the plan! I can't tell if they're truly frightened and trying to escape or if Otto has told them to fight. Lorenz screams at the top of his lungs. I can hear him from here! I think all of Warsaw can hear him. He kicks Otto in the shin while Stefan bites his hand. Otto hollers, grabs his shin, and puts his hand to his mouth. I stand up, ready to spring to their rescue. The boys sprint into the ghetto with Otto running after them. I find the guards in the binoculars. They're falling over laughing!

"Well done, Messiah," I mutter. "Well done."

That's my cue to get myself into the ghetto. No Nazi escort for me; I might be recognized. So I run down the side streets until I find the sewer I know will shortcut me through the ghetto.

I slip in and use my flashlight to light my way. I came down here on my own trial run yesterday and know just where I am. I'll zigzag my way and emerge close to the old piano factory, just two blocks from our rendezvous point on Pawia, and not far from my old home.

I'm careful to peek around before lifting the manhole cover completely off. The street is nearly deserted. I'm up and out in an instant, taking only a minute to spin the cover back in place as quietly as I can.

I duck into an alley and wait. I flash my light three times, waiting for Otto's two-flash answer.

Nothing. I look around and listen. Still nothing.

Then, from down the side alley behind the piano factory, a child's screech. Finally, three shadows emerge into the vague light. It's Stefan and Lorenz, running pell-mell toward me. Now Otto appears, chasing them and gasping for air.

I grab the boys as they zoom by me. Otto looks like he's run ten kilometers in full battle array. He nearly collapses at my feet. The boys are fighting to get free of my grasp.

"Stop, Stefan! Lorenz! What's the matter with you?"

"He, he . . ." Little Stefan stammers, heaving for breath. "He said to run and don't stop."

"He said run like hell. And we did," Lorenz adds.

Otto starts to laugh in and out of gasps. "It's true. I did. But I never told them to stop."

I lead the way through the back alleys to Pawia Street, my old haunt. The snow has piled high on the sidewalks, with narrow, dirty paths carved through the heaps of garbage and rubble. We weave through groups of people, bundled against the cold, hurrying home or perhaps finding shelter before curfew.

Our old building seems to sag even more under the weight of so much snow and humanity. How many people are jammed in there, I wonder. I flash on that once-splendid and dignified building housing a wealthy, proper Jewish family. Now, a ghetto within a ghetto. I look at the bottom floor, where my mother once entertained, my father once lectured, I once studied, Ruthie once played.

"I've seen slums. But nothing like this," Otto says, looking around.

"You should have seen this district just a few months ago. You've got to hand it to those Germans. They can build a slum overnight." I shake the image of what this home— my home—used to be, once, a million years ago. "Come on, Messiah. Let's get these boys hidden."

"Are you sure there aren't people living in the cellar?" Otto asks.

"Not as of yesterday. Anyway, you're the one in a uniform, *Obersturmführer.* Use your rank and kick them out. That might be my old home, but you outrank me here."

"I'm really, really cold," Stefan says.

"Pipe down. And start looking like a starving brat," I chide.

"I am a starving brat!"

"Not like children here are." I push him ahead. "Come on. We'll go into the side cellar. Can't get there from upstairs." I lead them down the walkway along the side of the building. The snow is high and untouched. Even my tracks from a few days ago are covered.

The coal chute is completely buried. All the better. We work fast and quiet to uncover it and snap it open through a thick and stubborn grip of ice. We slide down the chute and close the two doors behind us.

I signal them to wait and be quiet while I explore the cellar, shining my flashlight into all the black corners. Even though I was here to set things up, it can all change in a minute. I know this place so well! The huge bins for the coal are empty, of course, leaving a black, dirty pit under the chute. The coal was probably the first to go.

I flash my light into the first room. I smile, thinking of what my mother used to call it—her rainy-day room, stocked with preserves and canned goods. Everything there is long gone, too.

The second room is where Papa had the little school. I flash my light inside. The small desks and chairs are gone—kindling, I'm sure. The three other storage rooms are also clear. The wooden barrels and crates once stored in them have been broken, the goods pawed through.

"It's clear," I say to Otto. You can settle the boys in over there." I flash my light into the third room. "I found some bedding and stashed some food and water and a piss can there. Deck of cards and some books."

"Lord, it's cold down here," Otto says. "I sure could use a toddy."

"Toddy?" I remember the root cellar, but surely someone has found that, too. Every other corner of this house has been cleaned out. But maybe . . .

"I'll be right back."

The room farthest into this abyss is the mechanical room. The boiler and water tanks are in here. I remember how warm this room used to be, how comforting when I was playing here or hiding out. The root cellar is a hole in its floor, even lower than the actual cellar and held together by its namesake. I yank open the icy door and flash the light inside. This is where my father stored his collection of ritual wine and fine liquors, all reserved for high-ranking guests and special occasions. I found this secret stash when I was eleven and raided it regularly after that.

Well, look there. It's untouched. I have to laugh at all those people living upstairs. All this liquor and what those people would give for a strong drink. The dusty, icy bottles reflect the light of the flashlight. I step inside and wipe away the cobwebs and root tendrils hanging down. If nothing else, we can drink our way to hell, I think. I look around, rub an icy layer of dust off the some of the bottles. If I can get these to the Aryan side, they'll be worth a Führer's ransom! What a find! No telling how long a stash like this can keep me alive.

In the corner, my light reflects off of something white wrapped around a bottle. I pull it down and take the envelope off. I feel a jolt deep inside me. It's addressed to me, in my mother's shaky hand.

I walk out of the root cellar and into the boiler room. I lean against the wall and slip down, sitting, staring at the envelope. I set down the flashlight. I pull off my glove with my teeth and see my fingers are shaking. I carefully open the envelope flap and pull out two pieces of paper—the two pieces of my birth certificate my father ripped in half so long ago. Mother kept them.

I look inside the envelope. There's more. I blow warm breath onto my finger, pull out the note, and unfold it. Tears spring to my eyes. I can almost hear her calm voice in the icy chamber.

Abra, my precious daughter,

It's all happening. The walls, the soldiers, all these people, the raids. Death everywhere. Me soon, I know. There's no more morphine, but my head is clear for my one and only act of defiance. I pray you will somehow find this. Yes, I always knew you stole from your father's wine cellar. Fathers you can fool— mothers, you can't. If you are alive, if you come home, if you find this . . . so many "ifs." I am sending Ruth to the seamstress, Mrs. Kerber. They say she is being allowed to stay here to mend officers' uniforms. She will teach Ruthie to sew and perhaps . . . a stitch a day will keep them alive, G–d willing. I must hurry and let Ruth hide this before your father gets home. Mrs. Kerber is here, waiting. I will love you forever.

Mama

"Ruthie," I whisper, running my sleeve under my nose and taking several deep breaths. I read the note again. "Ruthie, Ruthie, Ruthie . . ."

I stuff the note and birth certificate halves into my pocket and grab a bottle for Otto. My heart is thudding and I have a hard time catching my breath. I've come so close in the last few weeks to giving up, walking away, saving my own hide. But now . . .

"Good God, Arab. Have you seen a ghost?"

I snap out of it. "Yeah, about a million of them."

"What are you holding?" Otto asks.

"Here. Here's your toddy. Look, get the boys settled. I have an errand to run."

"An errand? Like what, the beauty parlor? Not that you couldn't use it," he says, ignoring my gift. I put my glove back on and wrap my muffler over my hat. "I mean it, Arab! Look, we have to stick to the plan. We have less than a week to get all the children over here and set it all in motion."

"I'll meet you tomorrow and we'll bring Mrs. Praska's older children over. After that, the rest of our gang." I head for the coal chute.

"Arab, where are you going?"

"I told you. I have something to do."

"I warn you, Arab, we don't take any chances here. Whatever your errand is, it better not jeopardize all I've been working for or I swear I'll—"

"Careful, Messiah, you're sounding like a Nazi," I growl. "You'll get your damn Polish Scout merit badge."

The dim light of my flashlight casts shadows on his face. What am I seeing in his eyes? What is he seeing in mine? I climb back up the coal chute and he follows.

"I warn you, Arab."

"Close that chute and pack some snow on it. I'll meet you tomorrow."

I don't wait to hear his protests.

II.

"RUTH WHO?" MRS. KERBER GASPS, THROUGH HER CRACKED-open front door. "Who are you? Go away! It's after curfew!" She tries to close the door, but I push it open even further.

"I'm Abra Goldstein. Where's my sister?"

She inspects my face in the glow of a foul-smelling carbide lamp.

"You're not Abra Goldstein! She had long blonde hair, a fair face and—" She raises the lamp higher. "Dear God, it is you. After all this time."

"My mother left a note saying Ruth was with you."

She pulls me inside, looks around outside, then closes and bolts the door.

"She was, at first. But I couldn't hide her. She wouldn't stay quiet. She wouldn't hide. Twice she kicked a soldier dropping off his uniform. Threatened to shoot him. Such a child! Where does she get it?"

Her eyes land on me. She smiles, and I have to return it.

"But she could have gotten us all killed. So I had to send her away. As long as I sew and my Anna . . ." She indicates the rooms upstairs. "She entertains the soldiers for our freedoms. God forgive us both." She nods toward the parlor filled with German uniforms hanging in various stages of repair, and gleaming black boots standing at attention along the wall. "So many of the children have already been taken away, Abra. God only knows where. They said to safe schools, but, oh God, they never come back."

"Where is she, Mrs. Kerber?" I'm trying to keep my voice down.

"There's a den. We call it a den. There are some children there. We take food and see to their needs. We try our best. Some are very ill. Some have died. We can only do so much!"

"Mrs. Kerber, please. Tell me."

She looks at me and sits straighter. "The Minerva Theater. Two streets over. In the basement. But the patrols, Abra. It's after seven and past curfew. They shoot on sight! I've seen them do it."

"I know all about patrols and curfew." I head for the door. She follows me.

"For God's sake, don't jeopardize the other children," she pleads. "Please, Abra! Ruth is safe. Go back to wherever it is you've been!"

I don't even take time to thank her. I leave, keeping well inside the deep shadows of the buildings, dodging a group of soldiers enforcing curfew.

My Luger bangs against my thigh. A street arab knows to travel light, but never unarmed.

I remember the Minerva Theater well. I used to sneak into plays and movies here when I was a kid. For all the coughing I hear, I know Ruthie can't hear me. I see a sliver of light coming from the layers of theatrical curtains hanging from the rafters. Old movie posters are hammered up along the walls. Painted sets of tropical seas and snowy mountain tops give the place an almost gay atmosphere. I hear someone reading out loud. I carefully step closer until I can make out six little children, wrapped in blankets, lying around a girl, about twelve, who is reading to them.

I see Ruth's head of curly hair, knotted and wild, willfully escaping her filthy scarf. She holds the doll I gave her when I last saw her, forever ago.

I clear my throat, louder this time. Now the children spring to their feet and the young caretaker whips a large knife from her skirts, ready to do battle on behalf of her charges. Ruthie, on the other hand, runs toward me, yanking aside a curtain. But she stops cold when she sees me. I've forgotten how much I've changed. Even in my heavy coat, I'm thin. My face is dirty and scar-nicked; my eyes are red and sunken.

"It's me, Ruthie! It's Abra!"

Her doubt grows into a huge smile and she throws herself into my arms, wrapping her arms around my neck, her legs around my body as though she's latching on for dear life.

I twirl her around and around, holding her head safe and close to mine. We both cry each other's names over and over. Had someone told me that morning, as I helped little Stefan bandage his hand, as I padded Lorenz's coat with cigarettes to sell, as I made my way through the sewers to test an escape plan for children I hardly know, that I would be holding my baby sister that evening—well, I wouldn't have believed it.

"It's okay," I say to the girl in charge. "I'm Ruth's sister. It's okay."

Her knife comes down and I carry Ruthie aside.

"Mama said you'd come back," she says, her arms wrapped tightly around my neck. "Take me home, take me home, take me home," she chants in a nervous whisper. "I want Mama. I want my mama."

"Sh, Ruthie, sh," I hold her head next to mine. "I'm here. I have to leave again, but I'll be back in just a few days."

She leans back and looks at me in the face. "No! Don't go, Abra, don't go! You always go away! Take me with you! I want to go with you now. Now. I don't like it here."

"I know, but you're safe. I promise. And this time I really, really do promise. Stay here with your friends and I'll be back to get you. For forever this time. Promise me you'll be good and stay here and wait for me."

She places her forehead on mine. "Are we going to go home?"

"No. We're going far away."

"To find Mama and Papa?"

"Maybe we will. It's going to be fun, but just our secret, okay?" She doesn't need to learn the truth about our parents. Some truths can wait forever; others can fade away.

"Why?" she whispers, looking over my shoulder at her den-mates.

"Well, we don't want those mean soldiers to come and ruin our fun, do we?"

"I hate them! One told me I was going to die because of my bad foot. I stuck my tongue out at him and he hit me really, really hard. I want to kill those soldiers. I want to kill them dead!"

"I'm going to find a place where there won't be any soldiers. Won't that be fun? A nice place, far, far away. Where we can all be safe."

"Okay," she whispers. "Can I bring Sofia?" She points to her doll, propped lopsidedly up on a blanket.

"Sure. You can bring Sofia."

I carry Ruth back into the room. "Don't worry. Okay? Your hiding spot is safe," I tell the courageous girl with the knife. "I'm going to be back in two days to take Ruth. Be sure to tell the adults who check on you. Ruthie will be coming with me."

It's even harder now to put Ruthie down, tell her good-bye, and leave. My heart is filled with both love and fear.

III.

"HALT!" HIS WORDS CUT THROUGH THE CHILLY NIGHT AIR. His flashlight is weak on my face.

I squint. I try to catch the color of his uniform. Who am I up against this time? I know life and death can hang on first impressions.

"Good evening, officer." I'm hoping any fragments of femininity in my voice smile through. My eyes adjust; seeing the glint of his badge, I know I'm not up against a killer. Ghetto security. But armed, indoctrinated, well-trained.

"It's past curfew! Identification!" His Polish is lopsided. Hmmm. Now they have the Krauts working these Polish security jobs.

"Certainly." I shove my hands into my pocket, fingertips grazing the steel of my Luger. I pull out a folded wallet. I know I was careful to choose a gentile female's identification for tonight's intrigue, but I'm damned if I can remember her name, age, or occupation.

Another police officer comes up. I should have remembered they always travel in pairs. The first snatches my identification, screws up his eyes, and hands it to his partner. "This is in Polish. What does it say?" he grunts. His hands shake, and I figure he's just as cold and miserable out here as I am.

The second man looks carefully at it, then at me. The Kraut pulls a handful of crumpled papers from his pocket and, looking at them, he seems to be scanning a list. He leans his rifle against his leg. "Here, shine on this," he says, handing off his flashlight. He looks first at my identification, then at the papers. He jabs his partner. "Look. See? This is the same person. See?"

They debate the issue, German and Polish trading verbs, nouns lost in translation. And do I detect a bit of one-upmanship between them? Then the flashlight beam comes back to my face.

"*Nein, nein,* Alf. That's not her. Look at those eyes. Totally different."

My heart pounds. Her? Her, who? Oh lord, this can't be! I've just found Ruthie and now I'm going to be arrested, hauled away, put up against and wall . . . and then it doesn't matter whose identification I have. We'll both be dead.

"Yes, yes, look here," says the first to his partner, his German accent thick as he struggles with abbreviated Polish.

I shift my weight and the second officer flashes the light on me again, ordering in Polish, "Don't move!" I wish I could see their faces. On the streets, sometimes faces speak louder than words.

"*Ja, ja,*" the first says, pointing to the papers. "See? Here! Arab. This girl here, see? Look, it's her, I tell you." He comes closer to me. I can feel the heat of his flashlight on my face. My smile vanishes as I run through my options. What options? What's an option here in the ghetto with two armed soldiers—even if one is a fellow Pole?

The second officer looks at the paper and squints. "You're crazy, Alf. That photostat is old and faded. This is just a common whore, probably making a house call."

But the first officer isn't so willing to let it go at that. "Or making a call to the Jewish resistance. You know our orders. Round up all suspicious people."

"Well, I have my orders, Alf, from my hausfrau. She out-ranks everybody here in Warsaw. Be late again and no dinner, and no after-dinner mints." He gives his partner a shove.

The German comes closer and pushes my shoulder. "Why are you out here?"

I venture a small smile. "A girl has to make a living somehow."

"What did I tell you? Come on, Alf. Let's go. I'm frozen."

The German hands me back my identification. "Crawl back into your hole." Then, to his partner, "But we still have to report this."

"*Danke, danke.*" I lower my head humbly. I can seethe later, after I've crawled back into my hole.

They start off. I let out a huge sigh, hearing their boots crunch in the snow as they walk into the night. But the crunching stops. I turn. Damn! One is coming back! I reach for my Luger. Maybe it isn't over after all.

I have the Luger halfway out by the time he stops.

"Abra," he whispers. He puts the flashlight to his face.

"Gustaw Winicki?" I whisper back, letting the gun drop back into my coat pocket.

He hushes me, saying, "Alf thinks I'm finding out where you ply your trade."

"You're working for the Germans?"

"What choice do I have?"

"Winicki? You coming?" the other soldier calls out from the darkness.

"*Ja, ja!* Abra, listen. You can't be seen here. You can't be seen anywhere," he says, his voice low and urgent. "That was you on the German's list of agitators and felons. If it had been daylight, he would have hauled you in. You are wanted, Abra. You better go into hiding."

"I will. Thank you."

"Winicki?" the German calls out again. "Get your after-dinner mints at home!" He laughs, then coughs, spits.

Officer Winicki puts the flashlight down. "This is the last time I can warn you, Abra." His voice is now hard, Nazi-like. "If you stay in this district and I find you, I'll have to arrest you. There are no choices anymore."

He turns and disappears into the darkness.

It takes me a few moments to get my breath and my wits back. I fade into the alley and tell myself, what do I care about any Gestapo list? I know I'm marked. I even have my file somewhere. It means nothing—because now I've found Ruthie! Or wait. I stop and stare down at the sewer cover, gushing steam up into the frigid air. Does it mean everything because now I've found Ruthie? Yes! The reason I'm still alive is to save Ruth. All my close calls, my minute-to-minute survival, my cunning and luck and planning and curses and blessings are all for this one purpose—saving Ruth.

I emerge on the Aryan side, making my way to my basement home hole. It'll be morning soon and my close call in the ghetto reminds me to stick to the back streets, the alleys, and the plan. No matter how weary I am.

I use the piss can. I swear my pee is freezing as it hits the bottom of the can. I chip away some newspapers from the frozen stack in the corner, flap them out to make layers of defrosting blankets. I pull out a can of something from the stash inside the wall. I fall onto my bed of rags, pull the papers over me, and close my eyes. Sleep, Arab, sleep, I have to chant to myself. Sleep. Silent Night. Holy Night. All is calm . . .

IV.

I spring awake, not sure where I am. I'm shaking with the cold and I need something to eat—something warm to eat. Everything comes back to me. Now that I've found Ruthie, I have a reason to live. But as much as yesterday was a miracle, it's also a warning. They're circulating a photo of me. My Gestapo file must be the only thing in Warsaw getting fatter. All that's missing is a big red stamp: EXECUTED.

I poke my head out of the basement door. The sun is almost blinding on the snow. My watch has stopped and I have no idea what time it is, but the sun is low in the west and that means I've missed my connection with Otto at our meeting place, blocks away. There are soldiers milling about everywhere. I remember Fritz's warnings of increased searches, of roundups and deportations. I layer on another coat, check I have everything, shoot out of the building, and run through the back alleys to our rendezvous.

"Where the hell have you been?" Yankev growls, coming out from behind a snowdrift.

"Did Otto make it back in one piece?"

"Yes, and he took Michal and Golda back with him during this morning's shift crossing into the ghetto. But he should have been back hours ago! Where the hell have you been? Don't you know my mother is probably crazy with worry by now?"

"What time is it?"

"It's after three o'clock!"

"All right, let me think."

"I knew this wasn't going to work!"

"Shut up, Yankev! Okay . . ." I walk around as I talk. "The plan was, if something went wrong, we'd meet at our hideout in the ghetto."

"You and your damn ghetto! I tell you, it's insane to go there! Insane! I've been against this from the beginning! What if Otto got stopped?"

"Otto can take care of himself."

"Then why isn't he back?"

"I don't know. Let me think!"

"Meanwhile, I have to go home and tell my mother that we don't know what went wrong, we don't know where Michal and Golda are! Hell, they could be on some cattle car halfway to Auschwitz or Łódź by now! I should have known better to put our lives in the hands of a Kraut and a *lesbijka*!"

I've been called worse than a lesbian. I know he's drawing my fire, but I don't have time for his wrath and insults. "At least you have your lives, Yankev. So you go back to the factory. Tell your mother everything is fine. Just lie, damn it, Yankev. Can you just do that this once? Lie?"

"Where are you going?"

"Back over. Look, I'm sure everything is fine. They're stepping up the deportations. Things are crazy out there. But just do like I'm telling you!"

He glares at me as though he might, just might, take a stand against me. Then he turns and runs off.

I get back over as fast as I can. Same sewer, same line, same quick dashes around corners, into shadows, and finally down to our cellar hideout, just as we planned if something were to go wrong.

I look around before going around to the cellar. There's no answer to our knocking code. I lift one of the coal chute doors and slide down, Luger at the ready. I don't see any light from one of the lanterns we have. I don't hear anything, either. I step lightly and pull out my flashlight.

Nothing. Each corner is dark and empty. Then, I see a black pile of clothing in a corner. The light reflects off the brass buttons. Otto sits next to the pile, arms encircling his knees, drawn to his chin. He doesn't even respond to my light. In the room behind him are the faces of four children. Silent and frightened.

"Otto?"

I come closer and see he's dressed in a rumpled old suit I recognize as one of my father's, from the pile of rags. "Otto. What's this?"

"I'm never putting it on again," he says, pointing to his SS uniform.

"What happened?" I kneel down and see his face is white, his hands are shaking. God, has he been crying?

"I'd . . . I'd just brought in Michal and Golda. I was on my way back. Then, another soldier sees me and shouts, 'Trouble! You! Come quick!' It was chaos, Arab. You know how it gets. Some Jews were, I don't know, I guess acting up or fighting back or something." He runs his hand over his face and takes a deep breath. "They had them lined up against a wall. I was ordered to shoot." He turns his anguished face toward me. "Arab, I killed four people. An old man, two women, and—oh God, Arab, I killed a child! Four people! Dead!"

"You said you've killed before," I say, keeping my voice low and calm.

"I've killed the enemy. People who needed killing. Not innocent people. Not a . . . not a child. Oh, God forgive me."

He looks to the rafters and I see tears escape the corners of his eyes.

I'm not sure if I pity or admire him for thinking of forgiveness or even God at a time like this. I sit next to him, light a cigarette, and hand it to him. Suddenly, he looks so young, boyish. In another life, a normal life, he should be celebrating a university degree and departing on a grand tour of the world.

"Good luck with God's forgiveness." I light my own cigarette.

"Don't you ever think about that?"

"What? Forgiveness?" My gut tries to issue a laugh, but seeing the anguish in Otto's eyes makes me think carefully before answering. "No. I mean, I did. At first. They say girls get forgiven more easily. After all, we're just poor, weak, ignorant females. Maybe we don't know better."

"How many have you killed?" he asks, looking down at the glow of his cigarette.

"I don't keep count," I lie. "What's the use? If I'm going to hell, I'm going for a good reason."

"Is that what they teach Jewish girls?"

"With all the battles Jews have fought, you'd think they'd teach more about an eye for an eye and a tooth for a tooth. I just look at the bodies up there, one on top of another." I stop and look into the rafters, as though those bodies might come crashing down on us any minute. "Someday, when this is all over, maybe . . . if we live through it, which I doubt we will . . . we can bask in the luxury of guilt. Spend the rest of our lives on our knees. Praying for forgiveness."

"Four innocent people, Arab," he whispers. "I guess it's true what they say—die now or die later." Slowly his hand finds mine. "Four people."

I take a deep, shaky breath and look at his hand on mine. I can't lose Otto now. He's everything to this plan. I squeeze his hand and nod toward Stefan, Lorenz, Michal, and Golda, huddled across the room now, playing with a top.

"Four lives for four lives. And more to come, Otto. I beg you, put the uniform back on. We have to get back. The roundups, the slaughter. And then they'll start clearing the ghetto. You told me, Otto. You told me their plan. We only have a few days until we take them out. Please, Messiah . . ."

"Don't ever call me that again!" He gets up and crushes out his cigarette. "I'm no one's Messiah."

Again, I point to the children. He shakes his head. I return his doubt by nodding. "You are."

Otto takes the SS uniform and disappears into the darkness. He comes back fully changed again. Maybe it's the uniform, but he seems straighter. I see a determined set to his jaw.

"You know, Otto, I have a few lives to redeem, myself," I say.

He pulls on his heavy black coat and sets the lapels straight. "How do you redeem a life?"

"Maybe avenge is a better word."

He looks at the children in the corner, now starting to argue over taking turns with the top. He goes over, kneels down, takes the top, and sets it to spinning with a fast twist. It hums across the cement floor.

"Look at it go!" little Stefan cries out, joined by the three others.

Otto tousles Stefan's hair. "You be good, you hear?" Stefan ignores him. We leave Lorenz, the seasoned, bossy ten-year-old, in charge.

Otto and I go out into the night. The early evening sky is a black veil speckled with brilliant stars.

"I'll get over to the factory and set Mrs. Praska's mind at ease," he says.

"Be ready for Yankev to give you a hard time. I tell you, Otto, he worries me."

"We have bigger things to worry about." I'm set to go back outside, but he pulls me back by the arm. "Look, Arab. About . . . you know . . . back in there."

"As you said, we have bigger things to worry about." He smiles, and I return it before I pull my muffler back around my face. "I'm heading over to the Solec District. Got a hidey hole there. Left a good stash of cigarettes and supplies, if no one's raided it yet. We're going to need everything we can get our hands on to bribe our way out of this war."

"Meet at the factory?" I can't see his face now, thanks to the shadows. But he raises his arm in farewell.

"Tomorrow," I say.

V.

I MAKE MY WAY DOWN THE ROWS AND ROWS OF APARTMENTS, shops, and small factories toward my hole. I haven't been to this district for weeks. Interesting how desecrated and desperate everything looks. A building takes on a whole different personality when it isn't holding life. This area once had such bustle and commerce. Now, nothing.

This hiding hole is a half-crumpled home. A bomb must have shattered half, leaving the other half standing. A room off the kitchen has stubbornly survived the shelling and makes for a good hideout when I'm in this district. I don't see the remnants of anything other than rats, and maybe some raccoons who've escaped someone's box trap, skinning board, and cookstove.

I find my knapsacks of vital lifelines in the floorboard of a lopsided closet. I find cans of caviar—the Krauts will pay top dollar for these. And cigarettes, probably stale but still valuable. A small section of mirror still clings to the wall, and I step into its cloudy reflection.

"God, look at you," I whisper. All of us in Warsaw are looking the same. Sunken, vacant eyes; pale, thin skin; scratches and bites that fester and can't heal. Loose or missing teeth. Thinning hair, scrawny arms and legs. I don't know—maybe it's seeing how horrible I look. No, understanding this might be the best I'll ever look . . . I sink down and lean against the bathtub, my legs out in front of me. I catch my own smell. Everyone in Warsaw reeks, but here, alone, sitting on someone's ice-cold, bombed-out bathroom floor . . . did children once play in this tub? Did a mother once primp in that mirror? Did a father once shave in that sink?

I pull myself up and slip out, my knapsack slung protectively around my front. As always, I have my switchblade and Luger on me. One in each coat pocket. After all, a girl should never go out unless properly accessorized.

I make my way north. There's a café I used to frequent. Just a little workman's hole in the wall, but they serve real coffee, not that corn coffee most of Warsaw is reduced to drinking. Also, the owner always looks the other way when he should be looking at armbands and yellow Stars of David. Who needs papers with those bull's-eye targets sewn on?

I step to the counter, rummage through my pockets for some money, and order a coffee, hard rolls, and a slice of cheese—light on the mold.

"Identification?" the man asks, blandly.

I show him a two-*zloty* note with the red stamp, indicating German currency.

"Counterfeit?"

"Of course. Pass it back to the Krauts."

He takes the money, then nods toward the window. I look in the reflection in the glass separating the counter from the bakery beyond. There are several German soldiers across the street, heading this way. He puts the money in an envelope under his till and nods his head toward the back of his shop. That's my cue. We're all masters of glances, nods, and winks. I grab my bag and dash out the back door.

I feel safe enough to stop and eat a block down the road. I lean against a wall at a tram stop, just starting to get some early morning rays of light. A man, bundled against the cold, walks toward me, hesitates briefly as our eyes meet. He continues on.

I stop chewing and feel a thud deep in my chest. I know that face!

I watch him walk away. That gait, the swing of his arms. Then, as though he's just figured out who I am, he stops, turns, and looks back at me.

It's him! That crooked nose, those scarred lips. Sniper! We stare at each other, as though waiting for the other to make a decision, a move. Or no decision, no move. Another group of soldiers comes up behind me and I obediently step aside to let them pass, never letting Sniper out of my sight. He smiles and tips his cap at the soldiers as they approach. God, he could be signaling them about me right now!

Sniper shoots me a lopsided grin as I turn and quickly start walking in the opposite direction. I hear his footsteps coming fast behind me. He catches up, grabs my elbow, and whirls me around to face him. He looks ten years older.

He stares closely at me. "Arab," he whispers. "For the life of me, I can't figure out how it is you're still alive."

"Not for your lack of trying!" I yank my arm from his grasp. The soldiers have turned and are coming toward us. I feel my mouth go dry. Sniper releases my arm.

"Any trouble here?" one of them asks.

At this, Sniper throws his arms around me, then kisses me on the forehead. "No, sir, no trouble at all," he says in clumsy German. "My long-lost brother."

They look us over carefully. If they ask me to empty my pockets, I'm dead.

"All right. On your way then. No loitering," the soldier says. Sniper tips his hat as the soldiers leave.

Sniper takes my arm again, his grip tighter this time. "Come on. I'll buy you a drink. Who doesn't need a drink?"

Any more disturbances and the soldiers might come back, suspicious and demanding papers. We cross the street to a café and go inside. I sit down, but keep to the edge of my seat so I can make a fast escape.

"I can't tell you what a surprise it is to see you." He signals the man for two beers.

"Warsaw is nothing but surprises."

"Still selling your cigarettes and little trinkets?"

"I get by." I keep my hands on my lap. I can't let him see how they are shaking inside my gloves.

"I see that. Tell me, what else are you selling to get by?" He reaches over and moves my head scarf aside. "Because I am still definitely very interested in buying. In fact, we clean you up a bit . . ."

Fear ricochets through my head. How am I going to get out of this? This café is on a busy street, Sniper isn't too much bigger than me, and maybe he's grown a bit soft in the cushion of his new trade. Can I outrun him?

Our beers come and I raise my glass to Sniper. "We've come a long way since our old gang days, eh, Sniper?"

"I don't go by that name anymore. I'm Jarek Paluch. Those penny ante days are over."

"Are they?"

"Yes. In case you haven't noticed, it's a new world. Those who adapt win. Those who don't . . . hell, people have to stand in line just to die." He chuckles.

"I heard you've been doing quite well." I finger his lapel, then grab him a bit closer to me. "Selling souls, you fucking schmuck!"

He leans back, as though offended by my sewer-breath, but not my insult. "Surviving any way I can, *Liebchen*."

"So, how much is it by now? Does a bounty go up in value over time, like everything else these days?" I ask, looking him square in the eye.

He pulls a small black book out of his vest pocket and flips through some pages. "My, my. One thousand German deutsche marks. Coin of the realm. You're considered, let's see, enemy of the Reich, black marketeer, counterfeiter—I'd like to talk to you about that. Love to get into that racket. What else, smuggler—and oh, look here! Jewish to boot." He looks at me over his book and winks. "There's a nice bonus." He casts me a crooked smile, showing off a shiny gold crown.

"You sold me out twice, Sniper!" I growl. "I got sent to Vienna the first time and damn near got hauled in by the Gestapo the second time."

"Third time's the charm. Told you we should have teamed up. I don't like being told no." He tosses some coins on the table, finishes his beer, and stands up.

I know by his cocky smile, his stance, his treasonous black book, where I stand with Sniper or whatever he's calling himself these days. He leans over as though to kiss my cheek, but I pull back.

I watch him walk away with a confident stride. I know what I have to do. Even Jews know what a Judas kiss is. The two soldiers who approached us earlier are chatting over a cigarette across the street and Sniper is heading straight for them. He'll collect my bounty a second time—in a heartbeat. I know any chances I have of getting Ruth out of Warsaw will die with me.

I follow him. My switchblade bounces off one leg, my Luger off the other, beating a tattoo of courage.

Damn! A policeman stops me on a corner as some official Nazi cars zing through the intersection. I try to keep Sniper's hat in my line of sight, but lose him in the crowd. By the time we're allowed to cross the street, it's hopeless. He's gone.

I catch my breath and look around. Where am I? Some park or yard? My head jerks back as my scarf is yanked from behind. Off guard and off balance! He pushes me toward a wall.

"I always knew we'd have our day of reckoning, Arab, but I never thought it was going to be so sweet." I turn to face him and my scarf tightens against my throat. "But first . . ." He crushes himself into me and puts his fleshy, scarred lips over mine.

I shove him away, loosen my scarf, and catch a deep breath. He catches his balance and comes back toward me. "Come on. Let's do this the easy way."

"No easy way, Sniper."

"Sure there is." He pushes me back and kisses my face. "Come on. I know you've always wanted to."

"Okay, just stop, Sniper. Let me get my breath." I try to make my voice soft. "All right. Let's work a deal."

"I'm listening."

"What do I need to do to get that page out of your book?"

"Everything." He runs his hand down my chest.

"Team up again?"

"We'll see. You haven't been very nice to me lately. You'll have to prove your worth. Got to be worth more than a thousand deutsche marks."

"Well, this is hardly the place to . . . continue our discussion," I say, adjusting my scarf. He looks at me very carefully, as though searching for—what, treachery? Lust? I blink softly and offer a small smile. "In spite of what you see, I am a lady, you know."

"I'll be the judge of that." He looks around, grabs me by the arm, and pulls me to his lips. "You're just as valuable to me dead as alive. You just remember that, Arab." He yanks me around. "Let's go." I feel his grip relax a bit as a group of women walk past. He tips his hat, then pulls me along and into a darkened alley.

I know it'll have to be the knife. No noise, no alarm.

Sniper creeps toward the street. His grip is strong on my hand and he pulls me along. "Keep up!" he growls.

I struggle to pull out my knife with my other hand. I stop and he loses his grip. I click the knife open. He whirls back to face me—and it's done.

"I said, keep . . ." He looks down at his gut where the knife sticks out. He looks back at me, horrified. He gasps and clutches his middle, but doesn't seem to fully realize what's happened.

Slowly, his face contorts and he sort of shakes his head. "No . . ." He staggers a few steps toward me. "Fuck you! Fuck you!" He stumbles back out into the daylight of the street. "Police! Help! Police!" he screams, falling now on his side. Then up to me, "Arab . . . help . . . fuck you!" But his words are suddenly weak, his breaths coming deep and hard. People pass, but look the other way and speed along, skirting around him rather than getting involved. Being a witness can get you killed. He reaches up toward a man passing by. "Help . . ." he whispers.

"Save your breath, Sniper. The last thing you care about is a dying Jew."

I haul him back into the alley and wait for his last shudder. Blood drains out of him and pools on the frigid pavement. His final breaths are weak puffs of steam. "And this, Sniper, is what a man without blood looks like," I say down to his lifeless form.

Once again, I rifle through his pockets and take his money, his papers, his pinky ring, his switchblade, and— most precious of all—his black book. It's hard to say for certain if my face is the last thing he sees. It's always strange with dying people. They can look right through you. German or Jew, we all die the same.

I leave him in the alley for the rats to find.

I hop on the back of a lorry heading west. I take my silver lighter and hold it to each page of Sniper's bounty book, one by one, watching them all flame up and float away.

Guilt? Hell, no. Guilt can get a girl killed. Sniper's memory is just as it should be. Another X'ed out hash mark. Another life avenged.

VI.

I stop when I see the horse. Didn't know horses had such good memories. Hummel sees me, lifts his head, and nickers a hopeful hello.

"Arab," Fritz says, dismounting. He looks more dashing than ever in his long black wool riding coat and white muffler.

"Hello, Herr *Obersturmführer*. Thought maybe you'd be trotting Hummel at the head of some fighting unit by now. Didn't I hear most of you cavalry men were getting into the thick of it?"

Fritz smiles and strokes his horse's neck. "What? And risk the life of this magnificent animal?"

"Which magnificent animal? You or the horse?"

We chuckle slightly, neither wanting to be seen looking too friendly with the enemy.

I open my jacket, displaying cigarettes. "Smoke?"

"Not sure what the point is anymore. Last ones I bought from your boys were just a puff of smoke wrapped in a post-age stamp." He shrugs and takes a cigarette, all the same. I go for the silver lighter in my pocket, then remember whose it is.

"Got a light?" I ask.

He brings out another lighter from his coat pocket, uses it, then tosses it to me. "Aw, don't tell me you lost your pretty silver one," I say, lighting up and handing it back to him.

Our eyes meet. "Someone pinched it."

"No. Now who would do that?"

"Just about anyone here in Warsaw. Including most of the men in my unit."

We smoke and look over each other's shoulders. Such a habit, by now, for both sides of the war.

"Hummel's looking good. Thought someone might have pinched him for steaks by now."

"I guard him with my life." He runs his hand along the horse's well-groomed flank.

"Good friends are hard to find here in Warsaw." Damn, I didn't mean that to sound so wistful. Feminine.

"Maybe in the whole world." He's sounding a bit wistful, too.

Again, our eyes meet. Both of us are showing too much vulnerability. Quick, I need to change the subject.

"Oh! I found my sister!"

"Did you? Where?"

"In the ghetto! Hiding in . . ." I stop short, knowing I am about to break my own "trust no one" rule.

Fritz smiles softly and crushes his cigarette out, "I'm glad for you, Arab. I hope you can keep her safe." He nods east. "Over there."

"I'll guard her with my life. Like you guard your Hummel here."

"You know, Arab . . . it won't be long . . . until . . ."

He catches my eyes, which suddenly feel damp. Why? The softness, the pity, the utter despair in his warning? The sorrow in his glance? My own fear?

"I'll keep her safe." I hold Hummel's reins as he mounts.

He looks around. "Arab, sometimes I feel . . . you and me, we're . . . well, we're so different, but so . . ." He stops, nodding to some officers approaching. "It's as though we're all on a huge sinking ship. Some are in first class and others are in steerage. But we're all going to drown."

"Except those in lifeboats. *Nur für Deutsche.*"

"There are no lifeboats," he whispers.

"Is that what they teach you in Nazi school? Just go down with the ship?"

"Yes, as a matter of fact, they do." He pauses. The officers come within earshot.

"You have enough cigarettes, Herr *Obersturmführer?*" I ask.

"*Ja, ja,*" he replies curtly, as our dance around this sinking ship of his demands.

The officers pass. Fritz leans down to me. "I'm in command of my unit's night patrols and roundups, Arab. Not just here on the Aryan side, but over in the ghetto, too. I give you fair warning."

"People in the ghetto are already rounded up. Why . . ."

Again, our eyes meet. "Work will set them free," he quotes, as though reading it from a billboard.

"Bullshit."

"If you or your sister or any of your urchins are caught in my net . . ." He looks down at me and is suddenly every bit the SS Nazi he's been groomed to be. "There won't be anything I can do to save you."

"Understood."

"You need to be very careful."

"When am I not?" I ask.

He laughs. "Just about every time you get near a gun."

"I'll take your warning and give you one back, Fritz. I'll do anything I have to do to save my sister."

"Understood." He snorts a laugh and shakes his head.

Hummel is sniffing my pockets for his treat. I pull out a fuzzy piece of half-sucked candy cane and offer it to the horse. His gentle crunching of the offering seems to be the perfect ending to our awkward friendship.

Fritz gathers up his reins, turns Hummel, and walks away, dispersing pedestrians as he rides through a crowd.

The snow has started up again with a vengeance.

VII.

I CAN'T SHAKE FRITZ'S WARNING. AND ALWAYS IN THE BACK OF my mind . . . Fritz knows what I've done. Twice. He could get a fine bounty for himself. I need to get Ruthie out, *now*.

I make my way to the factory, where I find the remaining Praska children and the rest of our gang gathered in a corner, bundled, each holding a ration of bread. Otto comes out of the factory door. He walks toward me, looking down at several photos of children to match with the papers we've forged.

"Otto, if we're going to do this, we've got to do it now. The snow's really coming down."

"Our thoughts exactly," he says. "We have to move now. Get the children into the ghetto and out your rat hole. My connections are waiting for confirmation."

He points to a small cage housing three pigeons. "Mrs. Praska, please tell the children those aren't toys."

"They're probably hoping they're dinner," she grumbles. "Children! Away from those birds!"

"How soon can you have everything ready?" I ask Mrs. Praska.

"Everything's ready now."

"My big worry is the snow. The ghetto gates are getting harder and harder to close," Otto says.

"But if the gates are snowed shut," Mrs. Praska objects, "How can we—?"

"We? I thought you were going to stay here with your two youngest." I look at Otto, then over to Yankev, who just shrugs.

"And do what? Send them out to sell the cigarettes we have no tobacco to make?" She points to her babes.

Her eyes find mine and, for the first time, I see a hint of emotion in her glance, the tiniest of tears in the corner of her eye.

"Mrs. Praska, you know . . . you know we can't take them out of Poland. They're—" I begin.

"I know!" she cries. She takes her prayer shawl off, wads it up, and tosses it on the table. "Too young! Too young to die, too young to live. So I'm coming with you. To the ghetto. I'll do what I can for those you can't—or won't—take out of Poland. I can do more good there than I can here. At least there I can care for the children—and fight, if it comes to that. I've shot a gun before."

"Arab," Yankev says, "Mama's made up her mind."

"That way, if all goes well," Otto says, "You, me, Yankev, and Lizard can sneak back into the ghetto through your hole in the cemetery wall. We'll do it again until we—"

"You and your 'if all goes well' shit," I say, cutting him off.

"Well, it was your plan," Otto snaps. "Any other suggestions?" He squares off with me. He sounds so stiff, so . . . zealous.

"This whole insane thing was your idea, Messiah!" I snap back. "No skin off my nose if—"

"Quiet! Both of you!" Mrs. Praska shouts. "Bickering like children!" Mrs. Praska gives us each a hard, maternal look. Otto and I look at each other. I wonder if I look just as sheepish as he does.

"So, are we doing this or not?" Mrs. Praska demands, crossing her arms across her ample chest.

"Yes, of course," Otto says.

There's a moment of awkward silence between us.

I look around the room. "So where's Lizard?"

"He said he had a connection for a handcart," Otto says.

"What for?"

"You, Yankev, and Lizard will pull the handcart with the children and Mrs. Praska inside, and I'll walk behind with my rifle. Just like with the children. Only this time, I'll have flushed an entire family. All of us, and now."

I look around the room—the children, quiet and solemn; Otto and Mrs. Praska, resolute. Yankev, arms crossed and leaning into a corner.

Moments later, Lizard arrives and calls me outside to look at what he's hauled back.

"That thing?" I ask, looking down at the rickety cart.

"I won't tell you what I did to get it." Even he is sounding harder.

Within minutes, we're loaded and ready to go. Identifications in pockets, Stars of David sewn on, cart filled with children and what belongings we can tuck into the corners.

The snow makes for difficult going, and we have to lift the cart over obstacles along the way. Who knows what sort of things—even bodies—the snow covers? The going is easier on the more-traveled roads. Still, it's an hour's trek.

I defy anyone to recognize us, wrapped in layers of clothing. Still, I have my false identification in case we get pulled out of line for a closer inspection. This time, I silently chant the name, birthdate, and occupation of my identity.

"Now what?" I whisper over to Otto. We've been stopped while the guards direct a work crew to shovel snow to open the tall wood gate. It's bricked in on both sides, and the snow is forming high drifts as fast as they can shovel. People from both sides mill around, grumble, stomping feet to stay warm, anxious to just move.

"I don't know," Otto whispers back. "The snow is winning."

"Maybe we should try another gate."

Just then, a guard announces over a blaring loudspeaker, "*Zurückgehen! Das Tor ist eingefroren! Zurückgehen!*"

"The gates are iced over," I whisper to Lizard and Mrs. Praska. "They want everyone to go back. All the gates are closing."

Then, in fractured Polish read from a floppy book, the guard calls out, "Go home! Go back to work! Go! *Zurückgehen!*"

Otto approaches one of the guards. "So what am I going to do with these Jews? I have my orders. I can't just let them go. It took me all day to smoke them out!"

"Shoot them, for all I care! But if you do, line them up behind each other to save bullets. You've heard the orders to conserve ammunition," he barks back.

My head pops up at the guard's suggestion. Otto growls some swear words and comes back to our cart. Mrs. Praska has the younger children under her arms like a hen protects her chicks under her wings. She's ready for trouble.

"There's been a change of plans," he mutters to me.

"When hasn't there been?" I mutter back.

"Turn this cart around! Hurry! Do you want me to freeze out in this?" he orders. We move to comply, but the cart has frozen in place in just the short time we've been stopped.

"Can't we just go back?" Yankev asks. "This is insane! We'll all freeze to death out here!"

I look behind us and the crowd fills the whole street, on the sidewalks and spilling into the side streets and alleys. I start moving.

"Where are you going?" Otto calls after me. I always have a backup plan and I'm walking toward it.

"Sewers," Lizard replies, carrying one of the children, who's hurt his ankle falling out of the cart. "Come on. It's fun."

"Maybe we should try another gate. It's too dark. All this snow and ice, and these young ones," Otto hedges, catching up to me and spinning me around.

We look back at the guards. One in the tower has cast his spotlight on us. "Careful, Lieutenant, you're letting your colors show," I tell Otto. He whips around as a guard comes our way.

We all stop. Otto's face hardens as walks over to meet the guard, and they exchange some angry words. Then he comes back to the cart. He has his gun drawn and is motioning for us to turn and go off onto a side street.

"Otto, what's happening? You're scaring the children with that gun, you know," I say out of the corner of my mouth.

"Just shut up and keep walking."

Lizard shoots me a glance and I know what he's thinking, because I'm thinking it, too. We round the corner and are out of the guards' sight.

"Otto!" I move to grab the gun. "What the hell are—?"

He pushes me away and Lizard goes for Otto's gun, now held high in the air. I have my own Luger halfway out of my pocket. Then Otto empties his gun into the air. The sound echoes off the walls of the narrow street and chunks of ice and snow pelt down on us. The children scream, huddle together, and begin to cry.

He holsters the gun. "He ordered me to shoot you," he says. "You're all officially dead now. Come on, before those guards come to take a head count and pick pockets!"

I have to take some deep breaths. The icy air stings my lungs. "Otto, I . . . I thought . . ."

"Forget it. I know what you thought. Now, where is this sewer of yours?"

Lizard and I exchange glances. We really did come this close to . . . I can't think about that now. I look around to get my bearings. "Come on! This way!"

We bring the cart around and I lead the way. The snow is blinding now and we'll freeze if we don't get shelter soon. Where the hell am I? I look around.

"Don't tell me you're lost," Yankev growls.

Everything has changed with so much snow. Finally, my eyes fall on the telltale steam rising from a sewer grate. "There!" We crunch our way across the street.

I pull out several lapel pins I've bought off a street vendor. They're phosphorescent, and they glow in the dark. "Here. Put these on everyone." I hand them to Lizard and stick one on myself.

"Look at me!" one child chirps, flapping her arms. "I'm a firefly."

Otto seizes the child. "Look at you, you're a target for a sharpshooter!"

We dig down through the snow to find the cover. Frozen shut. We chip away at the ice while Yankev holds the flashlight and the children stare down, their feet freezing to the snow under them.

"I'm not going down there, you know," Yankev says, staring at the sewer cover.

"Then you're not going," I say, backing up. I feel no sensation from my frozen fingers as I try to get a grip on the manhole cover. "Come on, Otto! Help me with this thing!"

"Why can't we just try again tomorrow?" Yankev says. "It'll be warmer and lighter and—"

"Our connection is waiting, that's why! I've already sent six birds and have just these three left!" Otto snaps back, pointing to the cage, well hidden in the cart. "Our transport is out there someplace right now. If the damn truck hasn't frozen to the road. If they haven't been discovered and shot!"

Yankev backs away, staring as we wheel the manhole cover aside. A gush of warm, moist, and foul-smelling air greets us. The children look down, their faces a mix of disgust and curiosity. Except Yankev, who backs up even further.

"You think about it, Yankev," I say looking up at him. Then, to the others, "Come on! Hurry!"

Lizard goes down first and we pass the younger children down to him. Then Mrs. Praska.

"When I was a girl, my brothers dared me to do this," she says, carefully gripping the handles of the ladder. "I wish they could see me now," she adds with a nervous mumble, her head disappearing into the black hole.

Then Otto. I turn to Yankev. Even in the dim light, I can see his face is the color of the snow around us. "Those children, those little girls, and even your mother, Yankev," I say, pointing down. "Come on! Get down there! Hurry!"

"I can't."

"Yankev!" his mother shouts from below.

Yankev backs away, looking like he's going to be sick. "I can't. I hate small places."

"Do you know how small a grave is?" I offer him my hand.

"I can't. I just can't."

"Get down there or I swear I'll leave you! You won't see any of them again, Yankev! Think!"

"No. I'll meet you in the ghetto. I can make it there on my own. Not down there, not down there." He keeps backing away, staring at the black hole in the street.

"Yankev, for the love of God!" his mother cries out. Her words sound otherworldly, a muted echo from the underworld.

"Hurry!" Otto shouts up.

"Yankev!" I say. "Pawia 322. We won't wait for you. Pawia 322!"

I scramble down the ladder. Lizard and I pull the manhole cover back over us, and I let my eyes adjust to the dark, take the flashlight, and lead my charges away. I hear Mrs. Praska trying to stifle her tears as she warns the children to stay quiet no matter what.

It's never easy going through the sewers. The children are deathly quiet, considering where they are. I wonder if children recognize a life-or-death situation better than adults. Lizard has made it a game of Follow the Firefly Leader with the flashlight.

Sounds echo in the sewers and we don't dare holler from a stubbed toe, or screech as the flashlight reflects dead, nibbled-out eyes, or whimper when cold, slimy globs of God-knows-what drip down on us. Even the pigeons are quiet in their cage.

I am first up through the sewer grate on the other side. I'm praying some soldier isn't there to greet me with a gun pointed at my face. I circle the area with my flashlight. Clear! In moments we have everyone up and out and in a line, heading for our hideout, just a few blocks away.

Still strangely silent, we bring everyone down the coal chute and inspect faces. Mrs. Praska takes charge immediately and gets the children unwrapped and settled. Otto does a head count now that we've all made it over, excepting Yankev—twelve children, four adults, three pigeons.

Mrs. Praska keeps looking up, perhaps wondering if her Yankev might have followed after all. Our eyes meet.

What can I say? I wonder if we're both worrying about the same thing.

We give the children something to eat and some warm water. Soon, Stefan and Lorenz are showing the other children the interesting things they have found in their time exploring the cellar. As they warm up and find their beds, settle in, and fall asleep, I feel as though the entire cellar is encased in an atmosphere of . . . what? Peace? Not excitement, not tension, but—yes, I guess that's it. Peace.

VIII.

At first light, I head out to check the wall and start searching for my gravestone. The snow is even deeper now, maybe about fifteen inches. The drifts are huge. I don't see any fresh tracks, so at least that's good. It seems pointless to cover up my own tracks around the cellar entrance. Judging by the dark clouds overhead, the snow will begin again soon. Besides, only idiots like me are out in this weather. I walk close to the wall, now even more of a mountain of snow and rock. I almost expect to see kids sledding down the snow bank the wall creates. So hard to tell what's under all the fluffy, white lumps—a car? dead horse? child's bike?

It's hard going and I'm thirsty and exhausted after only a few blocks. I turn to head back and then I see it, a streak of red smeared down the wall. Blood frozen on the snow. I trudge closer and carefully poke my foot into a snow-covered lump at the base of the wall. Something half hidden and gray catches my eye.

I look around, then kneel and swipe carefully at the snow. The gray cap is frozen stiff, and I have to pull it loose from the grips of the icy snow. I know this cap. I dig a bit deeper, fearing, but knowing what I'll find.

"God . . ." I whisper. I gently uncover Yankev's face. He looks for all the world like a sleeping child. "No . . ." I swipe away ice crystals from his eyes and realize they're his last tears. "I'm sorry, Yankev," I whisper down to him. I pack snow around his head, then pull out a handkerchief to place over his face.

The sound of a horn honking several streets over reminds me where I am. I cover Yankev with more snow, encasing him entirely. I'm not a good Jew. If I ever knew the prayer, I've forgotten it. So instead, I sketch in the snow, just above his head:

Die with Honor

I stuff his cap into my jacket and return to my quest—finding our escape hole in the wall.

I look in both directions. Except for the streak of blood marking Yankev's snowy grave, it's all just one long, low mountain range. My chances of finding that one spot are . . . Damn it to hell! It's hopeless! What was I thinking? I pace along the wall, kicking at the drifts. I look up at the trees, hoping I might recognize something from that work party so long ago. It's . . . it's hopeless.

Defeated, with Yankev's cap tucked inside my coat, I make my way back to the cellar.

"Otto, I have to tell you something," I say. I try to keep the urgency out of my voice. Mrs. Praska is watching me very closely.

"Jesus Christ!" Otto says. "There are sixteen of us." He runs his hand through his thick shock of hair. "No, seventeen, when Yankev gets here!"

"One more, when I get my sister. Remember, she's the whole reason I'm doing this. But Otto, come with me. We have to talk."

"Go ahead and ration out something to eat, Mrs. Praska," he says. Then, to me, "Okay, what is it?"

"Lizard, you need to hear this, too." I lead them to the root cellar, where I know we can't be overheard. I shove the ancient door closed and light a candle.

"Jesus, Joseph, and Mary!" Lizard says, looking at row after row of bottles. "We can bribe our way out of Poland with this stash! Arab, you been holding out on us?"

"Lizard! Listen! There's been a slight change of plans," I say. "Otto! Put that bottle down! Yankev is dead."

They stop eyeing the liquor and look at me. Silence while that sinks in.

"What? How?"

"I saw him at the foot of the wall. My guess is he tried to climb over. Was spotted and shot." I exhale, wondering how I'm going to tell Mrs. Praska.

"Poor Yankev," Otto says.

"May he rest in peace," Lizard says, crossing himself.

"Yankev isn't the worst of it," I say, low.

"What else?" Otto asks.

"There's no way I can find my rat hole. The whole wall is covered with snow and frozen solid."

"What do you mean you can't find it!" Otto bellows. He points toward our covey of children. "We risked all those lives bringing them here, and now you can't even find your fucking surefire can't-fail rat hole? Your famous gravestone?"

"Arab!" Lizard jumps in. "Then how the hell are we going to get . . . Arab!"

I don't know what else to say. They're right. My plan has failed.

"Oh great!" Otto hollers. "Just perfect! Hell, what made me ever think this could work in the dead of winter? Look, I'm thinking about delaying everything for a few weeks."

I point up. "Okay, I take total responsibility for the weather! But, Otto, we can't wait! You've seen it up there! How many people can they cram into the ghetto? How much longer do you think we have? We can't wait until the spring thaw. We have to come up with something, and we have to do it now."

"And how are we even going to feed all those children? How long before someone upstairs turns us in?" Lizard says. "Hell, for all we know, there are bounty hunters—maybe even Sniper—just ready to cash in on us! We'd make quite a haul, wouldn't we?"

"Sniper's the least of our problems," I say. I've kept that to myself, too. I turn to Otto. "Another thing. The Krauts will level the ghetto at the first sign of that resistance you say is germinating out there."

"Otto, go over this plan again. Only leave out the part about the hole in the wall," Lizard says. He pulls out a bottle of something, yanks the cork, and takes a swig. "We're three reasonably smart men." He looks at me. "Sorry. People. We can figure this out."

Otto takes a drink from the bottle, hisses at the burn, then pulls out his multi-folded map. "By now, a transport has been delivered and hidden in a barn just outside of Warsaw—about here. They know we'll be there in the next few days, Arab." He points to the pigeons' cage, being kept warm in the rafters. "Once those last three go, we're committed."

"How far a walk is that?" I ask.

"Half mile. It's a bridle path most of the way. We've watched it and hardly anyone patrols it."

"You're going to walk those children a half mile in this snow?" Lizard says.

"We planned to walk through snow, just not this much," Otto says.

Lizard takes a pencil from his pack and starts to draw a circle around Otto's "about here."

"No!" Otto grabs the pencil from him.

"What?" Lizard demands.

"Having a map is one thing. Having a marked map is another. You should know that." He throws the pencil across the cellar.

"A truck will be waiting here." Otto points to the map. "But trucks are different sizes. That's why no more than twelve can go at a time. When I get as far as my connection here—a farmer and his daughter—someone else will get us to the next point. And then to here, then finally to Danzig, where we'll have a boat."

"Hope it's more than a rowboat," Lizard says.

"There's a tug and an old freighter. And someone offered the use of their yacht."

Lizard paces the root cellar. "Freighters! Yachts! I can't believe I got me and my boys into this mess!"

"You came along ready, willing, and able!" Otto says. I see his jaw tensing. "If you want out, fine! The fewer we take, the better our chances!"

"Look, gentlemen," I say, stepping between them. "This has just started. Let's not get into it now. Let's plan just one big fistfight when this is all over, okay?" That releases some tension. "Otto, go on."

"Then I come back after the children are safely delivered to the boat. Meanwhile, you and Lizard work to get more ghetto children lined up to go."

I point toward Danzig, far to the northwest. "A lot can happen between here and there."

"Which is why we do this in stages. We keep our lines of communication open, and we risk as few lives as possible at a time. But this weather, Arab. I tell you, it can ruin everything. No," Otto says, "a few weeks one way or another won't . . . I can plan this thing from now to doomsday." He turns to leave. "But I can't plan on the goddamn weather!"

"Where are you going?" I whirl him around by the elbow.

"I'm going to release those last pigeons and tell my connections it's a no-go. It's the only logical thing to do. Then I'm leaving Warsaw to reset everything, pick up more birds, and—"

"No, Otto! There isn't time! All those kids aren't going to die in the crosshairs of your logic!"

"*All* those kids?" Otto asks, a small smile coming to his face. "Thought you were in this just for yourself and your sister and your two pickpocketing boys. Arab, listen to me. We can't ask all those kids to walk a block in this weather. Let alone to our first connection!"

"But this road, here, it's well-traveled and might be easier going," I say, pointing to the map.

"No. Well-traveled means well-guarded," Otto returns.

"Wait. Let's stop. Let's think," Lizard breaks in. "Otto, you've been out there. Do they stop every truck? Every car?"

"They have checkpoints, yes. Sometimes roadblocks. But in this snow, it's hard to know what those Krauts will or won't do."

"Can you requisition a car or a truck?" I ask. "I mean, with all your papers and identifications, can't you get us transportation? Your uniform has already opened a few doors." I offer them both a cigarette and light them using Fritz's silver lighter.

"*Hitler* would be hard-pressed to get a transport in Warsaw right now."

"Well, Hitler might be hard-pressed, but I'm not," Lizard says, casually.

"Uh oh," I mutter. I recognize the expression on Lizard's face.

"Hear me out. I say we evacuate everyone at once. None of this 'a few at a time' business. That's just plain pressing our luck. I say we all go at once."

"How? Like circus clowns, we all just cram into our little truck and disappear into the bottom of the stage?" Otto asks. He points toward the outside and that elusive sanctuary destination at the end of our route.

"I can find us a truck," Lizard states. "Three trucks, if you want."

"'Find a truck!' Are you insane?" Otto says sarcastically. "Find a truck where? At the used truck store?"

"There are about six *Opel Blitz* trucks lined up, pretty as you please, on a side street off of Żelazna. All chained up for the snow. You know the street, Arab. Just a few blocks that way."

"Here in the ghetto?" Otto asks.

"Yes." Lizard exhales smoke rings and they vanish into the chilly air.

"Must be for the deportations. Jews in the front door, and out the back," I say.

"Are there any guards? Any soldiers?" Otto asks.

"Nope. Trucks just sitting there, minding their own business. Who would steal a truck here in the ghetto? How far could anyone get?" Lizard goes on, shrugging his shoulders.

"And Lizard can hot-wire a dead horse," I say, recalling some rides we took when we were kids.

"No. Can't hot-wire them," Lizard says flatly.

"You can't? You? Why not?" I ask.

"Because, Einstein, they don't even have keys. No military trucks do. You just hit the starter."

"Doesn't that make it easy to . . ." I stop and smile broadly. "Steal one?"

"Fine. So you get a truck. Then what?" Otto says.

"What would you say to three German SS men taking the children out of the ghetto?" I ask, my new plan forming fast.

"Who are the other two, Stefan and Lorenz?" Otto asks, issuing a pathetic grunt.

"Lizard and me."

"Lizard and you are staying here, remember? That was the plan," he adds, with an impatient snap. Then he cocks his head. "What are you thinking?"

"What if I told you I could get German uniforms for both Lizard and me? Three guards, a truckload of children, and just one big evacuation?" I say.

That's when they turn both on me—the men. "Well, I'd almost pay to see that," Lizard starts.

Otto joins in, chuckling, looking at me. "I've no doubt you've played many roles in your life, Arab. But really, a soldier?"

"I'm almost as tall as Lizard here, and he knows I can take him in a street fight."

"It isn't your height. It's your . . ." Lizard points to me and pauses.

"It's my what?"

"That pretty face of yours. Well, passable face." I hold back my grin, watching him fidget. "You're starting to look . . . female."

"And besides, do you know what it took for me to get this uniform?" Otto says, pointing his cigarette toward the SS uniform hanging in the rafters to dry.

"I tell you, I can get uniforms for Lizard and me."

"Forget it," Otto snaps. "I don't care if you sprout a beard and grow balls, Arab! You are not going to pass for a German soldier!"

"Well, now, wait a minute," Lizard breaks in. "I can pass, but I don't speak German. Why can't Arab be our interpreter or something? I mean, she doesn't have to be anything more than just a street kid you use to interpret your prisoners' Polish. Male or female."

Otto looks around the boiler room. "Lord, what am I getting myself into?" he mutters.

"You should have thought about that when you entered Warsaw," I say. Then, to Lizard, "What size pants do you wear?"

"The size I've just stolen."

"Give me an hour." I start to leave, but Otto calls me back.

"Arab, just remember: the more children we evacuate at one time, the more lives we risk in one go." He drinks again.

"When did you become such a doubter? I'm going to start calling you 'Thomas.'"

"There can't be any mess-ups, that's all. Everything has to go according to plan."

I laugh. "Since when has anything gone according to plan?"

"I mean it, Arab! Swear to God, we have to—"

"You know, Messiah, I can just go get my sister. That's all I really care about. Grab Stefan and Lorenz. It's all the same to me. I can take her and my boys back over to the Aryan side just as easily as I brought them here. So can Lizard. Mrs. Praska will figure something out. She's already beaten the odds. We'll all figure out a way to survive the rest of the war. We can all walk away from you, from your so-called connections, from your big plans to save the world! We'll muddle along somehow. Until your precious Americans come save us," I add with a look of disgust.

"I tell you, Arab, I have a plan, and I make the calls!"

"Well, your plan hasn't exactly worked, has it? Who got us here safe and sound?"

"And whose rat hole disappeared?"

"I can easily go back to the life before the Messiah's great second coming! And what good is a savior with no one to save?"

"I don't want to save the world! I just want to save all the children I can!" I don't like his finger pointing at me. I slap it away.

"Well, those are my children! So you either let me make the calls, or we walk!"

Is it a bluff? Would I walk? Which risk is greatest for my Ruthie and the rest? There's that damned amalgam of conflict—love, hate, peace, war. What'll it be, Otto?

"Arab," he whispers, stepping closer. "I don't want to lose anyone else."

"Then let me do what I do best."

He stares at me hard and long. "Okay, Arab. Okay."

I start bundling myself up again to head back outside. I need to be as invisible as I can.

Mrs. Praska has fixed up a small kitchen area behind the coal bins, where she can store and ration out our meager supplies. She comes out just as I'm heading for the chute. When she stops, our eyes meet.

She takes her prayer shawl from around her shoulders and puts it around my head. "He's not coming, is he?"

I can barely look at her. "No."

"He's dead, isn't he?" she whispers as she ties the shawl in a knot under my chin.

I take her hand, so close to my face. "I'm sorry. I should have told you first thing, but I had to tell Lizard and Otto."

She nods and keeps fussing with the shawl. "He was my firstborn. First to die."

I pull Yankev's cap out from under my sweater. It's warm from being close to my skin. "Here."

She exhales a sigh of grief as she sees the cap, then takes it to her breast.

I have never made any pretense of liking Yankev. "He died a hero," I say, the words slipping fast out of my mouth.

"He did?" A little smile comes to her worn face.

"Yes. I saw it, when I went out this morning. He defied a soldier. He stood right up to him and died before telling him why he was running. He was running to find us. Wouldn't say where he'd come from or where he was going. He kept us safe."

"Where is he? Can I see him? Kaddish . . . I have to . . ."

I touch her arm. "There is no Kaddish anymore, Mrs. Praska. They took his body away. He's gone." Another lie. I nod toward her other children. "But now we have them to save. He died for them."

She nods thoughtfully. "Thank you, Arab."

"Yankev died rather than betray us. A hero."

"Yes. Yes."

It's the kindest lie I've ever told. And Mrs. Praska is kind to pretend she believes me.

IX.

"AND WHAT HAPPENS WHEN A SOLDIER COMES FOR HIS UNI-form and it's not here? Do you know how these goose step-pers cherish their boots? What will I say? What will happen? We will be kicked out of here faster than you can say *eins, zwei, drei*!" Mrs. Kerber states flatly.

"But all those uniforms. Don't you have some that have been here for a long time?" I look at the tags on some, check the names and drop-off dates. "Look! This one has been here for two months! You think this Corporal Huber is, what, away taking the waters at Wiesbaden? He won't be back if he hasn't come to collect this by now. He's dead. I'll take this one. And here, this one is old, too. One of these should fit Lizard. Now, boots. And good, there's some heavy coats. I'll need three—no, make it five! Just for good measure."

Mrs. Kerber pulls me back by the arm. "No, I can't chance it. I just can't. I have my Anna to think about."

I rummage through the rank insignias on her sewing table. "I'll take this one. And this."

"No!"

"Mrs. Kerber, I've stolen from you before, and I can do it again. If anyone comes for these, just say the neighborhood *gonif* took them. Tell them it was me, Abra Goldstein. File a complaint."

"I forbid it. I . . ." Her bespectacled eyes fall on the wad of food ration cards I'm holding in front of her face. "I . . .

we . . ." I pull out two tins of condoms I unearthed from someone's dresser weeks ago.

"And here. Take these for Anna. Do you know the penalty for a Jewish woman getting pregnant? By anyone, let alone a German officer?" I run my finger across my throat and hiss. "For the mother and the baby."

Her eyes come up to meet mine. "These are too late. Already Anna is eight months . . . What have we become?"

I pull out two papers from my coat. "Do you know what these are?"

"No."

"These are passes out of Poland. All you have to do is get someone to type in all the information." I point to the form. "If you can get yourself out of the ghetto, these just might get you both out of Poland altogether. If you don't use them, then for God's sake, sell them."

She takes my offerings and turns her back on me. I leave burdened with two uniforms, two pairs of boots, five coats, and insignia patches for Mrs. Praska to sew on for us.

X.

"Is there anything you can't get your hands on?" Otto asks. He fingers the uniforms I've returned with.

"Yes. Decent weather." I hand the whole armful to Mrs. Praska.

The sound of children coughing brings Otto's face around to me. "We're not just fighting the weather, Arab. Listen to those kids. Four woke up sick. How do we keep a kid from coughing? You might as well ask a baby not to cry."

"Meanwhile, we sit here? All these children? How much food do we have? I just gave away four of our ration cards! Do we even have any medicine here for those kids?" I snap back.

"Maybe we should go back to the factory," Mrs. Praska says, sounding defeated for the first time. "At least on the Aryan side there's more we can get our hands on. At least we have electricity now and then. The children can sell what cigarettes we have left."

"Medicine . . ." Lizard says, low and long. "Med-i-cine . . ."

"What?" I ask. "What about it?"

"Irenka," he says, smiling.

"Who?" Otto asks.

"She's Lizard's sweetheart," I say. In a way, I want to tease Lizard. But this is war. They're probably far more than sweethearts by now.

"She works in an infirmary. Maybe she can give us something for the children," Lizard says. He turns to Mrs. Praska. "Write down what we need."

"Just hold it!" Otto says. "Won't she wonder why you need all this medication? All the infirmaries are controlled by the Germans. We can't just trust her to keep her mouth shut. What if she gets caught? Then what about your 'sweetheart'?"

Good points, all. We look at Lizard for his answer.

"She's a good woman. She's helped us before. I think, when she knows it's for children, she'll do what she can. She doesn't like the Germans any more than we do."

"All right, but here's the thing: if she hesitates, even flinches when you ask her, get out and get out fast," Otto warns.

Lizard puffs a bit at that. He and Otto are squaring off more and more. "I know what I'm doing, and I know who I can trust. Now, do you want the medicine or not?"

"Yes, yes!" Mrs. Praska says. She looks at Otto. "What we don't need now, we might need later. I have some morphine and aspirin, and that's all." She turns to Lizard. "I'll make you a list."

Lizard starts layering on his clothes.

Lorenz helps Mrs. Praska rip seams and identifications off the German uniforms. Little Stefan steps into a pair of the high, black boots and entertains the other children with an amusing imitation of Hitler, complete with a coal-smudge mustache above his lip and well-measured little goose-steps. "You cry you die! You cry you die!"

I try to get some sleep, but it's impossible. There's so much running through my head. Images appear, one on top of another—trucks, medicines, uniforms, sick children, Danzig, and Ruthie. As soon as it's dark, I'll head out, scoop her up, and bring her back.

I look twice around every corner now, knowing they have horse patrols here in the ghetto. The snow is coming down in thick, fat flakes, muting all sounds and building even higher drifts around the walls. Easy in, easy out. The Krauts will be out guarding these walls with their shoot-first-ask-questions-later motto, so I stay as far from them as I can.

I make my way to the theater cellar, sparing my flash-light as much as possible. At least the snow makes things lighter in the dusk.

"Abra! You did! You did come back!" Ruth screeches, before I can hush her.

"Sh, Ruth! Quiet. We have to whisper all the time, now. Okay?"

"Okay," she whispers up at me. God, she seems even smaller now than just a few days ago.

"Good. Are you ready? Do you have any warmer clothes?"

She shakes her head. "Somebody stole all my clothes. My toys, too." She wears a light coat, several sizes too small. Her boots are unmatched, and they look worn and pinch-ing, adding to her already pronounced limp.

"Come on, then. We'll get you warmer clothes. You have to take my hand and be very quiet."

"You said I could bring Sofia," she says pulling away and dodging through the theatrical curtains hanging from the rafters.

"Yes, get your doll. But hurry."

When she doesn't come right back, I weave my way through the shrouds of curtain. There's a commotion of chairs, voices, coughing. I step fully into the room—and standing in a small, tight group behind Ruth are six girls and their older keeper. Each is wearing a coat and gripping a valise or a bundle. Ruthie grips her doll, Sofia.

I stare. I can't seem to say anything.

Ruth points to a child next to her. "This is Sofia. You said we could take Sofia."

"But, your doll, Ruthie. Sofia is your doll," I stammer, keeping my glance away from the hungry, empty, hopeful eyes on me.

"I know! I named her after my friend, Sofia!"

Then I recognize the children. All friends, and renters, and neighbors. Perhaps the only survivors from our old neighborhood. I stand speechless. God, now what? I clear my throat. "No, Ruthie. I can only take you. Your friends will be all right, won't you?"

Ruth's infamous pouty lip starts to quiver, and tears well in her eyes. "You said," she cries in a whisper.

The oldest steps forward. "We made a pledge when we came here. We all stay together. No matter where God points us."

"But you have adults taking care of you. You have someone checking in on you, don't you?" I recognize a losing battle when I'm facing one.

"No. Not for a long time now. I think we're all . . ." She covers the ears of the youngster standing in front of her and mouths the word: orphans.

I have faced gun barrels, Nazi inquisitors, policemen of all stripes, and even Sniper. They were all training grounds for what I'm facing now.

"I . . . I . . ."

Then little Sofia comes over and looks up at me. "We'll all whisper. We'll be good. We promise."

I run my hand over my face—maybe in the hopes that when I open my eyes, only Ruth and her doll will be in front of me. "All right. Now listen, every one of you. All hold hands, and if I hear anyone say anything or whine or cry or even a stomach growl, I'll beat you."

"No, you won't," Ruthie says defiantly up to me.

"What makes you think so?"

"Because that would make us cry."

How can I not love her? How can I leave her friends behind?

I scoop up the smallest so we can walk faster.

"Hold hands!" I growl down to the horde now following me out into the ghetto streets. The snow makes for difficult going, but the children keep to their word. Perhaps it's the war, the shortages, the indignities, the loneliness. But they are deathly quiet during our short trek over to our cellar hideout.

"We're home!" Ruthie whispers up to me as we round the corner.

"Only for a very short time."

"Can I have my room back?"

"No. Other people live in your room now."

"I want my toys back."

"What did I tell you about talking?"

She puts her gloved hand to her mouth and flashes me wide eyes.

I knock out our code on the coal chute door. Otto knocks back, opens it, and I grin sheepishly as the eight new faces peer down.

"There's been a change of plans," I say as I pass down a child to Otto.

Once the children are all inside, Mrs. Praska stands, hands on hips, as they instinctively pool around her. I can tell she's counting heads as they shyly peek out from under their hats and scarves. She's just as speechless as I was earlier.

Otto pulls me into the root cellar. "What the hell have you done?" he cries.

"What the hell would you have done?" I bark back, throwing down my gloves. "The little blonde, that's Ruthie, my sister. The little brat conned me! What could do? I couldn't leave the others."

"Hell, we're not going to need a truck, Arab," says Otto. "We're going to need a goddamn bus!"

"What would you have done?" I bark again, taking a long drink from the bottle closest to me on the shelf.

Mrs. Praska lets herself in, grabs the bottle from my hand, and drinks. "Twenty-four of us," she says, shaking her head.

XI.

WE'VE BARELY INTRODUCED THE NEW CHILDREN WHEN Lizard knocks his code on the door. He comes sliding down, a wooden case strapped to his shoulder. He gets up, turns, and damn! A child slides down into his arms, followed by a woman laden with bundles.

Lizard immediately notices the new kids I've brought in. He looks at me, confused. "Shut up. You know exactly what happened!" I bark at him, nodding toward Irenka and her brother.

"Thank you so much for taking us," Irenka says. "Our parents were deported, and I've been doing my best just to keep us eating. But I haven't come empty-handed." Her hand holds on tight to her brother's. The little boy stands terrified and mute, two fingers in his mouth.

"I see that," I say.

"No, I mean I've brought medicine. And this. I stole it off a desk. You might be able to use it. I think it goes on a car or ambulance."

I unroll the fabric. It's a small pennant, but the red cross in the grips of a Nazi eagle says it all. "Throws me off," I say. "Swastika and red cross together."

"Never mind. It's a pass," Lizard says, handing it to Mrs. Praska. "Keep it with the others."

"Why were your parents deported?" Otto asks.

"Haven't you heard? Literature professors and cello players are dangerous enemies of the *Reich*," she says. Her chin is high and her eyes are dry. I look at her tight, gloved grip on her brother's small hand. I have no stones to throw.

By dinner, the cellar sounds like a tuberculosis ward with all the children in it restless and coughing.

"I suppose they'll all be coughing by morning," Mrs. Praska says. "Those tiny bodies can't fight off a bedbug bite, let alone a cold."

"Or worse," Irenka adds. "Whooping cough is going around. Thank God it's not meningitis back again."

Irenka sits now, a blanket wrapped around her shoulders. The glow of the lantern light bounces off her face. A slight pop of turquoise peeps out from under her layers of sweaters. Lizard sits next to her and shares his ration of bread and a sip of liquor. I can see why he's so infatuated. Love. Here, in the middle of a cellar, in the middle of a ghetto, in the middle of a war? Too bad, I think. Love can get a person killed.

I watch Otto pacing in and out of the shadows. He's a far more complex person than I first thought. He's obsessive about our mission, yet I've seen him break down with guilt, his anger at failure. I wonder if I'm seeing a man at odds with all those different passions. I wonder if he's thinking what I'm thinking: How do you choose? How do you say yes to one and no to another? Isn't that exactly what Hitler is doing? You, stay! You, go! You, live! You, die!

Otto cleans his glasses with a rag, something he does when agitated. He pulls me aside. "I tell you, Arab, this is far more complicated. We had a plan. We had an agreement." He whispers to me out of one side of his face as he casts a nervous smile toward the children's room. "Look how many we have!"

"What's a few lives more or less?" I shrug my shoulders in the universal gesture of a "so what?" I wonder which Otto is going to emerge.

"Fine. Crying babies, coughing children. Good luck with your 'You cry, you die' mantra here! Why not put up a big sign that says, 'Here we are, Adolf! Come and get us!'"

"I can get my hands on some neon, if you'd like."

He looks at me. "Neon?"

"For your sign? Good God, Otto, keep up, will you?"

We lock eyes. Finally, he smiles, slings his arms around my shoulders and pulls me into a rocking, almost stifling hug. He whispers in my ear, "What would I do without you? If I'm the Messiah, you're Joan of Arc."

"Terrific." I pull away from him just a bit. "You know how they both ended up."

"Look! A gift from heaven!" Mrs. Praska says, coming into the boiler room and showing us the case of vials and pill bottles. "We'll start by getting those coughs taken care of. Irenka and I quarantined the sicker children."

"Hopefully they'll keep their germs to themselves," Irenka says, shaking a thermometer.

"It's not as though it's the plague or anything," Mrs. Praska says. "They're children. They have colds. They'll be fine in no time."

"I gave codeine to a few and they're sleeping now," Irenka says. "Come see."

Irenka sweeps aside the hanging blankets that separate the quarantined children. Each face is peaceful as the children huddle together for warmth. Ruthie and both her Sofias are cuddled up, almost sharing the same breath.

I settle down into a corner and listen to the concert of breathing, snoring, and coughing. I try to remember the names and connect to the faces of twenty-six of us. Half quarantined. We social parasites might as well be imprisoned in one of those camps, Elsewhere, that Adolf F. Somebody is cultivating—dozens of them, with plenty of space for all us castoffs who spread political and Jewish contagion.

"Contagion," I whisper into the darkness. I think back on the German soldier I'd talked to as he herded people to Elsewhere. I grin as I remember his expression when I told him only Aryans can die from Jewish colds. Stupid Kraut. Wait a minute! That stupid Kraut with the cold said something about . . . where? Stutthof! Medical studies and experiments. Building three-legged women!

One of the children begins coughing. "Contagion!" I call into the darkness.

I pull my flashlight out and look at Otto's map of Poland—or what once was Poland—and the lines separating the new three sections: Germany, Colony, Soviet. I run my finger from Warsaw to the new Nazi camp in the northwest. Stutthof. Just a few kilometers from the Gulf of Danzig, where there are private yachts ready to sail the children away to safety. "Stutthof," I whisper. "Sick people! That's it!"

My mind is racing, and we're losing time. I am about to be either very, very clever or very, very stupid.

"If you keep having these delusions of grandeur, Arab, someone's going to put a net over you and take you to the nut house over in Tworki," Lizard says, sticking his nose back into the half-burned book he's resurrected. "Go away. I'm reading."

He waves me away, but then quickly rolls back. "What does Otto-the-Messiah-Kraut have to say about this plan?"

"I haven't told him."

"Well, from the way you two have been sparring over this whole fiasco, I'd say you better."

"I don't need his blessings, Lizard," I snap.

"Well, I think it's about the stupidest idea I've ever heard."

"No, listen! We make ourselves into something so vile, so feared, that the gates will open and they'll be glad to be rid of us."

"Like what? That Spanish Flu? Didn't that kill millions in the Great War?"

"No, it has to sound even worse. We have to come up with something that will stop them in their tracks. Something very contagious."

"What was that big plague?"

"Bubonic. Black Death."

"Why can't it be that one?"

"It can. But if we can come up with something new—so new it's not even in the medical books yet—we might get clearance all the way to Stutthof."

"Where's Stuffhof?"

"Just a little village close to Danzig. Where they just happen to have a camp. For Jews. Maybe even sick Jews. Three-legged women."

"Are you drunk?" Lizard asks, tossing a rag at me.

"Sober as a judge," I whisper, looking around the cellar and thinking. My eyes land on the secret bulkhead of my father's wine cellar. I'm remembering my schooling. Who knew more about plagues than Moses, having graced Egypt with ten of them? I run through all of them in my mind as I absently scratch a troublesome bug bite on the back of my neck. "I think we're dealing with the Plague of Moses here."

"The what?" Lizard asks.

"Better known as the Kinem Plague," I add, recalling Moses's third plague—the one with all the lice.

"Is there such a thing?"

"Could be."

"How do you get it?"

"From lice." I ignore the urge to scratch my head as Lizard's hand goes to his. "You die in three days."

"Lice don't kill you." He's skeptical as usual. He pulls out a nit and squeezes it dead.

"When they carry the Kinem Plague they do."

"You're making this up."

"Look, what do those guards know? If someone's breathing any plague on you, would you go running to your medical book, or would you wave them through? And oh, how the Nazis would love to find a new Jewish disease. Hell, they already blame Jews for everything from typhoid fever to toenail fungus."

"It's Jewish? Oh, good. Then I can't catch it."

I hit him squarely in the chest. "No, Einstein! It's not real! And even if it was, you gullible Catholics would be even more susceptible."

For a minute, I think he believes me. Then a big smile spreads across this face. "Let's tell Otto."

"No. Not yet. Let him sleep. He feels like shit. Besides, he'll probably just piss on it, like he has all my other brilliant ideas."

"Yeah, but isn't he in charge? Shouldn't we . . ." His words fall away when he sees my face.

I plug my thumb into my chest. "This whole thing is my deal! I'm in charge!"

"This better not be just another battle of the sexes. Not with all these lives on the line!"

I get up and rummage for my heaviest overcoat.

"Hey, where're you going?"

"I'll be back. Get some sleep."

XII.

I BUNDLE UP AND CREEP BACK TO THE MINERVA THEATER, damning the crunch of the icy snow. I carefully round corners, not turning my flashlight on until I'm safely in the basement. I hang it off a wire above and look around. Where to begin? How to begin?

I drag out two panels of scenery from the stack against the wall and slice the canvas from the wooden frames. Now, paint. The cabinets and cupboards are difficult to open, but I yank hard and search for paint that hasn't dried up or frozen.

I find two cans that slosh when I shake them. Black and brown. I mix them together. Then I rummage through the drawers and find an old crusty brush and—look here! Exactly what I need: stencils! I place the canvas panel on the floor; a menagerie of abstract painted faces laugh gaily up at me. I arrange the stencils to make sure I have enough room, then get to work. I finish panel one and hang it to dry, then work on another, identical one.

While waiting for my handiwork to dry, I explore the cellar of the old theater. When I was a kid, how many times did I sneak in here? I can still hear the echoes of laughter from the audience above, the steady *flip flip flip* of the film as it rolls, the hush of anticipation as the curtains rise. Will anyone, anywhere, ever hear those sounds again?

I slip into the room with WARDROBE written above the doorless jamb. There are clothes racks that were once crammed with costumes, but are now empty. There are heaps of burned and charred clothes on the floor. Who needs a Queen Antoinette wig or a cutaway tux when we're freezing here in the ghetto? The paste buttons off a chorus girl costume might become a baby's rattle. The cheap fur collar off a society matron costume might become a little girl's muff.

Along the walls are shelves, also ransacked and empty. The trunks along the opposite wall have been flung open, the contents rifled through and stolen. It's what everyone does here in Warsaw. We rifle, we raid, we rummage, we ransack.

I spot some high shelves, nearly hidden by ripped curtains. I stack some boxes, climb up, and yank open a stubborn cupboard. I check it with my flashlight, then reach in. "What the . . .?"

The boxes under me start to crack and I wobble. I grab the cupboard as the boxes tumble, leaving me hanging. Another crack of wood. Oh no! Now the damn cupboard—

After I hit the ground, I'm stunned but okay. My butt hurts from the edge of the box I've crushed. "What's this?" In my hand is the bundle I was reaching for. Looks like sheets—good. Sheets have street value these days.

But wait. These aren't sheets. What I'm holding is a thick stack of folded white uniforms, tied together with twine. I look at the card attached. NURSES ON PARADE. I flip through the folds and see each uniform has an identification tag: NURSE NAOMI, NURSE STELLA, NURSE MARJA, and HEAD NURSE LUCIA. I laugh out loud! "Damn!" Even theatrical characters have their papers in order! I clutch my find to my chest and struggle to get up, already feeling my back stiffen.

I don't believe in divine anything, let alone intervention or inspiration. I believe in being in the wrong place at the wrong time, like those first twelve Jews I saw executed—and I believe in being in the right place at the right time, such as here in the cellar of the Minerva Theater, holding a pressed stack of nurse stage costumes. Still, I give a nod of thanks to anyone from above who might be looking down on me.

I raid a box full of greasepaint and other things they use to make actors look like someone they're not. Anything that might make a healthy child look like death warmed up.

I'm frozen and exhausted. My butt hurts. The canvases aren't drying very fast in this cold. After another hour, I decide I'll just head back to the cellar. At least I can get warm there, and maybe catch some sleep.

As I leave the theater I breathe in the frozen night air, so cold it hurts my lungs and shoots some energy into me. Will it bring me to my senses, snap me out of this insanity, demand I just grab my sister, forget the rest, every girl for herself and her sister? Run away and . . . and then what? Vanish into thin air?

No. Not likely.

XIII.

I DON'T GET VERY FAR. TWO BLOCKS AWAY, I HEAR EERIE, FAR-away . . . is that singing? I stop and strain to listen. Singing? Here? It's such an unexpected sound. Has hunger finally gone to my head? It echoes off the snowed-in streets and gets louder. A low voice—male—off key. I can't hear words and I don't recognize the tune. Or is it even a tune? Then I catch a word or two of German.

I look around for cover—easy to find on these streets. I feel for my Luger as I sprint behind a burned-out car and listen.

The singing gets louder. I see shadows of men approaching! I take out my Luger and wait, listening for the muted crunch of footsteps on the snow.

I strain to get a better look. "Otto?" I whisper. What the—? They come closer. Otto and Lizard! Look at them! A couple of falling-down drunks! Otto is swaying and Lizard is trying to keep him on his feet.

I put my Luger away and rise up, but quickly duck back down again. I'm not the only one who's heard their drunken song. Two officers from the ghetto security are following them.

The police draw their pistols. Slowly, I edge closer, not sure what I can do if this turns nasty. Everything, all those lives in the cellar, all rest on Otto. And I'll hate to lose an old friend and partner like Lizard. I'm looking around, listening for sounds of even more trouble, calculating odds.

Lizard sees me and we lock eyes. He ever-so-slightly nods his head toward Otto. I pull down my scarf and mouth

"What?" And now I see by his scowl, his urgent eyes, that he's not drunk. He's in trouble.

I nod back to him, then dissolve into the shadows and listen.

"*Was ist das?*" an officer demands.

"*Nichts, nichts,*" Lizard says. "Drunk. *Ich bin . . . a . . . a—*"

Otto gives them a sloppy grin. "*Betrunken. Nur ein biss-chen.*" He put his fingers up to show "just a little," then nearly falls over. Lizard grabs him.

Otto grins at the policeman. "*Ich bin gerade Vater geworden.*" He cradles his arms and rocks an imaginary baby.

"*Ja, ja. Glückwünsche,*" the officer says, offering his congratulations. Then he asks for identification. Otto touches his uniform and steps back, looking offended.

Oh, please have your identification, Otto, I say to myself.

The officer keeps his hand held out.

Otto turns to Lizard. "They want our papers. Hope you have yours." His Polish is slow, broken, and slurred.

Both produce their cards. Thank God! One officer examines them under the glow of his flashlight. He shows them to his comrade. They exchange glances.

"*Gestapo?*"

Lizard catches my glance over the shoulder of his interrogator.

"*Betrunken?*"

Again, Otto looks like he's cradling a baby. "*Feiern!*"

The officer then looks at Lizard and asks, "*Mit diesem Polen?*"

"*Ja,*" Otto continues, now standing a bit steadier. I make out him explaining that "this Pole" is in his employ and has brought him the news of the birth since Otto was on patrol.

I know how the officers' minds must be working. What if this Gestapo clearance is real? What happens when this fellow German and his Pole assistant sober up and realize they were yanked off the streets like so much Jewish baggage? The officers confer, and I eavesdrop, catching snatches of their conversation.

"Gestapo pass? Could be forged."

"Out here, drunk, with this common Pole?"

"He reeks of the sewers."

"Middle of the night, in this weather?"

"And here, in the ghetto?"

"No, doesn't add up. Better to follow the book and take them in. Make some inquiries."

"Besides, it's cold and I want to get off these streets."

Both officers now have their Lugers drawn. *"Kommen sie mit uns,"* one says, taking Otto gruffly by the arm. Then, to Lizard, *"Du auch!"*

I watch and look at the odds—three Lugers between us, two policemen, Lizard and me, and one "drunk" Messiah with a Gestapo pass. Hell, even *I'm* curious how this is going to play out.

"Where are you taking us?" Lizard asks.

"Ja, wo es?" Otto asks.

I already know where they're going to take them—Pawiak Prison—now headquarters for the ghetto security and the Gestapo. God, what do I do? My first thought is Ruthie. I can just go back, grab her, take her with me, and . . .

No, I can't. I can't leave Lizard, Otto, the rest. Damn it! I should be thinking of Ruthie! What if I get killed? Damn it to hell!

I run ahead to beat them there, thinking of how I'm going to help Otto and Lizard as I run. I have only a few blocks to come up with my plan—any plan!

An out-and-out ambush so close to Pawiak is out of the question. One gunshot, and no telling how many inside will hear. Even at this hour, in this freezing night, search lights, guard dogs, marksmen will follow.

I have my knife on me and I know Lizard always travels with one. But I have no idea if he's ever used it for . . . this purpose. Does he have what it takes to make a stand? To do what he has to do?

And who knows if Otto has a weapon under that long coat?

Lights along the prison walls cast long, threatening shadows down on the drifting snow. The road into it is well-shoveled but shines with thick ice. The arched entry makes it look like a huge black mouth, open and ready to devour its prisoners and shit them out the back door.

I stop and hide inside an alcove in the wall.

Footsteps. What's my plan? It has to be from behind. Do I have the strength to slit a throat, clean through the muffler and the collar? And if Otto and Lizard don't spring into action exactly when I do so, I'm dead.

Lizard knows I'm out here somewhere. He looks down each alley and alcove as he passes. I hope the dim light coming from the prison walls will show enough of my face. Enough for establishing eye contact. For the nod of my head. Anything.

I take a chance in showing my forehead just as they pass. The officers have their mufflers low around their hats, holding in their breath. Otto sees me first. Then Lizard.

Otto stumbles, holds his stomach, and gags. "Uh oh, *spucken!*" He falls to his knees.

My cue. I dash up from behind and grab the muffler of one officer, pulling him back and off balance. I hear Otto and Lizard scuffling with the other officer. But I have my own problem! I drop to my knees, using my weight to pull the officer down, but the damn Kraut reaches around and grabs for my face. I bring my knife around jab it into the officer's neck. I hear him gag, then he whirls and goes for my knife. I strike at him again. Blood spurts from his neck. His hands go to his throat and he struggles to rise. I strike a third time, my knife taking a bigger slice just below his ear. He gurgles and pins me down. His face is close to mine. He struggles to speak.

"Otto! Lizard! Help me here!" I cry out, struggling now to knife the soldier in his back. He holds me down with rage. He's not dying! He's not giving up. "Otto! Help!"

I hear Otto in his own struggle with the other officer.

"Lizard!" I screech. "Help me! Kill him! Kill him!"

I struggle to get out from under him. Lizard tries to pull him back and up, but the officer is fighting like a madman. His hands strike out and pound anything he can find. "Kill him, Lizard!"

Lizard seizes the man by his hair and pulls his head back. He slices his throat. It makes a sickening sound. I scramble to my feet. And he still isn't dead. He rises, seizes his neck, then falls back. A thick, foamy blood guzzles from his throat. The man's face is shocked, disbelieving, even as his eyes meet those of his dead comrade, lying now next to him.

Lizard looks at me. His face is contorted with horror. He looks down at the dying man, struggling to breathe, trying to speak—praying, for all I know. Violently Lizard stuffs the officer's muffler into the gaping, gasping slit in his neck. He holds it fast against his struggles, suffocating him. When his gasping stops and the man is still, Lizard looks away, crosses himself with trembling hands, and stands up.

Otto, out of breath, stands, looking down at the two dead men.

"If this isn't resistance," he says, "I'd like to know what the hell is." He takes the officers' weapons, then goes through their pockets for their identifications and anything else useful.

"Come on! This way!" I call out. I lead them through the back alleys and to the safety of our cellar hideout.

I have avenged eleven of those first twelve lives taken at the Crystal Café. One more to go. And Lizard is now an official member of the Meet Me in Hell Club.

XIV.

ONCE WE'RE BACK SAFE IN THE CELLAR, I TURN ON LIZARD AND Otto. "What the hell were you thinking? Out there drunk and having a high old time? You nearly got us killed! What would happen to all of them if you'd—"

"Take it easy, Arab," Lizard says, pulling me around by my shoulder. "We weren't drunk, for God's sake! That was a ruse! Otto saved our asses out there!"

"Which wouldn't have to have been saved if you weren't out there!"

Lizard takes a long drink from a bottle of whiskey, then passes it to Otto. "I got to worrying about the truck," Lizard says. "I didn't know if I could get it myself, where to hide it, or what. Thought if the going got tough—which it did— thought I could use a good Nazi to help out. So Otto came with me—and it's a damn good thing he did, so keep your pointing finger out of my face!"

"Oh, so now you're doing the thinking around here," I return, poking his chest with my finger.

He slaps my hand away and we glare at each other.

"We knew we were being followed," Otto says, stepping between us. "They may have even seen us hide the truck in the piano factory warehouse. You don't think we'd be stupid enough to lead them here, do you?"

"That's when Otto said to just follow his lead," Lizard explains. "We had to come up with some sort of explanation.

Who we were and why we were out. So, turns out it's a damn good thing I had Otto with me!"

"So now we have two dead soldiers up there and like hell that's not going cause some problems!" I point toward the rafters.

"Now you listen to me, Arab," Otto says. "You were dead wrong to go making plans, risking everything without consulting me. I know a thing or two about trucks. And I speak German, you stupid little—"

I shove his shoulder but wonder if a slap across the face would have more effect.

"Stop it! All of you! Am I the only adult here?" Mrs. Praska says, taking a sturdy position between us. She points at me. "You! You listen to Otto!" Then, she turns on Otto. "And you! I'm getting sick of this little private war you and Arab have going! Now, it's four in the morning and I have sick children and I need it quiet!"

"I agree," Lizard growls. "I don't care who kings this whole damn thing! Let's just get the hell out of here!"

Otto sighs. He offers me a pull off the bottle. "Here. Peace?"

"No thanks. You have a cold. Contagion." That word brings Lizard's eyes to mine. "And you told him that, too, I suppose?"

"We're a team, Arab!" Otto says. Then he smiles at me. "And some members of the team are a lot more clever than others." He gives me a friendly shove.

"More clever or less stupid?" I ask, taking the bottle.

"Take your pick. Now, I don't care about the rest of you, but I'm tired, I have a head cold, and I need to get some sleep. I'm turning in." He looks a bit confused, then asks, "What day is this?"

"Tuesday. Very early Tuesday morning," Mrs. Praska growls through a yawn.

"Good. We have lots to do and only twenty-four hours to do it in."

Otto goes to his corner of the cellar. Mrs. Praska casts her eyes to the heavens, takes a drink from the bottle, and mumbles something to herself while she pads back to the children's section.

Lizard pulls the blankets aside and looks into our room of sleeping children. "Sorry I was so angry, Arab. Look, I've never killed anyone before. It was so easy for Otto. And you, Arab. How could it be so easy for you?"

"I don't know," I whisper, looking down at my hands, still shaking. He puts his arms around me and we rock back and forth. "I don't know," I repeat.

XV.

BEFORE TUESDAY'S FIRST LIGHT, BEFORE ANYONE HAS STIRRED awake, I go up and out and make my way to the cellar of the Minerva Theater, hoping the paint has finally dried. Of all the graffiti I've written, these two canvases are my masterpieces, these printed words my best work. I take my gloves off and gingerly test the paint's dryness. The word perfect doesn't often get uttered in the middle of a war in an occupation. But I say it out loud and proud. "Just perfect!"

The canvases are now half frozen so I pull them down and carefully start rolling each one up. I bind them with the line from the rafters and tie them to my waist.

I put all the greasepaint and stage makeup I've found into a rag satchel I've made. The nurses' uniforms get tucked inside my belt. No one will notice a slightly lopsided person walking with a stiff gate and carrying a filthy bundle here in the ghetto. Even so, as I head out I look around every corner before rounding it. These Germans are like hydras—cut off a head and two more appear. No telling what the retaliation will be when they find two of their own murdered and frozen, so close to the gaping maw of Pawiak Prison.

The cellar is warm and active when I arrive. I get everyone's attention and, with a flourish, unroll a canvas and hold it up. In block letters are two words—one in German, the other in Polish. It makes no difference which language. QUARANTANE . . . KWARANTANNA. The word quarantine is universal. And I'm hoping the reaction to that word will be just as universal.

I explain our plan, from the Kinem Plague to using the greasepaint to create a truck full of sick and dying children. All under SS guard, including three German nurses on a suicide mission. It sounds bizarre, even to me.

I turn to Otto. "Go ahead. Tell me I'm wrong."

"You're wrong," Otto states.

"Damn. Why?"

"You left out the umlaut."

"The what?" I demand.

Otto takes a smudge of blackface and applies the two dots on top of the last German a. "And you brag about your German."

"But drug the children?" Mrs. Praska asks.

"Well, yes. The younger ones. Like you did when they were all coughing," I say.

"I brought opiates and painkillers," Irenka says, going through the bottles in the box she brought. "Codeine, morphine, ipecac. I just emptied the cabinet. Even some ether. But don't ask me about the dosages. I'd just finished one year of nursing school when they made me work at the infirmary."

"Kinem Plague?" Otto asks, running the words over his tongue. Then, his face finally lights up. "Yes! The Nuremberg Laws!"

"The what laws?" I ask.

"Oh, just some little laws Hitler and his henchmen concocted to pave the way for getting rid of undesirables and defects. The incurables." He looks toward the room of sick children. "Incurables. And I'm sure the Kinem Plague, whatever that is, is quite incurable."

"And very contagious," I add.

"I love how your evil mind works," Otto says. "If we get out of this alive—which I doubt—but if we do, you'll always have a job with me."

"Big 'ifs,'" I mutter.

I hand Mrs. Praska the nurses' uniforms and the satchel of makeup.

"What's all this?" she asks.

"We ladies are going to wear these."

She takes a folded uniform off the stack, snaps it out, and holds it up to her chest. "I couldn't fit into this when I was twelve!"

"You'll have to make it work. And we'll be wearing long coats anyway."

Irenka goes through the stack, holds one up, and asks, "Do you have this in a fuchsia?"

Lizard gives her a playful shove. I turn to Mrs. Praska. "How are those Nazi uniforms coming along? Get the rank patches like Otto showed you?"

"Acting! Playacting! How can this ever work?" Mrs. Praska grumbles.

Almost as if on cue, a child in the back room starts to cough violently.

I nod toward the coughing child. "And your idea was . . .?"

"Not becoming a German nurse!" she says.

"If I can do it, you can." How long has it been been since I've worn a dress? Well, in this cold, I'm sure as hell wearing pants under it.

Mrs. Praska gives us her huge, seldom-used smile and holds up a uniform. "I wish to hell I brought my girdle."

She trundles off and sets the children to helping with sewing patches and cleaning uniforms. Games, stories, and naps pass the rest of the day—hopefully our last in the cellar.

XVI.

"WHERE'S OTTO?" LIZARD ASKS. "I CHECKED THE WHOLE CEL-lar. He's not here."

"He told me he couldn't sleep and was going out for a smoke," Mrs. Praska says. She looks at her brooch watch. "Come to think of it, that was some time ago. He left at seven and it's past eight."

Lizard and I look at each other. Strange. "If he messes anything up for us, I'll kill him with my bare hands," I grumble.

Knocks come on the coal chute door. "There he is," Mrs. Praska says.

He slides down, covered in snow.

"What the—?" I demand. "Otto!"

He stands up and starts to knock the snow off. "Sorry. I just went around the front to have a smoke, think about things, and damn, I tripped on a curb or dead something and fell into a bomb crater! Do you know how hard it is to crawl your way up on solid ice?"

"Did you hurt yourself?" Mrs. Praska asks, taking his heavy coat off him and shaking it off.

He rubs his shin. "The good thing about being frozen is, you lose all feeling."

"You could have ruined everything!" I bark. "From now on, no one goes anywhere alone!" I point a finger at him.

He points a finger back at me. "That goes for you too, Arab!"

"Oh look, a duel," Lizard says, yawning. "I'm getting some sleep. I suggest you do, too."

"I'll take the watch," I say.

"Wake us at midnight," Otto says.

Shortly after midnight, Wednesday—our day of exodus—I rouse the adults. We quiz ourselves on our escape plan, taking turns playing devil's advocate, trying to conceive of every wrong-turn scenario imaginable. We repeat any foreign words we might have to use over and over.

Otto writes on tiny scraps of paper and fumbles with the capsules on the birds' legs. They coo, as if they know they're about to be set free.

"Well, here we go," Otto says, attaching the capsules and returning each bird to the cage. I help him out of the cellar and follow him to the backyard. Ruthie's swing is frozen stiff at an odd and eerie angle.

"Won't they be too cold to fly?" I ask, noting the pencil-thin legs with the small metal capsules attached.

"Are you kidding? These birds have been cooped up in their own little ghetto long enough. They know what's about to happen. They can't wait to, well, spread their wings. Just like us, huh?"

"I didn't think birds flew in the dark," I say.

"Well, smart ones don't. But these old girls are proven night flyers. And they know just where they're going."

I stand guard while Otto pulls a pigeon out, kisses its head, and passes it to me for a kiss. "*Eins . . . zwei . . . drei . . .*" he whispers as he releases each bird to the sky. They fly up, find each other, circle, and are gone.

"What do their messages say?"

"Can I trust you?"

"Shut up!"

"All three messages are the same. '8-1-26.' We're leaving today, January eighth, and we're bringing twenty-six. That's all they need to know."

"Why all the same message? Can't one at least say 'send beef and brandy'?"

"Well, lots can happen between here and their home roost. Which is why we kissed them for good luck."

XVII.

BY THE TIME WE COME BACK INTO THE CELLAR, LIZARD HAS changed into his Nazi uniform. I resist the urge to tell him how dashing he looks as a Kraut. He and Otto stand side by side to compare. They look perfect, complete with the boots and the caps. I swear I feel a new chill in the air.

"Your turn, ladies," Otto says.

Irenka, Mrs. Praska, and I excuse ourselves to change into our new identities. The thin cotton costumes are simply white medical symbols covering up as many layers of warmth as we can get away with. First leggings, trousers, shirts, sweaters. Then the dresses.

"I don't know why we're even bothering with these dresses," Mrs. Praska mutters. "Oh look. I've lost weight," she says sarcastically, buttoning the uniform. We pin rank insignias onto the pockets.

"Is there even such thing as a Nazi nurse?" I ask Irenka. "A Captain SS Nazi nurse?"

"What does it matter?" she returns. "Soldiers salute the rank, not the person."

We all have gloves, mufflers, hats, and thick boots. Even Germans have to dress against this freezing weather. I hand out the woolen double-breasted greatcoats, and we pass them back and forth until we each have one that fits.

The five of us stand, looking at each other, turning around, adjusting, pulling, tugging, securing our ranks and our bright red swastikas. Our Aryanism complete, we present ourselves to our regiment of children.

The younger children edge nervously away as we walk into the room.

"That's all Nazi," Ruth says, pointing to our uniforms. "Look, Nazi," she informs her friends.

We put the children's fears to rest, telling them we're just playacting. "And soon you get to play, too, Ruthie." I kneel down to face her.

"I'm not going to be a goddamn *szwab*."

"Ruthie! You don't swear!"

"You do. They do." She points to Stefan and Lorenz, my protégés.

"Yes, but you don't. Mama would be mad if she heard about this."

"But I want to grow up to be like you, Abra."

I pick her up and hold her head close to mine. "No, Ruthie, never say that. Promise me you'll never be like me."

"I *will* be like you!"

I lean back to look at her. "Promise me, Ruth," I say sternly. "Now."

"Okay, I promise I won't be like you." I put her down and swear I hear her mutter, "But I will."

"And promise me you're going to be good. Do everything we tell you."

"Do I have to?"

"Yes," I say, pulling her knit cap down over her ears.

She yanks it off and throws it down. "I hate orange and green!"

I pick it up and cram it back on her heard. "Or else!" I give her a mean look, tucking her doll into the belt of her coat. "Now, you take Sofia and go back in there with the other children and listen to the stories."

It's one in the morning. Otto and Lizard leave to wire the quarantine signs to the canvas canopy on the truck, check the gas and tires, and make sure everything is safe and secure.

The cellar itself seems to pound with the collective beating of our hearts. The older children keep the younger ones busy with a pantomime game.

"Look at them," Mrs. Praska says. "Sometimes I wonder if they have any idea what's really happening. So easily they fall back into their games."

"I don't know," I say. "Sometimes I think they're just old, old people in those children's bodies. I heard Stefan and two others discussing the merits of being shot rather than dying slowly from starvation. Another wanted to know if it hurts to die."

I find Ruthie weeping in a corner. I go to her. "What is it, Ruthie? Are you frightened?"

"No."

"Then what?" I sit down next to her.

"I'm sad."

"Why? We're going on a great adventure, you and me." She's playing with her doll. A great, deep breath builds in her chest and she erupts with tears. "Oh, Ruthie, don't. Why are you sad?"

"You forgot," she whispers.

"What did I forget?"

"I left you something and you never came and got it. And you never left me anything else."

I have to think. "You mean in the mausoleum? That was a long time ago."

"But I remember. I left you something and you never came back. It was right before Mama . . ." She stops and heaves a heavy sigh. "Before Mama sent me away."

"Oh, Ruthie, don't cry. Tell you what. Maybe it's still there. Why don't I go out and look right now?"

"No, everything in this place is gone. The damn Nazis make people steal, and they take everything. They even burned my . . ." Again, a great, building sob. "My rocking horse."

She puts her head into her hands and muffles her tears. How many times have I told her not to cry?

I pull her into my arms and rock her tiny body to soothe her. "I'll get you another rocking horse someday. I promise."

She stops weeping, wipes her face. "No. I'm too old for rocking horses." She gives me a brave face.

"It's almost time," Mrs. Praska says. "Otto and Lizard are back. Everything is ready."

"I'll be right back." I jump up and grab a flashlight.

"Arab!" Mrs. Praska grumbles. "Why not put in a revolving door, the way people come and go around here!"

I'm out of the cellar in a second, crashing through the snow drifts en route to the mausoleum. The iron door has been taken, and snow has built up inside. I look around each crypt, wondering whose sleep I am disturbing. I chip away layers of ice in the corner where Ruthie and I made our exchanges. My fingers find a metal corner, and I dig out the snow around it. I tuck the box under my arm and run with it back to the cellar.

I go to a private corner and chip away the layers of ice sealing the box. I have to work its edges, but finally pry it open and pull out Ruthie's last offering. I set the box down and gingerly pull out the delicate silver chain, watching it glimmer in the candlelight.

"Arab?" Lizard calls out. I scramble for the box but Lizard and Mrs. Praska have already discovered me.

"Can't a girl have some privacy once in a while?" I bark. I run my hand over my face. Damn it!

"What's this?" Mrs. Praska asks, seeing the box.

"Yeah," Lizard chimes in, pointing to the chain now wrapped around my closed hand. "You lift someone's watch?"

I slowly open my hand to show them.

"I knew it," Mrs. Praska whispers, smiling at me.

"That's no watch," Lizard says, looking at the silver pointer at the end of the chain. "What the hell is that?"

"It's a *yad*. It was my father's."

"What's a *yad*?" Lizard asks, watching it dangle between us.

"Sacred," Mrs. Praska says. "It's used to point to the text of the Torah as it's read. See the little finger pointing on the end?"

"My father would have killed us for even thinking about touching this," I say, holding it by its delicate, serpentine chain as I raise it toward the light. There's a wooden disk dangling from it.

"What's it say?" Lizard asks, looking closely at it. "Oh, it's in Hebrew."

I look at the handwritten inscription.

"Can you read that?" Mrs. Praska asks me.

"Yes," I say, low.

I go back to Ruthie and I show her the *yad*. Her eyes get big. "You found it!"

"Ruthie, how did you ever get this?"

I know a lie is forming.

"The truth."

"It was a secret. I'm not supposed to tell."

"Tell me anyway."

She looks around, as if our parents are right here listening to her confession. She tips her head upwards. "Before Mama sent me away."

"He knew we were hiding things there in the . . ." I remember her silly name for it. "The masso linoleum?"

She nods her head. "But I didn't tell him! Honest! He just found out."

"And he told you to hide this there?"

She nods her head again, tears welling in her eyes. I take her into my arms again. "It's okay, Ruthie. It's okay."

"Can I have it?"

"Well, it is mine."

Her lower lip twitches, indicating a pout is on its way. "Well, okay." I slip the long *yad* chain around her neck. "You can keep it for me. Just for now, okay?"

"Okay!" She holds the *yad* up close to her eyes. She points the finger on the end toward me. "So what are you going to give me? Your turn!"

What a little opportunist, I think. "I am going to give you the biggest, most exciting day of your life! How about that?"

"I wanted candy," she says.

"Go on. Go find the others and do as you're told."

She throws her arms around me, and I'm reminded why I'm up to my nose in this insanity. I watch her limp away, still stunned at what I've found. And finding it here, now, in this place, stirs something deep inside. Something I'm not prepared for, and yet, something I've waited for all my life. I know what that *yad* meant to my father. He'll never know what his inscription means to me:

A PRIZED POSSESSION FOR A PRIZED POSSESSION.
I WILL ALWAYS PRAY FOR YOUR FORGIVENESS,
MY PRECIOUS ABRA.

XVIII.

HERE WE ARE: THREE NURSES, TWO GERMAN GUARDS, A FULLY-gassed Blitz truck, and twenty-one children, soon to be dying of my Kinem Plague. We've packed only what's absolutely necessary—but how can we know what might be on the road ahead? I put together my own survival essentials in a knapsack. Cigarettes, cash, some Luger magazines I bought on the black market, and my two remaining passes out of the country, swiped so long ago. These I've reserved for me and Ruthie. Just in case.

We've sorted out all of our forged documents, matching ages and faces to the children. But our plan, our hope, is that no one will want to risk catching the Kinem Plague. That they won't dare to even touch, let alone inspect, our papers in the first place. We are banking all our lives on the lowest common denominator in the German war chest—fear.

Our final step is applying pallor and sickness to the faces of the children. Between the stage makeup and kerosene lamp soot, our gang of children look like death personified. The girls actually giggle as we work to transform them. Irenka donates her only tube of lipstick to smudge along their lower eyelids, making their eyes look weepy and bloodshot. We drill the children who are old enough to understand the importance of our mission.

"Shit, only girls wear makeup!" little Stefan pipes up.

Lorenz gives him a brotherly shove and tells him to shut up. I have to break up a scuffle. "But I don't feel sick," Stefan insists.

"I can fix that," I warn. Then, I bend down to him and look him eye to eye. "Stefan, you know how . . ."

"My name is Jaguar," he corrects me.

"No!" I hold up the card dangling from a cord around his neck. "Your name is Stefan Orinski and you are very, very sick."

"Okay," he says, closing his eyes to submit to the makeup. "But no lipstick."

We line the children up and go over the hand signals we've taught them. A finger under the nose means sneeze. Sticking out a tongue means cough. Grabbing a stomach means moan.

Otto lifts the coal chute door. "Let's start. Only a few at a time. And quiet. Remember, if anything goes wrong, we're just soldiers herding Jewish children into the night." He looks at Lizard. "Come on. Oldest first."

"How long does it take for this to work?" I ask, looking at Irenka, who's deep in thought as she reads the label of a medicine bottle.

"Not long. I hope. But how much to give the babies?"

Mrs. Praska takes the bottle and gives it a cursory glance. "I'll do it."

"You know about this?" Irenka asks, handing her a bottle.

She snorts. "I have given birth to seven children. Of course I know about tincture of opium."

"Opium? Do you think that's safe?"

"It's laudanum, and I know how much to give. You tend to the others."

She administers the medicine to her baby and the youngest toddlers, and before long they're sweet, sleeping bundles in our arms as we make our way up, out, and along the two frozen blocks to the piano warehouse where our truck is waiting. We put the sleeping little ones under the benches, some on the racks overhead. Mrs. Praska stays with them, while Lizard and I go back for more. Otto stands guard, weapon drawn, at the warehouse doors.

It takes four trips before we have our entire troop of drugged actors in the warehouse. Any children that start to whine, protest, or even chat are given a pinch and a tablespoon of cough medicine to make them drowsy. This is no school outing.

Irenka hands us adults the pièce de résistance to our own disguises—surgical masks. After all, the Kinem Plague is highly contagious. Brilliant! I never would have thought of that—and here it was the first thing our nurse compatriot thought of.

I look at the blue bottle Mrs. Praska holds. "How long does this stuff take to work?"

"Fifteen, twenty minutes. Maybe longer with water."

I call Stefan and Lorenz over. "Here. Take this," I order as Mrs. Praska pours spoonfuls from the bottle.

"What is it?" Lorenz asks, trying to get a glimpse of the bottle.

"Syrup of ipecac," Mrs. Praska says. "It will make you throw up."

"But I don't want to throw up," Lorenz whimpers.

Stefan steps in front of him. "I do! This'll be fun! Come on, Lorenz."

Lorenz complies, grimacing while he takes the medicine.

"I like it!" my precious Stefan announces.

We are ready. We look at each other.

"Well, this is it," Otto says.

"In case . . ." Irenka says, her voice trembling, ". . . something happens. Goes wrong. I'll always remember you and thank you for . . . for this chance."

"All right. Load up," Otto orders.

Lizard checks the road outside and opens the warehouse doors. Irenka climbs into the back of the truck, then Mrs. Praska, who turns to me and hesitates. "I . . . I just want to say. No matter what is out there, Arab, no matter what, you've saved us just as surely as Moses saved our people." She catches my eye, smiles. "I know, I know. You don't have a people."

I steady her step up. "If it makes you feel any better, may I be your ransom."

Her face comes alive at my Jewish blessing. "May you outlive my bones, my dear, dear friend."

I smile back, and then climb into the truck after her.

Otto climbs into the driver's seat. He puts the Red Cross pass on the dashboard. Lizard, who speaks very little German, rides as a guard in the cab. Irenka, Mrs. Praska, and I stay in the back, keeping Stefan and Lorenz close to the tailgate.

We rumble out into the icy streets, the chains of the truck crunching the snow and making for slow going. Since the weather is even worse now, we assume the same gates will still be closed, so we head for Leszno Street. The roads will be better—and hopefully clear—on a well-traveled street. For the same reason, we'll go north on Okopowa, which borders the ghetto walls. Yes, there might be more soldiers along that route, but we don't want to chance getting stuck on the less-traveled roads. Our hope is that even a German won't be caught dead out on the streets on this frigid January morning.

XIX.

THE TRUCK STOPS AT THE LESZNO GATE. I CAN FEEL THE COLlective heartbeats of Mrs. Praska, Irenka, and myself as the truck inches to a halt and we hear the crunch of the approaching guard's boots.

"I don't feel so good," Lorenz whispers up at me, rubbing his stomach.

"Wait," I order. His eyes fill with tears as he looks urgently up at me. "I said wait!"

I can't hear what Otto is saying to his interrogator.

When the canvas of the back of the truck snaps open, I stand up and look down at the face of the young policeman assigned to this post. I know by his blue uniform that he's Polish police, not a German soldier. That makes sense—the Polish police draw the worst shifts.

"Stand back!" I order him. "Don't touch anything!" I try to taint my Polish with a German accent.

"What is all this?" he asks.

"Can't you read?" I demand. "This is quarantine! You better burn that glove, Officer. For God's sake, don't touch anything!"

"What kind of quarantine?"

"It's the Kinem Plague."

"Never heard of it."

"You will. It's worse than the Black Death. And you know how the Jews spread that throughout all of Europe! Now, if you know what's good for you, you'll stand back. Cover your mouth." He takes a cautious step back.

Another Polish policeman comes around, his gun drawn. "I don't know," he says. "These papers are in German. Do you read German?"

"This nurse says it's the Kinem Plague," he says, pointing to me. The sounds of children moaning and coughing inside the truck make the second policeman also step back.

"We're taking these children to the Stutthof camp," I say. "For study. Kinem Plague is rare this far north, but deadly."

"Then maybe you should let them die here," the first man says, laughing with his fellow policemen. The steam from their laughter clouds the air. "Let all the Jews catch it, and we can just torch this place and all go home."

"We better call over to headquarters," one man says. "No one has said anything to us about this sort of thing."

"What is the problem?" a third man asks, holding a flashlight and shining it in my face. This one is a captain. The policeman hands him the papers. He looks at me again, then flashes his light into the back of the truck. "Take off that mask and let me see your papers!"

I give Lorenz a nudge with my knee. "You better stand back, Herr."

On cue, Lorenz throws up out of the back of the truck, making a tremendous howl of agony after holding back for so long. It's more than ipecac—it's almost a knee-jerk reaction to the smell and the sound, or brotherly competition—because immediately Stefan joins him, projecting several feet and soiling the soldier's uniform.

"I warned you," I say. "Herr *Hauptsturmführer*, you have to go burn that uniform now. And you, take off that glove and burn it. Burn anything that has come into contact with

any of us. Don't you know how deadly Kinem Plague is?
Haven't you read the orders? We need clear passage. I beg of
you, sir, get us through that gate."

"If it's so contagious, how come you aren't sick? Those
other nurses, they don't look sick," the soldier asks.

I give them a hard stare, wishing I could summon tears
as easily as my boys can. "I got the first symptom this morning." I run my sleeve over my eyes. "I'm dispensable, can't
you see? Why do you think I'm here?" I cough into my mask.
"And they'll get it soon." Still the policemen hesitate. "For
God's sake! *Himmelfahrtskommando*!" I cry out.

The captain steps back. "Journey-to-Heaven Mission?"

"The driver too," a guard reports to the captain. "He was
coughing up a lung."

The German looks at our forged papers again. "I knew
about the medical studies, but Stutthof? I thought that was
for political enemies. I think I'll make a call."

"I wouldn't do that, sir," I say.

"And a woman tells a captain what he should and should
not do?"

Now I understand. This is all about rank, not about passage or plague. "Well, I might be just a woman, but I'm
dying for the Reich. What are you doing, besides jeopardiz-
ing your men?" I force a serious coughing spell. I put a rag
under my mask and spit into it, sounding almost as good
as my boys. I drop the rag at their feet. The German takes
a step back.

"Excuse me, sir, I'm only trying to help," I say. "Our Red
Cross pennant is on the dashboard." My heart is beating
so fast I just might pass out and fall at their feet. The first
Kinem Plague death.

"Yes, I saw it. Easily made or stolen."

"Please, please, in Polish," the policeman says, looking very concerned.

"Of course," I say, switching back to Polish. "Sir, haven't you read the bulletins? The Stutthof Directive?"

I nudge Lorenz again and, on cue, he vomits. Not to be outdone, Stefan joins in. Even the sound they make brings similar moans from the woozy children close by. Now there are four little heads popping out of the back of the truck, puking.

The guards all take another step back. The German looks at me, the truck, and then the papers Otto has drawn up. "No one told me about this."

"Well, this is only the beginning," I chance. "Children are the ones hit first. There'll be more, mark my words."

I pinch Lorenz, who's still at my side. He moans and grabs his stomach, then starts to twitch. The little ham.

"Very well," the captain says, glancing down at his soiled boots. He hands me back the document. "But once you get through the gates, stay well away from Leszno Street if you know what's good for you. Open the gates! Let them pass!" He shouts out.

"I beg of you, sir, burn your uniform," I add as the truck starts to slip away, the children's puke still steaming on the snow at their feet. "If you catch it, you'll spread it! Burn everything!"

One of the policemen has already taken his gloves off and tossed them into the burn barrel they keep for warmth. The other guard looks at his glove as though it has snakes growing out of it. "How will we know if we . . . catch it?" he calls out to me.

"A horrible itch on your neck, and then all over your body," I call back down. "Then a cough that brings you to your knees."

"Then what?" the other calls, scratching his shoulder.

"Then, this," I say, indicating the retching children.

We have made it past the first challenge. We're out of the ghetto, now back on the Aryan side. But far from safe. I untie my mask and take in several long, deep breaths of frigid air.

Stefan looks up at me. "Hey, Arab. Want me to puke some more? I got lots left!"

I pull him to me and hug him, wondering how in hell we're all going to keep each other safe.

"No. Save it for later. You did damn great, Jaguar."

That brings Lorenz over. I pull him close and ruffle his hat. "You too, Lion. Damn great."

Even through their sick makeup I can see the Lion and the Jaguar beam.

I use my surgical mask to wipe the sweat off my forehead. It's one thing talking my own way out of something. It's another having all these lives relying on my cunning or my lying—or lack of both. Hell, two little boys puking on cue—they probably saved all of us. I sit down on the bench, nearly crushing the foot of a dozing child.

Ruth makes her way toward me. "You said 'damn.' I'm telling."

I pull her onto my lap and want to laugh. "You are, are you? And just who are you going to tell?"

She holds her doll, Sofia, on her own lap as I hold her. "Hitler," she says. She flips up Sofia's arm. "*Swine Heil* Hitler! *Swine Heil* Hitler!"

I hold her tighter. "Hush, Ruthie. Sh. You'll never say that again, okay? You and Sofia go back to Mrs. Praska now."

"Why? It's stuffy up there. We want to ride back here with you."

"We still have a long, long way to go, and you better just get used to it like the others."

"Or you'll make me go to sleep like Hanna?"

"Yes, if that's what it will take to keep you quiet."

She leans back into my chest. I look down at her gloves and see her thumb sticking out of a hole. "What's this?" I ask.

"Mrs. Praska made me a hole."

"Why?" But I think I know the answer.

"So I can do this!" She pops her thumb into her mouth.

"Big girls don't suck their thumbs."

She pops it out. "Mrs. Praska says better to suck a thumb than to cry in the dark."

"I see." I let her sit quietly. I've never felt more important than I do at this moment.

The truck slows down after a few bumpy blocks, and we come to a stop. The truck pants beneath us. "You go up to Mrs. Praska now, Ruth."

I stand up and venture a peek outside. There are only a few street lights on, but the winter whiteness makes Warsaw look like a crystalline war-torn wonderland. The snow covers so much destruction, so much death, that I almost feel a brief glow of warmth.

Mrs. Praska makes her way toward me. "Why are we stopped?"

"I don't know." Then the captain's words hit me. *Stay well away from Leszno Street.*

Footsteps coming toward us. I stand up, my Luger close at hand.

"Arab," Lizard whispers.

I pull open the canvas. "What's happening?"

"Roadblock ahead."

"We need to turn right. Tell Otto to turn right some-place. We can work our way north on the back streets."

"The damn truck is stuck!"

A gunshot rings out, followed by more volleys from three different directions. Screams. Shouting. Then silence. Now a German voice on a loudspeaker. *"Juden raus! Juden raus!"*

Lizard and I look at each other. "Another roundup," he growls. "Always the middle of the night."

I jump down from the truck and look around for an escape—an alley or any side road we can take out of here. A building across the street is on fire, and people are filling the street. Soldiers have guns on them as they pour out of the burning building. Guard dogs bark, nip at legs, and pull at coats. Children cry, women scream, men shout obscenities. A formation of SS Cavalry guards ride into the street, scattering the Jews. The breath of the horses clouds the air. Just like Hitler's victory parade a thousand winters ago, the unit seems to move as one.

It's a sea of confusion all around us. Even more cavalry units fill the cross streets, and they hold their formation. The horses have been through this before. Heads toss, tails swish, legs dance. Then, soldiers push the barricades aside and the riders urge their horses forward. Each rider has a cane. They swat at people if they get too close, if they try to escape. Coming from the opposite direction is a line of sol-diers, rifles at the ready. Corralled between the horses and the soldiers are at least a hundred people. Their circle gets smaller as the soldiers force them in closer.

I jump onto the running board. "For the love of God, Otto, get this truck out of here! Before they bring the flamethrowers!"

"I'm trying, I'm trying!" The engine grinds, the tires spin, and the truck inches a few feet forward. "Do you want me to just run these people over? Get your mask back up, Arab!" His words are muffled through his own mask. "Get out there and see if you can move people out of the way!"

Lizard and I go ahead of the truck, shouting, "Contagion! Contagion! Stay away! Contagion!"

An old man begins striking Lizard with a cane, and a woman spits on me. Now we're the targets in our Nazi uniforms. The courage of one spreads to many. They shout and swear and spit at us.

Have you no soul?

May you rot in hell!

Fuck you, and fuck Hitler!

Foot soldiers shove them along using the butts of their rifles.

Lizard scrambles back into the truck while Otto tries to turn. I go around to the back of the truck and a man, clothed only in his nightshirt, is trying to climb in. I grab his leg and pull. He kicks back.

"Get down!" I scream.

The canvas pulls back and Mrs. Praska appears, holding a wooden box over her head. She crashes it down on the man, who falls off and into the snow. She looks at me, then skyward. "May God forgive me."

"Otto! Move!" I scream. "Now!"

We rumble a few feet forward.

I climb back inside the back of the truck and I'm hit immediately with the children's questions and complaints.

"What's going on?"

"I don't feel good."

"I'm thirsty."

"I'm not afraid of any German!"

Then, from my own sister, "I want to see the horses." She inches forward and sits down close to the tailgate, clutching her doll.

I sling my knapsack around Ruth's neck. "Here. You and Sofia can guard my knapsack." I go back out on the running board.

Otto backs the truck around and we wait for the mass of people to be herded toward the center of the block. Then we ease forward. Shots are firing above heads—and into heads. A man fights hand to hand with a German soldier and they fall into our path. Otto slams on the brakes, but the truck starts to slide on the ice. It bounces up as it runs over the fighting men. Their screams are hardly audible above the din. We finally come to a hard stop against the corner of a building. Our cargo of children cry out. I'm nearly bounced off, but I hold tight.

"Oh Christ," Otto says out his window.

"You've got to back up. Get us out of here!" I shout.

"But . . . those men . . . they're under us."

"Otto, back up!" Lizard says. "Hurry!"

Otto grinds it into reverse. The chained tires spin and we back up, clunking again over the bodies. Otto searches for another gear, turns the steering wheel, and we inch forward. We travel only another half block, up a slight incline, and then start to slide sideways. I dash around to the back of the truck to see if anyone was hurt in the crash.

Ruth! I don't see Ruth!

I rip my face mask off. "Ruthie!" I pick up Ruth's friend, Sofia—she's curled into a little ball, tears falling down her face. "Sofia! Where's Ruth?"

"You said not to talk," she whimpers.

I shake her. "Where's Ruthie?"

"She's not here! God, Arab, she's not here!" Irenka says.

"Sofia, did you see Ruthie get out of the truck?"

She nods her head.

"What happened? Why?" Irenka asks.

"It's okay to talk, Sofie. Tell us what happened," I say.

"When the truck went 'bump,' she fell out. She was sitting right there, on the edge. Then she was gone! I screamed, but no one heard." Irenka picks the crying child up and holds her.

I have my Luger and my knife in my pockets, my identification in a pouch around my neck. That's all I need. "Keep going, Mrs. Praska. I'll catch up with you if I can. If not . . . shalom."

"You can't choose one over all, Arab! We need you." Mrs. Praska says, gripping my arm.

"She's my sister. I need her!" I nod toward her children. "You couldn't choose, could you?"

She loosens her grip. "Then go with God," she whispers in Hebrew, and she gently squeezes my arm.

I jump out of the back of the truck and pound on the driver's door to signal Otto. "Keep going!"

"I can't! All these people!" he shouts back.

"Lizard knows the roads! Go! Now!" I hit the door once again. My farewell.

I run back toward the commotion on the street behind us. A formation of mounted soldiers are splitting the crowd in half. Two soldiers blow whistles and motion the crowds to move right, move left. I hide behind a snowbound car and watch. A path is clearing for the truck. Our truck is free! It rumbles along then disappears around a corner. Gone! The soldiers on the perimeter urge the crowd back into itself, moving again as one.

I'm frantic! Calling for Ruthie is useless in this chaos. The rounded-up Jews are huddling closer and closer together. Surrounded now by soldiers, they quiet, as though just beginning to understand their predicament.

A soldier stands on the bumper of a truck, speaking into a loudspeaker, telling the masses to separate into two groups—women with the children, and men. "You will be going into the *Jüdischer Wohnbezirk*—the Jewish Quarter. There you will be given housing and selected for either work or deportation to other facilities. Remember, work will set you free."

I dash from alley to shadow to alcove, searching the faces of the crowd, now moving east, toward the Leszno gate. Ruth must have been pulled into the roundup. Maybe she grabbed some woman's hand, or scooped up by some kindly man, maybe followed another crying child.

The soldiers are ushering the two groups away. "Ruthie!" I scream out. "Ruth Goldstein!"

No one even turns their head toward me. What's one more voice pleading for help?

I catch my reflection for an instant in a shop window. I have on my German officer's coat and nurse's uniform over my trousers. But my surgical mask is gone. Damn! I lean back into the window. What should I do? Keep up the pretense, or quit my SS coat and strip the coat off that corpse in the street or . . .? I hear the crunch of horse hooves approaching.

I recognize the horse before I recognize its rider. Hummel. "Fritz! I need your help! For the love of God, Fritz, I need your help!" Even I don't recognize my voice.

He looks around, then sees me. That's goddamn whimsy on his face! "Well, what do we have here?" he says, tipping his cap. "No wonder we're winning the war. When did you enlist? And as a nurse, no less. Turn around. Let's see how you clean up."

"I need your help!"

"You? The famous Arab of Warsaw, who can get her hands on anything, needs *my* help? I think I'm flattered."

There are gunshots and Hummel skitters aside, startled. Fritz steadies him.

"My sister! She's here somewhere. She must have gotten mixed up with the crowds. She's only six! Please, help me!"

"Here? I thought . . ." He breaks off and looks around.

"Fritz, please! I'll do anything, just get her back! You're in command here. And you can do something! She's wearing an orange-and-green cap."

He stands in his stirrups and looks around. The soldiers are inching the crowd forward, beginning the march to the oblivion of the ghetto. The shouting, the crying, the swearing is now an inhuman lowing, like cattle. He looks back down at me. "I'm sorry," he says, his voice hard now. "What's done is done."

"It's not done!" It's only an instant, but it's all I need. I seize Hummel's bridle and yank it, pulling his head down, and then I have my Luger against the horse's forehead. "Drop the reins!" I order. "Do it or I swear I'll shoot."

"Arab, don't be a fool." I feel the reins go limp.

"Help me get my sister!"

"Look around you, Arab! There's nothing you can do now. You're good as dead."

"So is your precious horse!"

"Drop the gun. Let go the reins."

"I've kept your secret, Fritz. You know I have!"

He leans toward me. "And I've kept yours. Everything. Two dead soldiers!"

"I've trusted you!"

"Never trust the enemy!" he spits down. "How come you haven't figured that out?"

"For the love of God, Fritz. You have sisters! Don't make me shoot. I'll drop this horse under you, and then you on top of him. I swear I will!"

Three soldiers come running up. I pocket the gun and drop the reins.

"Everything alright here, Captain?"

"Get on with your work!" Fritz barks back.

They salute and run off.

"I can get you anything, Fritz. Enough liquor to last the war, every cigarette I can get my hands on. I'll give you everything I have—I have stashes all over Warsaw, I have—"

"Chopin's heart? Arab . . . save yourself. Get out of here! Save yourself!"

Tears now, damn it!

"Abra!" A screech echoes from across the street. "Abra!"

Fritz and I lock eyes. Most of the crowd has moved out and I can see Ruth's orange-and-green knit cap, her billows of curly blonde hair escaping. My canvas knapsack around her neck is weighing her down as she limps toward me.

"Your Ruth?" he asks.

I run out to get her. Fritz spurs his horse. He swoops down and scoops her up, pulling her clean off her feet. She screams. I stop. Between me and Fritz are the two officers' horses, charging now straight at me.

"Ruthie!" He's going to save her! He's going to bring her to me! He's going to—

I try making my way to Fritz, but the soldiers are coming straight for me. I turn tail and run, ducking into the shadows, now frozen, afraid to move. What's happening? Get back out there, I scream to myself. I look around the corner. There's no one. No Fritz. No Ruth. All I hear is the thundering, fading sound—iron horseshoes on packed snow. Gone.

Think, Arab, think! I have to get out of here. I have to find Fritz. Maybe he's keeping her safe. Or maybe he's . . . I look at the last of the rousted Jews, disappearing now down the street. What did he say about trust? God! How can I have trusted the enemy?

I dissolve back into the shadows and lean against a building. I don't even think I can stand, let alone walk. And walk where? Everything has vanished for me. I'm alone. I exhale and look up. The pink of the rising sun kisses the clouds far off to the east, over the ghetto.

"Come on, Arab. Think!" I scream as loud as I can. There's no one alive to hear. I look out at the street, now empty. Overturned carts, churned up snow, clothes strewn about. Bodies and blood decorate the snow, and the only sound is the faraway trill of a factory whistle calling people to work.

I turn into an alcove of a shop, sit on a step, wrap my arms around my legs, and rock myself to and fro. Everything plays over and over in my mind. What happened? What went wrong? It was all so carefully planned.

If I stay here, I'll either freeze to death or get shot. I have to use the handrail to pull myself back up. I feel like I'm a million years old. I slink back into the shadows. I walk the alleys to my nearest hole, pull out a stash of clothes, and change, numb inside and out. I crawl onto my cot and pull the heavy Nazi coat over me.

I can't sleep. I have to sleep. I can't cry. I have to cry.

Please, God, just let me sleep.

XX.

I SPRING AWAKE AND HAVE TO PUT TOGETHER ALL THAT'S HAP-pened. What's real? What did I dream?

I take a look around for something, anything I have of Ruthie. My one photo is now on her forged identification papers. I have nothing. I try not to relive what happened, but I can't help it. I keep seeing the charge of those soldiers. And me . . . running away instead of running toward Ruthie.

I have to shake my head to get the visions out. Eat, Arab, I tell myself. Eat and move and breathe. I pull together some things, cram down a piece of frozen bread, and head out.

I take side roads and alleys through town, planning my mission as I dash in and out of the shadows. I head toward the cavalry barracks. I'll find Fritz if I have to tear the place apart. I hide not far from the intersection where the bridle path from the stables meets the street.

Hummel sees me before Fritz does. The jingle of his bri-dle is almost musical. I step into the sun and the beautiful horse stops.

"Not again," Fritz says, looking around.

"Where is she?"

"Didn't I tell you to save yourself?"

"And you also told me to never trust the enemy! Where is she? Did you take her back to the ghetto? Did you put her on one of those trains to hell? Where?"

"She's been taken away."

"What do you mean?"

"I mean you never listen, do you? You think you know everything, Arab! You think you can outrun and outsmart anyone you come up against! I'm telling you, you can't! Why can't you get that through your thick Jewish head?"

"I want my sister!"

"Keep your voice down. Half my unit knows who you are and how much your bounty is."

"What did you do with Ruth?"

"I'm one step away from getting demoted and sent to the front! And you don't know how valuable I am right here in Warsaw!" He looks down on me, his face hard, his words clipped and angry.

"No, tell me. You ride your patrols, you round up innocent people and herd them into the ghetto and off to God knows where! You play polo, drink your Schnapps, read your *Don Juan*, and you brush your precious horse, you spoiled rich *faygeleh*!"

Silence.

"Just tell me where my sister is, and I promise you'll never see me again, Fritz." I keep my voice low, regretting everything and having nothing else to lose.

"She's gone. I had a job to do, and I did it."

"You and your fucking Nazi job! I hate you!"

"I'm the enemy. You're supposed to hate me." There's a tone to his voice I've never heard him use before. "Now, get out of here."

"Where? Everything I've done has been for her! You think I'm going to just let it go and walk away?"

More silence. It's as though we don't even know each other.

"You better, Arab. You damn well better walk away."

"No!"

"You're pushing your luck. You're going to get yourself killed. Don't know how you made it this long. And once you're dead, who can you save then? Think about it," he whispers. "Just let it be. Now, move aside. I'm on patrol."

"No!" I aim my gun at him. "Tell me!"

Hummel alerts us to more horses approaching. "That's my unit. You better vanish, Arab."

I pocket my gun and step back into the shadows I know so well. Another soldier approaches, his gun drawn.

"No need for that, *Obersturmführer*," Fritz says. "Everything's under control here."

"I have my orders."

"What orders?" Fritz demands.

"To arrest you."

"On what charge?"

He hands Fritz a piece of paper.

Fritz scans it, wads it up, and throws the paper down. He nudges his horse forward. More soldiers trot up, all guns drawn on Fritz. One man grabs Hummel's bridle. "Release that bridle!" Fritz orders.

The riders move in, surrounding Fritz. The horses rear up and toss their heads, snort, whinny, as Fritz tries to break free. A soldier reaches for Fritz's gun and Fritz pulls him off balance. More shouting and confusion, and now the others are on him.

A shot rings out.

Silence. Then, slowly, Fritz slumps, leans, then falls sideways, half off Hummel, who tries to balance himself. Fritz falls to the ground, making a hideous thump. Hummel stands his ground and sniffs his master's head.

Fritz . . . no . . .

The soldiers are arguing now. I pick out words of accusation and blame. Finally, one shouts orders to pick up Fritz's body. They lift him and sling his body over Hummel, his hands and feet dangling lifelessly. I have to turn away at the sight. Then, as quickly as they were upon him, they lead Hummel and his cargo away.

"Fritz . . ." I whisper.

I walk over and watch the unit disappear. I look down and see Fritz's blood in the snow. I pick up the paper and unwad it. "Order of arrest," I read. "Treason to the Third Reich."

I kick up snow to cover his blood. I don't know why.

XXI.

FOR THE FIRST TIME SINCE I RETURNED TO WARSAW ALL THOSE months and lifetimes ago, I don't know what to do. Where to go? And why? I'm right back where I started. Alone. No, even more than alone. Empty. Alone is alive. Empty is dead. With Ruthie gone, what's the use? I've lost something deep inside me—something I never knew I had. I'm empty.

How much room does a soul take up?

FEBRUARY, 1941

I.

It's been over three weeks now, and nothing. I can only assume Otto, Lizard, Mrs. Praska, and all those children have been caught, killed, taken Elsewhere, maybe frozen to death in Palmiry—or hell, drowned in the Baltic. For the first few weeks, I hung around Three Crosses Square— where Otto and I had agreed to meet back up if something went wrong. Well, everything went wrong, and I'm the only one here selling anything on the steps. And now I'm running out of cigarettes to sell.

I head over to the cigarette factory. We're having an early thaw, but now the slush and mud bog everything down. I know every corner, every alley, every side street, and every home—or what used to be homes—on every route to the factory.

I try the side door of the factory but the doors are swollen and iced over. I force the door open and slowly inch inside. There's a light coming from the hall that leads to the factory. Odd. Not like Mrs. Praska to have left any lights on. Not that she ever had an electric bill to pay. I listen. Just the drip of some melting icicles somewhere beyond the bricked-up windows.

I step into the factory. A single light dangles from the ceiling. I'm hit with memories—the smell of tobacco and cigarette smoke permeates the thick wood floors. I walk along the rolling machine, dip my finger into the spillover area where years of grease, dust, and tobacco have combined to make a thick goo. The side wall of the room, where the bales of tobacco were once stacked to the ceiling, is now piled with canvas sacks, brown wrapping paper, and twine—the only evidence of our once-thriving business.

In one corner I hear Yankev warning his mother it will never work; in another corner I hear Mrs. Praska swearing her revenge; in another corner I see Lizard, packing the cigarettes into bags to take to our sellers. And in the last corner, I see me—full of . . . what? . . . exuberance? The fast-talking street arab, full of ideas and excitement for the road ahead. Ready to take on all comers. Where is that Arab now?

I find a few cigarettes under the packing table and roll one between my fingers. I light one and it tastes horrible, but a smoke is a smoke—how many times have I said that to a customer? I watch the smoke rise over my head and disappear into the chilly air.

There's nothing left for me here. I switch off the light, pocket the cigarettes, and leave the way I came in. Out of habit, I cover up my footsteps. Don't know why.

It doesn't surprise me I've ended up here, in the ghetto. I walk the streets, searching the faces for one of my own maybe captured and tossed back in. Every little girl could be Ruth or Sofia, every little boy could be Stefan or Lorenz. Every bundled old woman could be Mrs. Praska, every thin young man could be Lizard. Every soldier could be Otto.

I have to stop wondering what might have happened to them. All our planning, my sudden strokes of genius, turned out to be just half-witted impulses. Failures. Stop it, Arab! Don't be a fool, I swear to myself. But God, the images all come back. Why me? Why am I the only one to have survived this hell? Of all the ones who should have died . . . I'm the one who lived.

I return to my cellar, still undiscovered and vacant. I search every nook, every hidey hole, every corner, looking for something in the cellar to anchor me—a sock, a half-smoked cigarette, a smell.

Nothing.

I sit down on Ruthie's little pallet and look around. The tears come fast and uncontrollable. Spasms of gasps. Who cares who hears me now? Let them hear! Let them come and get me!

II.

I WAKE IN THE DARK AND RUMMAGE IN MY POCKETS FOR A STUB candle and a match. I light my way through the boiler room and into the root cellar. At least I can barter some bottles of liquor up there in the ghetto. I fill my coat pockets and head up to do some trading. I rehearse my sales pitch, my banter:

> HAVE A DRINK
> GOT LOTS TO SELL
> LET'S ALL DRINK
> OUR WAY TO HELL

I don't get far. Coming toward me are two figures. A few blocks away I hear gunfire, explosions, shouting, and screaming. How well I know those sounds. Another roundup. They seem to come one right on the heels of another, as though clearing the ghetto block by block. Why? They just bring in more. Thousands and thousands more by the truckload. In the front door and out the back. All on trains to Elsewhere.

I pull my cap down lower to hide my eyes. Dressed the way we all are, I can't tell an old man from a young girl until they are standing in front of me. These two aren't lost, that's for sure. They walk toward me with a purpose, but slow, not being escorted or chased. Now I can tell—female. My heart picks up. Could it be . . .?

Careful, Arab!

They stop when they see me. Slowly, we search each other's eyes.

"Mrs. Kerber?"

She brings down her scarf. "Abra?"

"Yes. What . . .?"

"Thank God for a familiar face! Please, please help us. My daughter, Anna."

Anna shows me her face, contorted in pain.

"Why are you out here? I thought the Krauts kept you safe. You and Anna. The sewing, not to mention the passes I gave you—"

"Someone informed on us about Anna being pregnant by a goddamn Nazi! All my goods, my whole life, my machines—everything down to the last button and spool of thread. Gone! Us too, if we hadn't slipped away. Please, Abra! Please!"

Anna grips her stomach. "Mama!"

"She's gone into labor, Abra. A soldier tossed her down and . . . for god's sake, help us. We need shelter."

"Can't you find a midwife or . . ."

"She's in labor! We have to find shelter!" Mrs. Kerber shouts. Anna doubles over in pain.

Damn! I look around. She can't just stand here and drop her baby! "All right. But I warn you . . ." I stop. Warn them what? Mrs. Kerber and her baby are doomed no matter if I help them or not. "Come in. It's not far."

I lead them to my hideout and help slide Anna down into the cellar. "There. That room over there is the warmest," I say, pointing to one of the side rooms where we had our little infirmary of sick children. The blankets still hang and the pallets are still side by side. I help get her settled and bring what rags I can find.

"Do you think you can get some water boiling? We're going to need water and—"

Anna screams out. I remember the rooms full of people upstairs. "She has to stay quiet, Mrs. Kerber. Others might hear and rat us out."

"I know, I know," she says.

"I'll try, Mama," Anna says, stuffing a rag into her mouth to stifle another cry.

Mrs. Kerber dabs her daughter's forehead. "It will be soon. Soon, my precious. Soon. Breathe, breathe."

I do the best I can with what I can find. There is still enough clean snow to melt for water and I rip out pages from a few books from my father's collection of first editions to fuel a fire. If he could see them now. I'm able to get the water to near-boiling, and I bring it and the cleanest rags I can find to Mrs. Kerber.

I'm paralyzed. I've never seen this before. Anna's bare knees now point to the ceiling, and Mrs. Kerber is sitting on a crate at her daughter's feet. "Push, Anna, push," she whispers. "I'm right here. It's going to be okay."

I bring the water over. "Set it down there, Abra. Take her hands. Help her sit up, and let her grab onto you."

Another scream through the rags. I sit behind Anna and let her lean against me. I take her hands, and she squeezes mine.

"Push, darling. I have the head. Come on, one last push! You can do it, Anna!"

I hold her while she strains against my grip. Her strength amazes me. I lean into her, as though my own strength can help her push.

"Now! One last push!" Mrs. Kerber says, her hands reaching between her daughter's legs.

It's like all three of us women push that baby out. A huge gasp for breath from all of us while Mrs. Kerber pulls the baby up into the faint lamp light. She takes the rags and quickly begins to rub warmth into the baby.

There's no sound. "Is it—" Anna asks. "Is it—"

Mrs. Kerber sits back on her heels and holds the baby upside down. She clears something out of the baby's mouth, then slaps it gently on its backside. "Come on! Come on!" she chants softly. I can see the umbilical cord, pink and twisted and still connected to Anna.

"Mama?"

"Come on!" Mrs. Kerber commands the baby.

Then, finally, a huge baby gasp, followed by a small gurgle, and then crying.

Mrs. Kerber hands me the towel-wrapped baby. "Watch out for the cord," she says. "Come on, Anna. One more push! One more!"

Anna falls back on the bed and gives it her all.

"There we are!" Mrs. Kerber says. She takes a pair of scissors out of her apron pocket and holds them up to me. "I hid this from the Krauts! I knew I'd be needing it." With that, she snips the umbilical cord.

I look down at the wrinkled pink-and-white baby, now starting to squirm in my hands. This little miracle, here in this cellar! "You're number twelve," I whisper down to the tiny, puffy face. This one new life avenges that last death.

Anna is sweaty and breathing hard, but she sits up and reaches for her baby. I hand the child to her. "What is it?" she asks.

"A girl," Mrs. Kerber says. "A beautiful, perfect girl." She looks at me. "And I think Abra should be the one to name her."

I blink in surprise, but my choice comes to me immediately. "Ruth," I whisper.

Mrs. Kerber touches my hand, her eyes seeking out mine. "Of course. Ruth."

She sits next to her daughter and granddaughter. "Put her to your breast now, Anna. The baby will know what to do." Sure enough, the baby latches on tight.

Anna smiles down at the tiny face of her child. "Ow. Are they all born hungry?" she asks her mother.

"Of course! She's in the ghetto!" Mrs. Kerber says. Her eyes fill with tears. "A life . . . here in the middle of all this death."

I leave them to their moment and go back to tend the fire for more hot water. I can hear the muffled whimpers of the newest resident of this old house . . . a baby named Ruth. But now what? I ask myself. Here I am again, in this cellar with three more lives to look out for. "So, what's the plan now, Arab?" I ask the steaming kettle of water.

As though to answer, the baby lets out a huge scream. I want to scream right back. So why am I smiling? Oh yes, I remember! My own Ruthie screamed just as loud when she was born.

MARCH, 1941

I.

THIS EARLY MARCH THAW HAS BROUGHT OUT NOT ONLY THE scavengers and the vendors, but also even more patrols and roundups. The baby seems to be thriving. At least someone is getting fed around here. I sell and barter the liquor in the ghetto, but people have so little to give or trade. A cup for a loaf of bread, a swig for a slice. We give what little food we can find to Anna. She needs her strength for the baby.

Sometimes I don't know if it's a mercy, protecting them here, or a curse. Because we all know it's only a matter of time. You'd have to be deaf and blind to not realize the Nazis' plan. This whole ghetto is nothing more than a corral to hold in Jews and other undesirables. Just a stop on the way to the next destination . . . Elsewhere.

Still, I go outside to scope things out several times a day. The snow is now muddy slush and every eave drips with the melt-off. There is a small hint of spring in the air, but I try to ignore it. I know winter isn't over by far. It's much too early to look forward to spring. But the streets do have a bit of color, no longer the stark black, white, and gray that cold weather seems to bring. Someone's red coat, blue handcart, green hat, all stand out now, seductions of spring.

I look at the ghetto wall, only a block away. When it was covered in snow and ice, it was easy to forget the coiled barbed wire and pieces of glass cemented in to its top. I walk the base of the wall, the snow no longer crunching under my feet, but making sucking sounds of deep, thick slush. I see the lump at the base of the wall. Oh God. Yankev, now only partially covered with snow. I throw a rock at some crows showing an interest. Thank God Mrs. Praska isn't here to see this.

I keep walking until I get to the ravaged cemetery. I think about my old plan to dismantle the weak spot marked by my own gravestone. Big dreams, fantastic plans. Stupid! I want to laugh, but my face hardens when I spot it. I wipe away the slush from the edge and see my epitaph is right there. GONE AND FORGOTTEN.

I grit my teeth. It's like that stone is laughing at me. "Fooled you, Abra Goldstein!" it seems to shout. I whip off my gloves, toss them down, and grab my gravestone by the edges, pulling with all my might. I lose my grip in the slippery ice and fall back and down.

"Oh yeah? I'll show you!" I scream at it. I get up and break a limb off a fallen branch and bash it again and again to break the ice from around the edges of the stone. I pull at it again. Still solid. It enrages me.

"I'll get you out, goddamn it!" I growl. Then I stop. Arab, what are you thinking? So what if you get this thing moved? What then? What makes you think Mrs. Kerber, Anna, and the baby will be any better off on the Aryan side? Where can you hide them?

"Stop it, Arab!" I screech out loud. "Think of yourself! There's nothing you can do, so just stop it!" I take the tree branch and whack it hard against my gravestone. "Stop thinking!"

Whack! Whack! Whack!

Slowly, the damn gravestone falls forward and thunks to the ground, splashing my pants with icy slush. I stare down at it, half expecting it to fly back into place.

But it doesn't move.

II.

I QUICKLY WORK TO PUT MY GRAVESTONE BACK , GEARS ALREADY turning in my brain. I pack snow all around it, then run back to the cellar. It's going to take some more work, but damn, we have an escape route if Mrs. Kerber and Anna will have the courage to take it.

"How's Anna doing?" I ask Mrs. Kerber when I come down the chute.

"She's weak, but that baby! Abra, she's so beautiful."

I look at my three guests. An undernourished, middle-aged seamstress; her daughter, weakened by childbirth; and her beautiful grandbaby, screaming her lungs out.

Mrs. Kerber offers me a cup of tea. "So," she says, "what do we do next?"

"I found an escape hole in the wall. It's a small opening, but I think you and Anna can get through. But it's risky."

"While you were out, I heard commotion somewhere above. I think they caught someone still in hiding. Abra, we'll be next. We have to chance escaping now. While we can."

I sigh. "Well, I can find you a place to hide on the Aryan side, but you'll be on your own. You do know that, don't you?"

She touches my hand. "I know. You've already risked so much."

"I mean, maybe I can find you a sewing—" I stop.

She reads my face. "What is it?" she whispers.

"Sh. I hear something." I lean closer to the coal chute and listen. Footsteps in the snow above and outside, coming closer. I grab my Luger.

"We've got company. Get Anna and the baby in the root cellar. Close the door. And for God's sake, keep the baby quiet."

Slowly, the hatch to the coal chute opens. A soldier slides down and before he can rise to his feet, I have my Luger to his head.

"Why do you always pull a gun on me?"

I'm so stunned, I can't move. "Otto!"

"Do you mind?" He takes his finger and moves the tip of the gun down.

"Where—What—Where the hell have you been?" I finally sputter.

He pulls me into an embrace, rocks me, and whispers in my ear. "We made it. All of us. We made it."

I break away from his embrace. "Well *mazel tov*! It's been over two months! So where the hell . . .?"

"There's so much to tell you!"

And there it is again—Otto's famous, optimistic grin. The same grin he shot me so often when he first tracked me down how many lifetimes—how many lives—ago? I seethe at that grin.

"We got back to Warsaw just yesterday! Lizard and Irenka and I drove the truck back, no questions asked."

I put my Luger back into its hiding spot. Anything to keep from looking at him. I should be thrilled he's back, that all went well, but . . . I just can't.

"I'll tell you, it's far easier to get in than it is to get out," he goes on. "Of course, we took down the quarantine signs. Well, the whole exodus took a little—okay, it took a *lot* longer than we planned. Weather, broken truck, sick children."

I step away. I don't want to see his face. I don't want him to see mine.

"Oh, Arab, I wish you could have been with us! God, the close calls. Sure could have used you a few . . ."

"I had my own problems here," I say over my shoulder.

He pulls me back around. "I wish you could have seen the faces of those kids when they saw that boat anchored out in . . ." Our eyes meet. His words trail off.

"Did you walk on water out to the boat?" I snap, glaring at him. "Messiah."

"What? Arab, I thought you'd—"

"How about a little of that raising the dead you do so well?" I grit my jaw and fight back tears.

"Oh," he whispers. "Ruthie." He steps closer and puts his hand on my arm. "Arab . . ."

I cast off his hand. "The fucking irony is, the only reason I did any of that—that whole—whole—idiotic suicide mission was to save her! And she's the one I lost!"

"What happened?"

We lock eyes. I don't care now if he or anyone else sees me cry. "That fucking bastard Fritz Von Segen took her that night! I had her, then I lost her! I had her!"

"Arab." He grabs for my hand but I pull back further. "Arab, don't—"

"I tracked him down and he gave me that whole 'never trust the enemy' bullshit! Well, I did trust him, but you can be damn sure I won't trust anyone else again!"

Otto looks down as he takes his gloves off. "Fritz was a good man, Arab, and—"

"Don't give me that bullshit! I was a fool to trust a goddamn Kraut and . . ." I stop, cock my head toward him, and narrow my eyes. "You said 'was.' How do you know Fritz is dead?" His face grows dark. I seize his arm. "How?"

He pulls away from me. "God, you know better than to ask so many questions!"

"How could you know? You've been gone all this time!" I shout.

"Can't you just believe me if I say I just can't say?" There's that conflict again in Otto's wavering voice.

"Maybe all you Krauts are the same. One way or another, you're going to get your victories. Well, you know where you can put them!" I walk into our little kitchen area and start moving a few dishes around.

"Arab," Otto says, following me. He sighs heavily. I know that sigh. I turn around and face him. He takes the cup in my hand and places it down. "Do you remember . . . when we first met . . . how I said resistance comes in many forms?"

"Yeah—and you also said die now or die later! 'Now' is looking better and better to me, Otto!"

"Well, I'm going to choose later. Arab. Will you look at me?" I turn back around.

"Arab, we've all lost people we love. But come with me. Let's avenge your loss. Let's get more children out." He takes me by the shoulders now and looks into my eyes. "Think of the other Ruthies out there, praying for someone to come and save them," he whispers.

"Where is it written that I have to risk my neck, over and over again, for people I don't even know?" I manage to spit out.

"It's not. But even your Ruthie stood up for her friends. She was willing to risk her neck for their safety."

Tears burn my chapped cheeks. I run my sleeve over my face. He hands me a linen handkerchief.

"So let's do what we can, Arab. Let's save as many as we can."

"Why? Why should I?" I use his handkerchief and hand it back.

"Simple. Because you can." He grins at me as though that's the most logical reason in the world.

What can I say to that? I shake my head and look down. I see blood stains on my boots. I can't remember whose.

Otto breaks the silence. "Here. I brought back some black-market cigarettes. Picked them up in England."

He lights my cigarette. The flash of silver and the sharp sound as his lighter snaps closed pull my attention. I know that sound. I grab his hand and seize what's in it. It is! It's Fritz's lighter! "How did you get this? It was in my knapsack. Ruthie was carrying it!"

"I can't tell you," he says again, pocketing the lighter. He glances around the cellar. "So, how long have you been back hiding here?"

"Don't change the subject, Otto."

Our eyes meet. He's never figured out I can read his face like a book. Slowly, I feel a smile creep onto my face—the first since that horrible night. I set my cigarette down and reach into a box to pull out a bottle of scotch we've been using as disinfectant. "Here. Have a drink."

He takes a long swig from the bottle and hands it back to me.

"Now, tell me about Fritz's lighter, Otto." I take a drink myself.

He takes his second drink. He sighs. "I want you to know I took an oath," he begins.

"Bet it isn't first oath you've broken."

He looks around, crushes out his cigarette, and sighs. "Have you ever heard of *Lebensborn*? It's this . . . program . . . where orphans are taken in and given to German families for adoption. Usually, the illegitimate children of German officers, or other high-ranking officials." He pauses.

I feel my jaw tighten. "Go on."

"Or, sometimes . . . children who can pass for Aryan."

I feel the hairs on my arms rise up. "Ruth?"

"Arab. For God's sake, how do you think I ever found you in the first place?"

"What do you mean?"

"Fritz Von Segen! How do you think I knew about you? Knew you were keeping boys alive on the streets? Knew where to find you?"

"Fritz?"

"Do I have to draw you a picture? Remember I told you about my own family opposing Hitler? *Widerstand?* Fritz's family works to unseat the Nazis, too. Fritz and I even trained together in England! *Lebensborn!* Fritz's family takes in children, Jewish children, who can pass for Aryan."

I have to walk around while I let this sink in. "Are you saying Ruthie is alive?"

"I am saying Ruthie is alive," he states slowly.

I still can't grasp this. I want to believe it, but do I dare? "But how did Fritz get her out? And so quickly?"

Otto stops my pacing and takes my hand, slipping Fritz's lighter into it. "Arab, there's a network. Very small, but there's a network. Someday, Ruth will have an exciting story to tell at cocktail parties."

I'm speechless. I look down at Fritz's lighter, now warm in my hand. I'm envisioning Ruthie, all grown up, dressed to the nines, chatting gaily at a cocktail party.

"The Von Segen family," I say, shaking my head, taking all this in. "Their son dead, because of . . . us." The photos in the locket are engrained in my memory. I look down at Fritz's lighter, rereading his mother's inscription . . . *carry the fire.* Tears spring to my eyes again.

"Well, they may have lost a son, but they've gained a daughter."

"What does that—?"

He plunges his hand into his pocket and pulls something out. "Here, been hanging onto this for you. Quite the good luck charm, turns out."

It's—oh God, it's the silver *yad* Ruthie wore around her neck the night of the escape.

I finger the wooden tag bearing my father's words of forgiveness, and I smile through my tears. "I'm surprised the little con artist gave it back."

It's all so much. I sit down where I stand. Otto kneels down and looks me eye to eye. "You know, Arab, it takes quite a man to do what Fritz did." Otto takes my hand. "Our Fritz had to live two separate lives. Three, if you knew—"

"I knew," I whisper, remembering his copy of *Don Juan*. His Henri.

Fritz was Ruth's savior. All along. And any way I look at it, I killed the savior. God, what happened that day? Was he creating a diversion? Protecting me?

"And someone found out? Turned him in?" I remember the order of arrest. ". . . treason to the . . ." I flash back on the scene of Fritz's death. I exhale a long, tired breath. "God, Otto, this is going to be hard to live with."

"No, Arab. *Lebensborn* wasn't the reason they wanted him. It's a very secret operation."

"Then what?"

"Consorting with the enemy."

I have to glance away. "Me. I'm the enemy," I whisper. "We used to joke about—"

"No, not you. Me." Otto says, offering me his hand and pulling me back up. "I'm the enemy."

"I don't understand."

"Arab, I didn't go out to smoke a cigarette before we left that night. I went out to call Fritz from one of the German offices in the ghetto. Tell him our plan. So he could be ready, in case anything went wrong. And, well, our call must have been intercepted. I hate that we lost Fritz. But he knew the risks. Gladly accepted them." He catches my eyes. "Like you and I do."

"Please tell me he didn't arrange a roundup just so we could escape. All those people . . ."

"No, those are planned in advance. Jewish holidays and such. But I think he's the one who moved people off the street so we could make it out of that alleyway. Remember how the crowd suddenly parted?"

"So the Nazis know about you, too. What if they go after you?"

"I'll just throw myself off that bridge when I come to it." He swishes the air with his hand as though it bats away that little problem.

I have to laugh. He would say that. "So, Lizard? And Irenka?"

"Hiding on the Aryan side, just waiting for me to return with new plans."

My heart feels even fuller. "Stefan and Lorenz?"

"Probably driving their adoptive family in England crazy by now. I tell you, if we're still at war when they get a little older, I'm going to recruit them!" He pauses. "Sometimes I think our biggest success will be Mrs. Praska."

Just the mention of her name brings a smile to my face. "How so?"

"She got her children to England and we set them up with a small factory. She's going to supply us with more cigarettes for children to sell. There'll always be more children, you know."

"Yes, I know," I say, nodding.

"So let's not stand around jawing. Let's get to work, huh? I'm in the mood for some good old-fashioned avenging. Come on. So many children waiting."

There's a faraway shrill. Otto straightens up. "Sh! What was that?"

I can't resist teasing him. "I've been trapping rats. Can you stay for dinner? Follow me." I lead him through the boiler room and open the heavy wooden door to the root cellar. The small candle light reflects off the faces of the Kerbers. Just then the baby lets out a howl. Otto looks at me. Oh, his expression!

"It's okay, Mrs. Kerber," I say. "Come on out. He's a friend. A very good friend."

Anna follows her mother out, shushing the crying baby. Otto's mouth falls open. "What's . . . I mean, who—?"

"You know better than to ask so many questions, Messiah," I say, giving him a jab.

I walk over to Anna and she hands me the bundled-up babe.

"I guess it's true what they say," Otto says. "The great Arab of Warsaw can get her hands on anything. So, just who is this?" He puts his arms out.

I hand him the baby. "Our next customer. Her name is Ruth."

SEPTEMBER, 1946

In red paint, hastily splashed upon a sagging cellar wall
in the heart of the Warsaw Ghetto:

WE WEREN'T THE LAST
WE WEREN'T FIRST
WE WEREN'T THE BEST
WE WEREN'T THE WORST
WE RESCUED KIDS
ONE-THIRTY AND FOUR
WOULD THE LAST ONES OUT
PLEASE SHUT THE DOOR?

—*The Arab of Warsaw*

Acknowledgments

WITH ANY WORK OF HISTORICAL FICTION, THE AUTHOR TAKES great care in research. A part of that research is finding experts in certain areas and asking for their help. I started researching *The Girl Who Wouldn't Die* in 2004. In that time, I have relied on several people to point me in the right direction and answer certain questions, the answers to which were not readily found elsewhere. Since much of my research was from first-person accounts of that time period, many of these people have, sadly, passed on. Of these, I wish to acknowledge Helmut "Brownie" Braunsteiner, whose name I have borrowed. Brownie showed me and all those he came into contact with what true heroism is.

Several names of those alive and well stand out and I wish to acknowledge them here: novelist B. E. Andre for her knowledge of Warsaw and her kind and appreciated assistance as a beta reader; RJ McHatton, videographer and writer, for pointing me in the right direction in locating certain experts; artist Lawrence Kamisher, for also connecting me to people who had firsthand recollections of the period.

Thanks also to my agent, Andy Ross, who believed in this book from the beginning—and there were a lot of versions! Lastly, my team of editors at Sky Pony Press for sharing that faith and for holding my feet to the fire when it came time for revisions—Julie Matysik, Adrienne Szpyrka, Kat Enright, and especially Rachel Stark for her yeoman's duty.

All of you—thanks!